My Father's House

a novel

Rose Chandler Johnson

Printed in the United States of America

Cover picture of house by photographer Brian Brown, www.vanishingsouthgeorgia.com

Cover design by Amber Lanier Nagle

Author's photograph courtesy of Branch Carter

Library of Congress Control Number: 2016903315

CreateSpace Independent Publishing Platform, North Charleston, SC

ISBN-13: 978-1530040391
ISBN-10: 1530040396

In loving memory of my aunt, Mary Frances Elliott Frazier,

and, as always, for my children.

Chapter One

"**G**o on, Darling, and see about the colt," I said. He stirred a cup of steaming coffee, and then handed it to me. When my hands wrapped around the warm ceramic mug, he leaned down and gently pressed his lips to my forehead. I closed my eyes, grateful for his touch.

"I love you," he said, while taking me by the shoulders and gently pulling me into the circle of his arms.

I laid my head against his chest and felt its rise and fall.

"Go," I whispered. "I'm going to take a walk and look at the gardens."

He rubbed my back in wide slow circles.

"I'm grateful she died in the spring."

"I know," he said. "I won't be long. I imagine I'll find you sitting under the magnolia when I return."

"Uh-huh."

"Wait for me there."

I followed him out onto the porch and watched him walk to the truck, stop, and turn. He fixed his gaze on me, and I knew he didn't want to leave. I smiled then, and he nodded before getting in and backing down the driveway. He waved, and something about his smile and the gentle blue of the sky strengthened my heart. I watched him disappear down the street before I turned and walked back inside.

Yesterday we buried the woman who raised me, tethering my heart strings to both heaven and earth. Full of simple goodness, her love never let me go. She wanted to be buried next to her husband, and so she is, and before we lowered her body into the red Georgia clay, we read the 23rd Psalm. The words flowed like a soothing balm.

Surely goodness and mercy shall follow me all the days of my life: And I will dwell in the house of the Lord forever.

This morning the words are whispering to my soul, and I can't help remembering.

***

Looking back, I see the goodness and mercy of God. Along the way, when I lost Daddy, and then through all the turmoil and pain with Manny, I couldn't see it. But it was always there. I tried so hard to make sense of my life— grappling with shattered ideals and the self-inflicted wounds of my own naiveté.

I had to painstakingly piece those years together like one of Aunt Martha's patchwork quilts. Little by little the pattern became clear and made as much sense as ever can be made of mistakes and misunderstandings, loss, and good intentions gone wrong. Now I hug the memories close to comfort me when I need them or kick them back and forget them when I want to leave them there . . . in the past.

I was born on April 10, 1964 in our little Georgia town during the most beautiful time of year. It was Easter, much to my father's delight. That time of year when the earth flourishes with color and fragrance. The dogwoods and azaleas bloom, and irises and lilies nod their pretty heads like well-behaved children. That's how I came to be called Lily Rose.

Daddy made everything perfect in my world. To his way of thinking, Mama and I were the best things God had ever created. Because he believed in me, I believed too.

Memories of my childhood kept hope alive through the hard years, but my childhood reality was such a different place from where I later found myself, sometimes those memories made life even harder. When life hurt, I floundered.

My early world consisted of my daddy and mama, my brother, and me. James Michael was born ten years before me and Mama adored him. She lit up like a Christmas tree whenever he walked into the room.

"Hold me, Jimbo," I'd say to my brother when we played. I'd reach as high as I could stretch on tippy-toes. He'd swoop me up and carry me in his arms. There I could pick plums from the highest branches at the edge of the woods behind our house. He'd run fast pulling me behind him in his red Radio Flyer wagon. I liked nothing better than sitting on his bicycle handlebars, holding on tight and riding around town and on the bumpy dirt roads. But, holding tight couldn't keep him from growing up and going away too soon.

James Michael loved Jesus. Mama said he would be a fine preacher one day. As soon as he graduated college at the age of twenty-one, he traveled to France with a mission team, then to Africa, and back to France again as a pastor and church builder. Along the way he met his wife. She was about as plain and simple as a baguette, but Daddy said she would do him good . . . said she was a gift from God.

But Mama said, "What does he want with that little mouse who can't even speak English?"

He brought her home to meet us right after they got married. Within a few years, they had two little boys. And Mama cried.

"James Michael won't ever be coming home again," she said.

Although I missed my brother every day after he went off to Bible College, by the time he left for the mission field I was used to his not being there. I suppose I knew he was gone from my life. But Daddy was there, as sure as sunshine.

Daddy was our high school's history teacher. He knew everything there was to know about the Civil War, the Great Depression, the World Wars, about so many events and faraway places. He'd been in the Pacific in World War II and traveled across the entire country by bus and train. He didn't talk about that much. He said it best to keep all those memories and nightmares locked in his green army trunk. He talked politics and called presidents by their last names like they were his personal friends. Like they smoked pipes or chewed fat cigars together under the old oak trees outside the American Legion. He talked about the time Grandpa advised him to come out the Democratic Party. I loved his stories.

When I was thirteen, Daddy was awarded Teacher of the Year. I went with him to the banquet. Just me, because Mama couldn't go. After James Michael went away, Mama seemed to go away too. She missed him bad, and when she realized he wouldn't be coming home again, she lost interest in all else. Daddy found the best doctors to treat her, but to his sorrow, they only seemed to make her condition worse. From morning 'til night she rocked on the front porch not saying a word to a soul.

"Come on in Emmy," Daddy would say. "Supper's 'bout ready. I've fixed you a glass of sweet tea and Annie Ruth has made some corn muffins just the way you like 'em."

But Mama kept right on rocking in that big oak rocker like she hadn't heard a word he said.

Daddy would walk over and wait beside her. Reaching down he gently held her elbow like it was a baby bird. Sure enough, she'd rise as if empowered by invisible wings. They stepped side by side across the weathered porch, letting the screen door slam behind them. Daddy would smile then, and look at me and nod.

"It's gonna be all right, Lily Rose," he'd say. "It's gonna be all right."

At that time I didn't understand that something was wrong with Mama. Just that she was too quiet and she rocked for a long time on the porch like she was waiting for somebody. Daddy was the only one who could perk her up besides James Michael. She never seemed to notice me.

Mama called Daddy "Daddy." They got married when she was seventeen, he twenty-nine. A baby boy was born dead, and Mama reckoned she'd never have another child. Then James Michael was born. Every year on my brother's birthday, I heard my mama say, "I was born the very minute James Michael took his first breath."

My arrival was unexpected. Mama was thirty-five and Daddy was forty-seven. Mama's depression set in then. They didn't call it postpartum in those days, just "depression." That's when we got Annie Ruth. Right after I was born Daddy brought her home to take care of us five days a week. She was about Mama's age, but childless and unflagging. She kept the house running like clockwork. Besides my daddy, she was the most perennially pleasant person I've ever known. I don't know what we'd have done without her. Even more so, I don't know what I would've done. She never left us.

My childhood was like a bright star more radiant than all the others . . . until the moment it falls from the sky. Flashing through the purple night . . . making you stand still, and wait and watch . . . wondering if it's really gone, or not, and if it had ever really been there at all.

My sixteenth summer started with a pool party at the country club. People Daddy worked with, church folks, Mama's sister, Aunt Rachel, and my cousin, Maggie—all gathered to celebrate. After sunset, burning bamboo torches and hanging lights cast a magical glow over the laughter of friends. After the party, Maggie came home with us. The two of us giggled and whispered in my four-poster bed long after everyone else was asleep.

"Shhh . . . ," Daddy whispered as he tapped lightly on the door. As we listened to his slipper-shod feet shuffling down the hall, our giggles faded, and sleep settled in.

A couple of weeks after the party, on a hot day, I lay sprawled in bed looking at the ceiling through the spinning blades of the fan. Lifting one leg then the other, I admired the frosted pink polish on my toes. Listening to Mama and Daddy talking downstairs in the kitchen, serenity embraced me. Hearing Daddy chuckle and Mama's voice real low caused love to fill my heart.

I got up after the voices quieted in the kitchen. By the time I walked downstairs, Daddy had just started the lawn mower.

"He's waited too late," Mama murmured to herself more than to me. Barefooted, in baby doll pajamas, I rolled the cellophane bag back down in the Rice Krispies box.

"It's too hot out there," she grumbled.

She sipped coffee from a mug cupped between both hands as she watched Daddy through the screen door. The mower's engine choked. In the silent pause, I heard the wall clock ticking like it always had on the wall beside the kitchen table. Daddy wound it up every Saturday night. *Tick, tock, tick, tock . . .*

Mama gasped, and then let out a yelp that shot a jolt right through me. The coffee cup slipped from her hands and shattered at her feet. Coffee splattered onto the wall and shot out across the floor. She bolted through the door, calling Daddy's name.

"*Michael!*"

I stared at the shards of glass and the coffee creeping across the floor. A wrenching turmoil seized me and pinned me where I stood. I strained to pry myself from its grasp. And then, freed, I ran out too.

Daddy lay on the grass in the middle of the yard.

"Call 9-1-1, call 9-1-1!" Mama shrieked.

I don't remember making that call.

When I crouched down beside him, Daddy looked like he was sleeping in Mama's arms. His face was flushed beet red. I leaned over to kiss him and tasted salt on my lips. Mama grabbed my arm, digging her nails into my skin, and pulled me into her place. She slid Daddy's head onto my lap, then jumped up and ran to the house for some cold water.

It seemed so strange to me. I didn't know she could run.

Daddy's eyes, barely open, looked directly into mine. Sweat glistened on his face. A quivering movement fluttered across his face and lips. I bowed my head as close to his as I could to hear his voice.

"Lily Rose," he whispered. "Lily Rose, you're gonna be all right."

Right there in that moment, nothing existed in the whole wide world but my daddy and me. I held him in my arms; his eyes held me. Then his eyes closed. His chest lurched once followed by a long heavy sigh.

"Daddy?"

The medics said he was gone when they got there. A massive heart attack. I couldn't figure it out. He took his last breath in broad daylight, lying on the grass in our own backyard. How was it the sun continued to shine?

"Stop the sun from moving across the sky," I wanted to scream. I tried to make them stop. *Leave my daddy alone. Don't take him away from me!* The incomprehensible cruelty crushed me. I crumpled to my knees. Silent screams tore out of me from deep inside my belly, threatening to turn me inside out as the gurney rolled over the half-mowed lawn. Then, I heard screams . . . screams from far, far away. But I couldn't tell if it was Mama or if it was me.

The rest of the summer drifted in the clouds somewhere across that summer sky. My high school days sort of passed away too. They dragged on with an inertia that pulled me down and had it not been for Annie Ruth, I would have ended up right there rocking on the front porch beside Mama.

Annie Ruth took care of me. She and Mr. John drove up in his dusty old pickup truck every morning at six o'clock. She got out and came in, bringing her life and soul into the house. Daddy had seen to it through his estate that she continued to do exactly what she'd always done for Mama and me. We were her cherished charges, and I was like her own.

"There ain't nobody ever been like Mr. Cates," she'd say, shaking her head and murmuring to herself. And whenever Annie Ruth saw the need, she'd have a talk with me.

She'd say, "You jus' sit down and listen 'cause I'm gonna tell you the things you gotta know. Ain't nobody else but me can do it."

The solemn way she put it, she had to explain things and why people are the way they are. She explained why Mama took no notice of me in ways to help me understand her sickness, so I wouldn't personalize it and punish myself. It helped me not to blame her for my loneliness and loss. Annie Ruth was no nonsense and genuine, like Daddy. When the time came, she told me I had to go to college because that's what my daddy wanted for me. I listened to Annie Ruth. With one exception, I always listened.

So, when the time came, I went off to university. During those years I began to feel like myself, *me*, before I lost my daddy. "You can do anything you set your mind to," Daddy had said. I began to feel like maybe it was true.

But, the truth is, those college years weren't near enough to heal my heart. Before I knew it, we were graduating, and I was on my own. Childhood had passed. Yesterday was gone.

Chapter Two

With a month to go before college graduation, a subtle, yet growing sense of unease settled on my chest. My roommates, Julie and Vicky, got more excited about the future with each passing day, but dread seemed to hover over my part of the neat three-bedroom stucco we'd shared for the past three years. No one else seemed to share the feeling, so I kept it closed inside. Maybe I thought I could deprive it of oxygen and snuff it out, like a candle's flame.

But as they inevitably do, the fears came to light. Julie failed to come home one night just weeks before graduation. I knew she was in love with our French professor, and he with her, despite the broken rules of that relationship. I lay in bed, worrying, wondering what had gotten into her.

"Where is she?" I said aloud. For heaven's sakes, neither Julie nor I had ever stayed out all night.

I'd held onto hope all through the night. Hope that the door would open, that she would sweep in and everything would be as it had been. But when the morning sun rose and still Julie hadn't come home, I anticipated the worse.

I thought I'd be able to catch her after our morning classes. With that in mind, I jumped out of bed, splashed cold water on my face, and brushed my teeth. Grabbing my cornflower print dress draped across the chair, I slipped it over my head, fumbling with the buttons on the back of the neck. I applied some lotion and lip gloss, and a few hard strokes of the brush, letting my long brown hair fall full and soft around my shoulders. Finally, I strapped on my favorite platform sandals.

As I poured myself a cup of coffee, I glanced at the clock, spilling the coffee. With no time to spare, I grabbed my keys, hurrying to make it to my statistics class. I nearly broke my neck tripping over Vicky's book bag left in the pathway to the door.

Scenarios and conversations played in my head, obliterating the professor's words. So many, "what if's." Normally the coffee kept me alert as the professor droned on. That day, my wild imaginings and thoughts of Monsieur Combier and Julie moving away to some remote place in Canada kept me wide awake. Her moving away—that's what I dreaded. I didn't want our lives to change.

Julie and I had extensive plans. Graduation, then on to every major city and museum North America and Europe had to explore—New York City first, then Paris, and Rome. We'd visit them all, and the great art museums as well—the Metropolitan, the Louvre. Julie would sell her sketches to support our bohemian lifestyle. I would perfect my language skills, all the while writing clever travelogues. More like sisters than friends, we'd have the time of our lives. If only their passion hadn't laid waste to our well-made plans.

When class dismissed, I popped from my seat. Almost stumbling down the stairs of the Math and Science building, I rushed towards Taylor Hall, hoping to meet Julie coming out of her French class. We needed to talk about everything—graduation, my anxiety about being alone, her *thing* with the professor. If only it wasn't too late . . . .

Julie had hinted for weeks that she'd rather run off and get married than confess her relationship to her mother, who would most certainly declare the unsuitable nature of a marriage between her daughter and the university's French professor.

"And if I run off," Julie said one morning over coffee and cheese grits, "I'll save my daddy the expense and hassle of the elaborate wedding my mother will orchestrate."

I changed the subject or feigned disinterest every time she started talking about how much she loved the man. I wanted to avoid any discussions that might uncork my own emotions. If she married, where would that leave me?

Running across the campus that morning, I regretted not talking to my friend. A gnawing concern settled in my empty stomach.

A sheet of notebook paper was taped to the door of the French class. Scrawled across the paper in Julie's lovely script were the words, *Un jour férié—les élèves français! à lundi. M. Charles Combier.*

My breath caught. Dizziness fluttered through my head as I grasped the meaning of eight foreign words to his students, declaring he was on holiday, and would see them on Monday.

After a moment's pause, I headed for the student union, praying there wouldn't be a line at the pay phone. I dialed the number to the house and waited, muttering, "Please Lord, let her answer."

"Hello?"

"Vicky, is Julie there?"

"No, I don't think so. I haven't seen her this morning."

I told Vicky then that Julie hadn't come home, and what I feared.

"I'll be right home," I said.

Five minutes later I pulled into the driveway. By then, panic—a combination of anxiety and grief—had risen in my chest.

As soon as I turned off my rattling Mustang, Vicky threw open the door and stood with her arms wide, holding onto the door frame. She was smiling like crazy and nodding her head.

"Yes, yes," she yelled. "They ran off and got *married* . . . last night by the Justice of the Peace in Savannah!" For a few seconds, I watched Vicky bouncing joyfully in place.

The tightness in my chest erupted with a burst of tears. I slumped forward onto the steering wheel burying my face on my folded arms.

"Lily!"

I sobbed shamelessly. Vicky did all she could to comfort me.

I leaned against her as we walked into the house, then I slumped onto the floral sofa, curled up, and smothered my face in the back cushions. Vicky's soft words couldn't penetrate my tears. Any measure of self-assurance I'd gained over the previous three and half years washed out of me that day. When the tears dried up, I felt like a fraud. Until that moment I hadn't realized how much I relied on my friends.

I was grateful that Julie wasn't there to see me crying. Besides my own humiliation, I didn't want to take away from her joy or taint Vicky's happiness either.

When I finally got over the initial outburst and pulled myself upright, silent tears continued to trickle down my cheeks and neck. Vicky sat beside me and draped her arm around my shoulders, reassuring me that we all would be fine. But my heart didn't believe her. Her words didn't sooth the hurt made all the more painful because I didn't understand it myself.

"I don't know what I've been thinking," I said as I swiped my hands across both cheeks. "Julie's the best friend I ever had. I . . . I guess I wasn't ready for this."

"I know. We've all felt that. The two of you had some great plans too. But they're in love. They want to be together."

I nodded, but said nothing, realizing that to her, it all made perfect sense.

"Let's freshen up and go over to Le Bistro," Vicky said. "Come on. After a couple hours chatting and sipping our favorite peach tea, we'll have this thing all figured out."

"Okay." I managed to silent my sniffles.

"We need to get out of here for a little while—enjoy this sunny day, sit on the terrace, watch the people go by."

Reluctantly, I agreed to go. But I didn't say the words that kept running through my mind. What would I do without my best friends? Julie and Vicky both would be leaving. I'd be alone . . . again.

My mood brightened a bit after we got out amongst friends at the café. We sat on the terrace, and whiled the afternoon away, chatting about our university days, retelling silly stories, and musing about our dreams for the future.

As soon as we got back to the house from the café, we fell into our routine and waited for Julie to come home.

"They should be home by eight," Vicky said. "That's what Julie said when she called this morning."

Vicky lay propped on the sofa with an oversized chintz pillow under her head, flipping through a magazine.

I sat at Daddy's oak desk and tried to concentrate on my final research paper. As I took sips of iced tea, I stared out the window, watching light play on glossy gardenia leaves.

"Listen to this," Vicky said, "from People magazine—'college-educated white women who have not married by their 25th birthday have only a fifty percent likelihood of marrying thereafter.'"

"Really?"

"'Those who turn thirty without having wed have only a twenty percent chance.'"

Our eyes met. We wrinkled our noses and made faces at each other before saying at the same time, "Old maids." Somehow, that was painfully funny. I tossed my head back and laughed until my sides hurt.

Still grinning, Vicky admired the small marquise diamond that graced her left hand. "I can't believe it's only forty-five more days until Scott and I get married."

"Seems like only yesterday you waltzed in here waving that diamond in front of our eyes."

"It's been nearly two years."

A car door slammed in front of the house, immediately followed by the sound of another closing. Vicky and I stared at one another, listening intently. Julie's laughter rang out, and we jumped up at the same time and rushed to the door.

Vicky reached her first. As they hugged, swaying like daffodils in the breeze, I glanced at Charles Combier. Pride and joy lit up his face. Then my friends stepped apart just long enough to pull me into their circle. We embraced for a long moment before stepping apart. Julie's eyes found her husband's and she reached for him.

Charles stepped forward and gently pulled Julie to him. He framed Julie's face in his hands. They gazed into each other's eyes.

"I'm going to leave you in good hands, darling" he said before slowly pressing his lips to hers. "I love you."

"I love you, too," she whispered.

They continued to stand there, looking at one another, holding each other gently, saying nothing, while Vicky giggled and I stared awkwardly at the newlyweds.

I was relieved when Julie's new husband left. She had to continue living with us for another few weeks. Discretion was a must. Our women's university would be scandalized by the elopement, and Monsieur Combier's career could be jeopardized.

"Ah Lily, we couldn't be happier," Julie said as we walked, arm in arm, into the house.

She looked at me, and I smiled. Tears threatened to spill over again, but I willed myself to put on a happy face.

"You know I'm happy for you, Julie. I am. It's just been a bit of a shock."

Yes, that was it. Shock. My best friend eloped without telling me. Shock. The plans we'd worked on for over two years, null and void.

In an instant, all my senses burst into a full blown memory—the hot summer sun beating down on me, Daddy in my arms, the smell of fresh mowed grass, the taste of salt on my lips. My daddy . . . gone.

"Lily," Julie called my name. "Lily?"

I blinked in answer. *How* had I forgotten *that*?

"You'll adjust in no time, Lily. You will."

"I will. I'll adjust in no time." *Maybe this was the way Mama felt when James Michael moved away.*

Somehow I held back the tears that stung my eyes. I kept up my end of the conversation and listened as Julie replayed the events of their secret engagement, the ceremony at City Hall, and their plans. I made it through the evening without making a fool of myself.

"Good night Lily," Julie said, and then firmly planted a kiss on my cheek.

She turned to Vicky. "It'll be your turn soon." They smiled at one another, sharing a secret I didn't yet understand.

When Julie turned to look at me, I pointed to Daddy's desk.

"I'll be along shortly. I need to work on that paper a while before turning in. Sweet dreams y'all."

I watched them go down the hall to their respective rooms. Like so many other 'goodnights.' Somehow everything was different this time. When their doors closed, I let my heavy shoulders sink for the first time all evening. Hot tears filled my eyes and spilled down my cheeks. No one would see them. I was alone. So I let them fall in big drops onto the paper . . . blurring the black and white.

Chapter Three

Collage faded into memory. While I had graduated with a degree in journalism, my two best friends managed to get their M.R.S. degrees as well. Julie and Charles moved to Canada. Vicky returned home to Florida and married her high school sweetheart. Looking back, it seems like that summer was wrapped in organza and tulle. And at the end of it, I was alone.

I stayed on in the stucco cottage that had become home, worked part-time at The Flower Box, and wrote for the local newspaper. I adjusted in no time, like Julie had said. By summer's end, I had gotten used to the new routine.

By all outward appearances, my life was just fine. I enjoyed my work and woke up every morning to serene surroundings. The house, however, had lost some of its charm. The now silent rooms transformed the once nurturing abode into a right lonely place. Sometimes, without my girlfriends around, sad old memories and troubling emotions threatened to surface.

When my cousin Maggie called, urging me to come visit her in New York City, I jumped at the chance. We'd been great friends in childhood, but then we drifted apart. Maybe we could rekindle our friendship, I hoped. I contacted my Uncle Bill, the executor of my daddy's estate, to send me my quarterly allowance a bit early.

Maggie graduated high school the year before me, and then attended the Savannah College of Art and Design. Following graduation, she moved directly to New York along with several of her SCAD friends. On a muggy Monday in August, I flew up to visit.

On the flight to New York, I pressed close to the window, gazed at the perfectly clear sky, and tried to take in all of the exceptional view of the city upon approach. The aqua and teal blues of the water, contrasting with forest green patches, and the silver-gray of skyscrapers, made an indelible impression on my mind.

Throngs of people surrounded me in the airport which pulsated with energy. It fascinated me and I chuckled to myself. I couldn't remember Atlanta's Hartsfield or even Charles DeGaulle having such crowds. But, then again, I was only eight when my family and I flew to France to see my uncle's grave. My mother's only brother had died in France in WWII. Everyone said James Michael was his spitting image. Walking through the airport that day, I remembered walking through that other airport years before, holding Daddy's hand.

After being bumped along by the crowds, I found a restroom. As I exited the stall, a man sashayed in, looking neither to the left nor the right, and entered the one I'd just vacated. I had to pick my chin up off my chest. I scurried toward the line of sinks to wash my hands. Before I could get the liquid soap into my hand, a woman installed herself at the sink next to me, stripped off her blouse, and proceeded to wash her unshaved armpits. I got my butt out of there as fast as I could.

Maggie couldn't stop laughing at me when I described the scene.

"Well, Toto," she sputtered, when she finally caught her breath. "You're not in Kansas anymore."

"Okay, go ahead and laugh," I said, beginning to realize the joke was on me. Then I laughed too.

"Oh, Maggie, how silly of me. I hope you can put up with your country cousin."

A few minutes later, after our taxi hit the concrete jungle, the stop and go maneuvering through noisy streets had me pleading for caution. My life was in the hands of a total stranger. To make matters worse, I got car sick. I moaned with my head between my knees. By the time the taxi stopped in front of Maggie's building, I'd broken into a sweat and threatened to throw up right there in the car. Mercifully, I did not.

"My gracious, Lily, I can tell you're going to make this a memorable experience."

"If I survive," I managed to say through the moans.

All just a part of the New York experience, according to Maggie.

As soon as we got to her apartment, Maggie instructed me to lie down and she laid a cold cloth on my forehead. I sipped ginger ale while lying on her tiny couch. By some miracle, I found myself revitalized an hour later and ready to go out for the evening—to walk the streets of Times Square in "the city that never sleeps."

"Just look at you, Lily," Maggie said when I came out of the bathroom. "You look beautiful."

"What *are* you talking about? Me, beautiful?" I slipped my feet into the new high heel leather sandals I'd bought to wear with my white peasant top and cotton skirt.

"Yes, you," Maggie said. "Your hair has body and curl and you don't have to do a thing with it. It's not fair. You're like a Barbie doll."

"I wouldn't know about that," I smirked. "Remember, I didn't have Barbies. I played hopscotch or read with Daddy or Annie Ruth."

"Well," Maggie said. "I had a collection. You look like one. Let me think long enough and I'll remember the name of the doll." Maggie squinted her eyes and pursed her lips, "Humm."

I laughed and she did too. It felt good to laugh, and to be with family.

"Maggie, you're adorable. Daddy always did say you were cute as a button."

***

The next morning, as soon as we woke up and got ready for the day, Maggie declared our first stop would be for bagels and cream cheese. The streets were crowded with smartly dressed people, business-like and impersonal, rushing to and fro, clutching coffee cups and brief cases in their hands. I commended Maggie on her upscale neighborhood.

"Don't thank me," she giggled, rolling her eyes. "Thank Daddy."

The Metropolitan Museum of Art stood before us. I was as excited as a kid at the county fair.

"Take a picture of me here on the marble stairs. I want to send a picture to Annie Ruth." I handed Maggie my camera. "This place is amazing."

Once inside, I had to see everything. I gushed over the collections of fine art. "The Egyptian Collection is awesome. Julie would *love* this." One magnificent collection after another, each more inspiring than the last.

"Lily, haven't you seen enough?" Maggie sighed. "I don't think I can stand much more."

When she said that, I reluctantly pulled my eyes away from the art treasures to look at her.

"You're kidding! I could stay here all day. Don't you love this place, Maggie?"

"Of course, but you have to realize, Lily Rose, I've been here a dozen times, and my interest is primarily fashion." She looked at her stylish watch, and then lifted her hands helplessly. "We've been here almost three hours."

"Oh," I said, genuinely surprised. "I didn't realize. I had no idea, really." I held up one of the brochures I'd rolled into a paper telescope. "Just one more exhibit pleeaase," I said, drawing out the last word. "I have to see the Tiffany collection." She gave a little nod, and I hurried on ahead of her.

When Maggie and I finally headed down the grand steps to the sidewalk below, I was already wondering when I might come again. Next on our itinerary was iconic Central Park, south of the Met.

"Maggie, this is great," I said, breathing in the city air. "Thank you for asking me to come visit.

"I'm glad you're here, Lily." She wrapped her arm around mine. "It seems like old times."

"Yeah, it does."

"I'm glad you're back to yourself."

"Me, too." I sighed. I glanced at her, wondering if she was referring to my long grieving spell after Daddy's death, or my sadness over parting with my friends. Either way, it made no difference. It felt good to be alive. I fell out of step with Maggie to watch performers tumbling and chanting to the beat of African drums.

"Lily, look there," Maggie called, pointing to a man running with what looked like a film crew jogging beside him. "They're making a movie."

"Oh my. What fun!"

By the time we reached the Tavern on the Green, we were ready for a leisurely lunch in the Garden Room. Abundant flowers spilled from planters and vases all around. We lingered over crisp romaine salads topped with goat cheese, and then finished our meal with *crème brulée*. This time it was Maggie—who watched the veritable fashion show of stylish guests—who had to be coaxed to leave the place. We strolled over to 5th Avenue to window-shop, or more appropriately, as the French say *faire du lèche-vitrines,* which means "to lick the windows."

We practically drooled as we peered into the glitzy shops. Some were so extravagant we opted not to venture in. Security guards stood at shop entrances looking a bit tourist weary, but not so at Tiffany's. The friendly security guards loved my Southern accent.

"Like sweet magnolias," they crooned.

Emboldened by their gracious manners, I grabbed Maggie by the arm and walked in.

"Leave it to you to waltz us in this place," Maggie said, and squeezed my arm.

Not only did we look, we picked out rings as though we were princesses and were allowed to try them on. I chose a perfect one carat diamond set in platinum with heart shaped diamonds on each side. Dazzled under the crystal chandeliers, we admired each other's choice.

"This is the one for me," I said, fluttering my fingers like fairy wings. I felt like royalty . . . in reality, more like a little girl playing dress-up.

"I'd rather have a bigger apartment." Maggie pulled the ring off her finger and gingerly handed it back to the elegant lady behind the glass case.

"Oh, you're no fun," I teased, and pretended to pout.

When we finally returned to the apartment, Maggie made pimento cheese sandwiches.

I curled up on the loveseat—there wasn't room to do much else, and picked up the book I'd been reading on the plane.

"What are you reading?" Maggie asked as she poured us some iced tea.

"*Illusions of Love.*"

"That figures." Maggie rolled her eyes. "I'm reading *Elvis Is Dead and I Don't Feel Too Good Myself.*"

"Then you haven't wandered too far from your roots," I said. We giggled like silly teenagers.

The week was completely entertaining as far as I was concerned. Although Maggie, being totally over the New York scene, appeared bored at times. All the while I wondered who could be bored in a city like New York. I had stepped into a very different world from the small structured one I knew.

On Friday night, I got dolled up for our last night on the town. We were going to Maggie's favorite restaurant.

Valenti's was an iconic place in the heart of Little Italy. We requested a table in the garden café, a small courtyard with vine-covered walls. The atmosphere was idyllic. The service was exceptional. The waiter, divine.

Something about his presence excited me. Maybe it was the way he lingered beside me and caressed me with his eyes. It was hard for me not to stare at his smooth olive hands as they moved back and forth around our table.

I suppose I got caught up in the moment because without thinking, I asked, "Would you take our picture?" I held the camera out at arm's length to the dreamy eyed waiter. I smiled before saying "please" as sweet as pie.

"It would be my pleasure," he said in a voice as rich and smooth as caramel.

Maggie and I leaned close together, our cheeks almost touching side by side.

"Smile, ladies." Besides the camera's flash, I was dazzled by his eyes.

Then, he caught me by surprise. Instead of handing the camera back to me, he handed it to Maggie and said, "Now, take *our* picture?"

A thrill ran through every fiber of my body as he squatted beside me and slid his arm around my bare shoulders. His warm hand gently pressed my shoulder. I inhaled slowly, grateful to be seated since my legs had turned to Jello.

When he walked away, my eyes followed. Perhaps too long, because when I turned my gaze to meet Maggie's, her face bore a look of sheer astonishment.

She leaned toward me with her eyebrows raised. "What just happened here?"

"I don't have a clue," I said, while shaking my head and giggling with embarrassment. My mind had gone completely blank. No one had ever made me feel that way.

Maggie relished every morsel of the delicious food, but I barely tasted mine. It took all my energy to focus on the conversation. Each time the waiter appeared, my composure unraveled. And then, the unthinkable happened. When he brought us the check, not only did he wish us a lovely evening, he asked for my phone number.

I mindlessly reached into my purse for something to write on while he handed me a pen. I wrote my number on the back of a dog-eared business card from The Flower Box. Our eyes held on as I handed it to him, but neither of us spoke.

Maggie and I walked through the restaurant in silence. As soon as we stepped outside onto the magical street, we laughed in total abandon amongst the hundreds of strangers under the neon lights.

Almost thirty years have passed since that night. Even now when I remember it, I pause, close my eyes, and smile. A window opens in my soul, and a fresh breeze drifts over me. And for a moment, like that night, nothing exists but now and forever. No fears or sadness, no need to forgive, nothing to hold me back, just possibilities and passion to empower every dream.

Chapter Four

"Hey, Lily." Miss Elaine, the owner of The Flower Box, came around the large table where I worked arranging gladiolas in a tall vase. "What's going on with you?" She planted her hands on her hips and tilted her head to the side. I noticed the bemused expression on her face.

"What do you mean, Miss Elaine?"

"Well, look at you. Miss Sunshine. You've been flitting around here like a butterfly."

I giggled. "Oh. I was thinking about my trip to New York."

"Fun, huh? I'd love to go there myself one day . . . Central Park, Times Square . . . haven't seen 'em yet."

"You have to go. Gives you a whole new perspective."

"Well, you don't say." She spritzed the display glass with window cleaner and buffed it crystal clear.

"Yeah," I said. "I found myself contemplating . . ." I couldn't think of the right words. Then I blurted out "the mysteries of life."

"Well, in that case, I need to make some travel plans." She laughed. "But, I can't see getting my Harold to give up his weekends at the lake to visit New York City."

"I'll show you the pictures we took when I get them back. In fact, I'm picking them up tonight." I'd embarrassed myself by my childish choice of words.

As soon as I got off work, I headed over to the pharmacy. Miss Elaine was right. I felt lighter somehow since the trip to New York. Somehow those few days had changed my outlook.

I couldn't wait to look at the pictures. I'd made doubles so I could send some to Maggie, Julie, and to Annie Ruth. As soon as I got home, I spread them out on the desk. Which ones to send to Julie? The picture of me at the Metropolitan for sure. Picture postcard perfect—me, the smiling tourist on the broad marble steps. I picked up the one Maggie had taken of me in front of Tiffany's. We were so full of ourselves, I thought, remembering the rings we'd tried on.

Although deliberately looking at each picture, reliving the scenes, in the back of my mind, I was looking for one in particular. When I saw the picture of Maggie and me at Valenti's, I paused and looked closely. We looked radiantly happy and carefree. And then, I saw the picture of *us*. I studied the wavy black hair and heavy eyebrows, those deep brown eyes, his straight nose and square jaw. My *goodness*, he *was* handsome, and he looked so polished. As finely chiseled as Michelangelo's David.

I wrote the names of places and dates on the back of each photo. When I got to his, I paused and closed my eyes.

"Hello, my name is Manuel. I will be your waiter tonight." His caramel-smooth voice replayed in my mind.

I'd already turned out the light when I thought of him again. I couldn't rest until I got up and looked at the picture one more time. I stared at his lips, full and sweet. And those dark eyes . . . there was a story in those eyes. I pulled the picture closer. Something else was there. Was it sadness? Whatever it was, his eyes captivated me.

I climbed back into bed, ready to dream again of hot dog vendors, carriage rides through Central Park, and a certain brown eyed waiter, all the while wondering if he'd ever call me.

"Lily Rose," I said aloud in the dark. "He's already forgotten you and your silly little card."

The next day, I mailed Julie some pictures, including the one of me and the Italian waiter. As I knew she would, she phoned me as soon as she got them. We practically squealed with delight when we connected.

"So you went to New York without me. *And* met a man?"

"Oh, wouldn't you have liked to have been there," I teased.

"You know it," she said. "Now stop stalling. I'm all ears."

So I told her about my trip, including the intriguing photo op in Little Italy.

"It's just a souvenir of New York," I said. "He hasn't called, and I don't expect he will."

"Well, you never know," Julie said. "You never know. Remember how long it took Charles to let on that he wanted me?"

I made no response to her playful banter, but I was intrigued just the same. Warmth filled my body at the thought of Manuel wanting me. Julie and I chatted for an hour. She regaled me with stories about her marriage and their charmed life in Quebec City. I told her about my jobs at the newspaper and the flower shop. Her joy was contagious. All my qualms about her marriage evaporated. I was truly happy for her, especially now that I was beginning to understand so much more about life.

And love.

Chapter Five

I've often wondered what my life would have been like if I'd never met Manuel Valenti. Would I have experienced such sweet pleasures or suffered such cruel pains? I can't imagine really. The truth is, at that moment in my life, my heart longed for love. I grabbed hold of its promise like a drowning person grabs hold of a life jacket. It was vital for my survival. I flung open my heart, he walked in, and I grabbed hold.

He called a few days after my conversation with Julie. I was just unlocking the door late that Friday night when I heard the telephone ringing. I rushed to get it, but the caller had already hung up. I shrugged, got ready for bed, and watched a few minutes of Johnny Carson. I'd already fallen asleep when the shrill ringing woke me.

"Hello," I whispered in a voice hoarse with sleep.

"Hello. Did you have fun today?"

I struggled to find my voice. "Excuse me?" My voice shook. I felt confused.

"Oh no, excuse me," he apologized. "I've startled you." His tone was kind. I paused, shaky still, searching for sense on the edge of sleep.

"Don't hang up," he said. "This is Manuel Valenti. I'm the man who served you in Valenti's restaurant . . . in New York City."

I still couldn't manage to speak.

"You've forgotten?"

"Oh, no, I remember. You just woke me up," I stammered.

"I'm sorry," he said. "Should I call you back tomorrow?"

"I'm working . . . a wedding . . . but I should be home after eight."

"Good," he said. "I'll call. Go back to sleep, Lily."

I fumbled the phone hanging it up. Closing my eyes, I thought of his smooth voice. Already drifting back to sleep, the call felt surreal. Perhaps, maybe, I had only dreamed it.

The next day passed in a flurry of ribbons and rosebuds. I delighted in the dozens of tiny details needed to make someone's perfect day. But by the time I got home, I was feeling nervous in anticipation of his call. I pulled out the pictures and set the one of the two of us by the phone. I had just showered and fixed myself something to drink when the phone rang. My heart skipped a beat. I took a deep breath before picking up the phone.

"Hello." I listened, my breathing stopped.

"Now that's a nice hello." I heard the smile in his voice. "This is your midnight caller."

"Hi, Manuel."

"I'm sorry I called so late last night. I'd already called a couple of times with no answer, so I didn't expect to wake you."

"It's okay." I relaxed a bit then. "You're lucky I remember you called at all. I've been known to forget entire conversations I've had when awakened like that."

"Hmm, I *am* lucky." Somehow I knew he was smiling, and I imagined his face. "I intended to call you weeks ago, but work got in the way."

"Well, I can understand. That restaurant does great business. How long have you worked there?"

"Only all my life," he said.

"Really?"

"It's our family restaurant. My father opened it before I was born. Naturally, I grew up working there."

"Oh."

"Now, when I go home, it's still a thing I do, from time to time," he said.

"When you go home?"

"I go home a few times a year since my father died to check on my mother. My brother owns the restaurant now."

When he mentioned the death of his father, pain pricked a tender place in my heart. I understood his loss.

"I'm *so* sorry," I said. "How long ago did he pass away?"

"My father? Oh, two years ago."

An awkward moment of silence passed between us. Afraid I might have touched a wound and unsure of what to say, I diverted the conversation.

"Well, tell me, where do you live when you aren't in New York?"

"Detroit, I live in Detroit."

"Wow, another big city."

"Yes. I love the city. It's the only way for me to operate."

"And I'm a small town girl."

"You certainly are, Lily Rose. Innocence personified."

Warmth spread over my cheeks, and I was glad he couldn't see me blush.

"Are you in the restaurant business in Detroit?"

"No, no, that's an entirely different way of life. I'm an attorney."

"An attorney?" I didn't intend to sound surprised, but it came out that way just the same.

"An attorney," he said with a chuckle. "But I didn't call to talk about me. Tell me all about yourself. I want to know you."

We talked so long my ear was burning when we hung up. Conversation was easy between us. Everything in my life had led up to us knowing each other, or so it felt to me. He led a fascinating life. Yet he was interested in me. I found myself waiting for his next call. As it turned out, he felt the same way.

"I couldn't wait any longer," he said a few days later. "I had to hear your sweet voice."

From that time on, he called every night. I hurried home after work, so I'd be waiting when the phone rang. Every moment of the day, I thought of him, and at night I lay awake imagining encounters, creating scenarios of the two of us together. We shared our thoughts and told each other stories about our days. I felt like I really knew him well and that he knew me.

We talked about having Christmas together in New York . . . about waiting to see each other until then and how difficult that was going to be. The wanting turned to longing, making the interval seem impossible.

"Lily Rose, I dream about you. I want to see you, to touch you, to hold you in my arms." He filled me with a dreamy longing like nothing I'd ever known and I fell under the magic spell of desire.

***

One day in late September as I waited for his call, I opened a letter from the landlord. Since my lease was up at the end of October, I assumed the letter was regarding renewal. Instead, it informed me that the landlord wanted to move an elderly parent into the house and that I would need to move out by October 31. I reread the words—*move out.* They punched me in the stomach. *Move out.* That was the last thing I wanted to do.

When Manny called a few minutes later, I felt stunned and slightly sick. My head ached acutely.

"I can tell something's wrong by your voice. What is it?"

I told him about the letter. *Move out. Unsettled from my home, unexpectedly. I was being uprooted.* I burst into tears.

"Lily, don't give it another thought. I mean it. Let me think it through. If you need to move I will help you find the right place. I will personally take care of it for you."

A new feeling rushed to take the place of the anxiety I was feeling. I had not had a man to lean on for personal matters, since my father died. I had missed his reassuring presence. I sighed with relief. Manny was someone I wanted to trust.

The next day, for the first time in more than a month, he didn't call. I was baffled. Sure, I could have called him, but he'd always called me, so I waited. When no call came the day after that, I missed him terribly and prayed nothing was wrong. On the third day, when he didn't call, I fought nausea all day and regretted not having called him in the first place. Over and over I replayed our last conversation in my mind and regretted my tears.

Friday afternoon I unpacked a shipment of fresh flowers at the shop. Knowing this was my favorite part of the job, Miss Elaine left for the day, leaving the pleasant task to me. I sorted bunches of fragrant blooms into colored buckets in the cooler. Soft music played. In the cool stillness, I thought of Manuel. Tears had been close to the surface all day, and this moment was no exception. I reconciled myself to the fact that tears would fall. But, I won't let myself mistrust his love, I thought.

He loves me. I know he does. He has to. Please Lord, don't let me lose him now. I need him.

I was so caught up in my thoughts, I didn't hear the bell on the shop door ring, or the glass door of the cooler room slide open. Warm hands gently grasped the sides of my waist from behind. At the same moment, he spoke my name touching his lips to my hair.

"Manuel?" I leaned into him. "I dreamed you'd come."

My head rested back on his chest. I didn't need to see; I knew it was him. He cradled me there for a moment. Then, like some instinctive dance, I turned and encircled his neck with my arms. We clung to each other in an embrace that seemed to fill eternity. His lips found mine and he kissed me with such passion, my knees went weak. There was no hiding the emotions, my joy, my relief.

"Let's get you out of this cold room. You're trembling." He slid open the door and escorted me into the warmth beyond.

"What have you done to me?" He whispered, trembling too. We laughed at our wonderful crazy love and said our hellos with dozens of tiny kisses. It took a few minutes for our hearts to settle down.

"Can I take you home and then pick you up at seven for a proper date?" He smiled down into my face.

"That would be perfect," I said.

He gently held my cheeks in his hands and lightly kissed my lips. When I looked into his eyes, I could see our future . . . at least the part of it that we were to enjoy.

Chapter Six

It was just like Manuel to have planned every detail of that evening. The drive home from the shop seemed surreal. While he looked at the road ahead, I gazed at his clean cut profile and smooth tanned skin, and willed my heart to be still.

He took my hand, curling his manicured fingers around my slender ones.

"I can't believe you're here," I whispered. "I worried when you didn't call."

"I've been busy." He chuckled to himself.

I sighed. Handsome and tailored, he looked professional, in complete control, whereas I was as jumpy as a new puppy.

Neither of us moved for a minute when we stopped in the driveway. For a moment we were locked in a gaze. Then I reached for the door handle.

"Wait. Not so fast," he said. When he smiled, I melted. When he opened my door, he slid his arm around my waist in one fluid movement and drew me against him. His lips brushed mine, then returned to kiss more deeply. I kissed him back. We leaned on one another as we made our way to the door.

"Be back soon," he said.

"What should I wear?" I asked, suddenly self-conscious.

"Surprise me." He turned and walked down the sidewalk, then looked back and winked.

Oh my, and what is that supposed to mean? For the first time I felt completely out of my league.

"If I knew where we were going, I'd choose better." I called to him.

"No way, that's my surprise." He flashed a perfect white smile before getting into the car.

My heart beat in every muscle of my body—I felt each breath expand my chest. This was an entirely different milieu than schmoozing one another over the phone. I was accustomed to the sound of his voice, not to the flesh and blood man.

I dashed into the bedroom, stripping off pieces of clothing as I made my way to the claw foot tub. I turned the faucet on full force. The sound of running water soothed my nerves. Grabbing clumps of honey colored hair I wound it around large rollers before stepping into the warm bath. The scent of lavender swirled around me.

Moments later still damp from the bath, I opened the closet door and scanned the contents, then brushed aside each article until I came to the paisley teal dress I'd worn to Vicky's wedding rehearsal. Its spliced bodice crisscrossed in a low V, revealing just a kiss of cleavage. I smiled at the memory of how beautiful I felt with the silk draping my hips' gentle curves. And I wondered how he would like it.

The doorbell rang precisely at seven. When I opened the door, his eyes widened and his brows arched in an unapologetic appraisal. I caught only a glimpse of that expression before he bestowed a quick kiss on my lips. He reached for my hand and we walked in silence to the car. He opened the door for me and waited patiently as I smoothed my dress.

"Wow!" he exclaimed, sliding into the driver's seat and slamming the door.

I giggled at his monosyllabic expletive, tucked my chin down, and smiled sweetly at him. He threw back his head and laughed loudly, then spun out the drive. Neither of us spoke for a few minutes and I began to relax.

We drove past the university toward my favorite part of town. Gnarled limbs of ancient oaks entwined over the road. Magnificent historic mansions framed by lush magnolias sat back behind manicured lawns, flowering shrubs, and rose gardens. Landmark churches and historical markers dotted every street. I pointed out some of the places I'd already told him about.

"Where are you staying?" I asked.

"You'll see."

When we approached a shady turn he glanced at me as if he watched for my reaction. He squinted and smiled a tight-lipped smile. The thought crossed my mind—*he's teasing me.*

At that moment I had a fuzzy notion that I had underestimated Manuel Valenti. I was amazed to find myself, a girl who rarely dated, with a mature man like him—sophisticated, handsome, intriguing.

Then we turned into the drive of The Presidential Inn. I gasped.

"Manny. You remembered."

"Of course, my dear, I remember every word you've spoken."

I'd told him how I dreamt of staying there in the penthouse someday like celebrities and presidents had done in years past.

Someone was playing "Nobody Does it Better" on a grand piano as we walked up the stairs to the veranda—the trellis laced with tiny yellow roses. The scent hung heavy in the evening air along with the hum of voices and the clinking of glasses from other guests enjoying their *tête-à-tête* alfresco.

No fairy godmother could have created a more enchanted evening. Soft music played while we dined by candlelight. Romance and roses scented the air. I can't tell you what we talked about, exactly. An aura of intimacy and fascination made it seem we'd known each other forever, and that it would now be our constant delight to know each other more and more. The future unfolded as hopes and dreams were unveiled.

The hours passed like seconds. Beautiful desserts designed like works of art completed our romantic dinner.

"You have to taste this." Manny lifted his fork to my lips.

I opened my mouth for a taste of his chocolate raspberry torte while feasting my eyes on his perfectly handsome face.

Licking the chocolate from his lips, Manny straightened and pushed back a bit. Then, reaching inside his jacket, he brought out a small blue box tied with white satin ribbon and set it on the table between us.

My eyes leaped from the box to his eyes. He nodded as if replying to the unspoken question on my face.

Gingerly I reached forward, and he laid his hand on mine. He lifted my hand, turned it over, and pressed his lips to the palm. A tingle of delight ran through me, along with an inexplicable tinge of something else.

"Open it," he said as he released my hand.

Butterflies fluttered in my belly. With trembling fingers, I untied the bow. He didn't smile, only observed my face, my eyes.

"What? How is this possible?" Unmistakable surprise was in my voice.

"Is that the right one?" He smiled a self-satisfied smile.

"It's the same one," I whispered.

Diamonds sparkled in a magnificent square cut diamond ring with heart diamonds gracing each side. Exactly like the one I'd tried on in Tiffany's. Bedazzled, I couldn't take my eyes off the ring.

"How did you know?" I asked in amazement.

"Your cousin wasn't difficult to find. Then, after I told Maggie what I wanted, she didn't mind at all taking me to see the ring you'd chosen."

My mouth fell open. I can't explain my emotions— flattered, well of course, who wouldn't be. To think Manuel had tracked down my cousin based on the little story I'd told, and convinced her to accompany him. But, how had he convinced her, practically a total stranger, to go with him to Tiffany's in order to show him the ring that I'd tried on weeks before? I felt odd . . . strangely disconcerted, and I didn't know why.

"Well?" Manny arched a brow and waited for my response.

My heart and mind played a tug-of-war. "Oh . . . I'm amazed. It's gorgeous. I love it."

He brushed the back of his finger lightly across my cheek. "Not as gorgeous as those big green eyes that melt my heart."

"Oh, Manny, I don't know what to say."

"How about 'Yes'?"

I looked into his eyes, but no words formed.

A flicker of emotion passed over his brow. Impatience? How could I judge? I couldn't figure out my own emotions at that moment—it would have been impossible to figure out his. As it was, I felt shaky.

"I'm amazed at you," he said. "One minute you're a vamp. And the next minute you've transformed into an innocent little girl."

His words along with the suddenly stern look on his face confounded me. "Manny, I'm so surprised I can't think straight."

"It's quite all right, darling," he said, although I'm sure nervous giggles were not the response he desired.

He took the dazzling ring out of its box.

"Let's see how it fits." The perfectly sized ring slid onto my finger before I could utter a word. "You wear it this weekend while your little head settles."

I couldn't bring myself to say no. An awkward pause resulted from my struggles to form a coherent phrase.

It's funny how our minds work sometimes. If I'd had time to think, I might have realized the significance of what popped into my head the next moment . . . but he didn't give me time to think. I didn't have the good sense to take time.

"Manny, I promised Annie Ruth I'd come home this weekend. Would you like to go home with me?"

He shifted his position, put his elbow on the table, and propped his head on his fist.

"You mean I can meet your elusive family?" For a second I thought he mocked me.

"Elusive?"

"That's what I was beginning to think. You've said almost nothing about your family. You've talked all about your girlfriends, the university . . . ," He leaned closer and smiled. "And your visit with your cousin in New York."

"Oh." Memories hidden away. Remembrances too tender to talk about without unraveling myself.

Manny squeezed my hand and leaned closer. He'd recovered his charm. "I'm here all weekend. I'd love to meet your mother and Annie Ruth."

With that, I took a deep breath. My first sips of champagne rekindled the magic and more.

If I could bottle a moment in time, and pour it out when I need to feel romanced, I'd bottle that evening. On the dance floor, we melted into each other's arms. Our bodies touched and seemed to float as one in a paradise of earthy and sensual pleasures. By the time Manny's lips found mine for good-night kisses, a part of him had engrafted itself eternally into my heart . . . although my fanciful thoughts even then tried to figure out the unearthly pull he had on me.

Later, I watched the moonlight waltz across my bedroom for hours, replaying in my mind the magical moments we'd shared. My feelings were in a muddle. He'd asked me to marry him, so unexpectedly . . . although he hadn't actually asked me. He offered the gorgeous ring and said, "Say yes"—which seemed more commandeering than a proposal of marriage. Then again, he was soft-spoken and good-looking, rather spectacular really. One look at him caused all thoughts, coherent or not, to fly to the moon. He was here, he wanted me, and that's all I could think about.

***

We started the drive to my childhood home at ten the following morning. After we'd driven out of town, Manny looked out across the fields like we were in the backwoods of no man's land. I laughed.

"Manny, would you please stop up ahead at the produce stand, just ahead on the left. That old farmer always has nice fruits and vegetables. I wonder if there's anything left from the summer crops."

"You want to stop there?" he asked, nodding in the direction of the tin roofed shack.

"If you don't mind. I always pick up something for Annie Ruth. She loves everything homegrown."

"Oh, your maid."

"Manny. I never think of Annie Ruth as the maid. Our relationship is not like that at all. She's been a mother to me."

"Sure, okay." He shrugged. "I knew that. I'm sorry."

Manny pulled off the main road onto a dirt road at the corner of a big corn field. A substantial wooden stand lined with bushel baskets punctuated the scene. Signs made of rough boards painted with names of vegetables and fruits had seen better days.

"Hi there." I waved to the weathered old man in overalls and a baseball hat. Manny appeared disinterested, but he gave the old man a solemn faced nod.

"Hey there, little lady." He flicked a cigarette behind him and wiped his hands on his pant legs before
thrusting his hand toward me. "What'chu up to?"

I shook the farmer's hand and smiled.

"Oh, about five feet three. Let's see now what'chu
got. The corn's all gone. Too bad. You had pretty corn this
year. Vidalia onions. Tomatoes, still? Amazing. Umm.
Manny, smell this tomato." I held a tomato the size of a
man's fist to his nose. Not like those plastic ones for sale in
the grocery store." Manny smiled a tight lipped smile and
continued looking at the produce.

"How about some of those collard greens? A good
size mess," I said.

The old man put the vegetables in individual paper
bags while I made small talk. Then he put them all in a
brown grocery sack.

Manny had an odd expression on his face when we
got in the car.

"What?" I asked, leaning closer to catch his eye.

"Did you know that man?"

"No, I don't know him," I said, shaking my head.
"Well, I've seen him before when I've stopped there, but I
don't know him."

"You sure were talking to him like you did."

"That's how we do down here in Georgia, Manny.
It's a Southern thing."

"I see . . . must be." He gave me a sidelong glance,
then shook his head and smiled. When he smiled, I did too.

"Gee, won't Annie Ruth be surprised," I said. "I
didn't tell her who our guest would be."

We drove on under a big blue sky, past fields of cotton and dried up sunflowers. I was as happy as a little wren
and just as oblivious to any cares around me.

Our house was a large white clapboard Victorian with a wide front porch. It sat at the end of a dirt drive on the outskirts of town behind massive oak trees, pines, and dogwoods. I loved how the front door and the porch steps peeked out like a shy lady welcoming you as you approached.

Annie Ruth came out the front door and watched us drive up. Her sweet smile vanished when she laid eyes on Manuel.

I've never seen anything like it in my life . . . before or since. In a New York minute, that little old woman saw clean through to that man's soul, and he knew she had. Me . . . well . . . I guess I saw what I wanted to see, and he knew that too.

Annie Ruth met me as I got out the car.

"Oh, come here child, and give me a hug." She squeezed me tight, and then held me at arms' length by my shoulders, squaring me in front of her so she could look at my face. Annie Ruth's hugs always made me feel beloved. "You jus' get prettier and prettier. You sho' do."

"Hey, Mama." I waved to her. She stood up momentarily, still holding the chair arm, and then sat right back down.

"Annie Ruth, I'd like for you to meet my friend, Manuel Valenti." He smiled and stepped forward, putting out his hand to her. "We met when I was up in New York visiting Maggie."

"Good afternoon, Mr. Valenti." She took his hand. Had I been seeing clearly, I would have noticed her coolness. As it was, I just noticed polite good manners.

"Manny's a lawyer. He lives in Detroit. He's visiting me for the weekend."

"Well, come on in. I've been cooking for y'all all morning."

We climbed the steps and walked over to where Mama sat in the porch swing. She glanced up and reached out her hand to me like she was groping in the dark. When I took hers, she squeezed mine.

"Why, Lily Rose, aren't you pretty. You look like a grown lady."

I kissed her cheek, and said, "How you feeling Mama?"

"Feeling fine." She released my hand and resumed gazing out across the yard. You could never tell if she was looking at the trees, or the sky, or if she was gazing through an invisible veil.

"Mama, I want you to meet my friend, Manuel Valenti. He's visiting me this weekend." I stepped aside to allow Manny to move closer.

"It's nice to meet you Mrs. Cates."

"It's nice to meet you." Mama smiled, but didn't get up, only took that moment to push her heel across the floor and start the swing swaying.

"Y'all come on in." Annie Ruth held open the screen door.

"Y'all go on in," Mama repeated. "I'll just wait here 'til Daddy gets home."

Manny gave me a curious look.

"It's all right," Annie Ruth said in a low voice. "She says that most days. When she's good and ready, she'll come in." We entered the cool shadows of the house.

Manny followed, carrying the sack of vegetables. Suddenly, he looked out of place. I grabbed the sack to relieve the awkwardness, and handed it to Annie Ruth.

"We brought you some vegetables, Annie Ruth, from that produce stand up the road."

"Oh, bless your heart, you know how I love 'em. Let's take 'em on back to the kitchen."

"I'll help you finish dinner."

We walked into the spacious, sun-dappled room. Manny looked out at the pond down the hill past the back-yard. Annie Ruth took vegetables out the bags and pressed them to her nose before setting them down while I peeped under the lids of pots steaming on the stove. Delicious aromas caused my mouth to water. It smelled like home.

"Watch that grease, Lily Rose. I just turned it on."

I noted the black cast iron frying pan on the stove. Annie Ruth had fried a lot of chicken and catfish in that old iron pan.

"Lily, why don't I walk down to the pond and have a look," Manny said. "I'll get in your way in here." He glanced at Annie Ruth and smiled.

"Sure, go ahead. What time will dinner be ready, Annie Ruth?"

"'Bout two."

I watched Manny walk across the back yard, past the plum trees, and down the hill. Annie Ruth's little dog Rascal ran up the hill to meet him, prancing circles around Manny's feet and bouncing up to his thighs. Manny gave him a little sideways kick, then looked back over his shoulder and smiled at me. I laughed at him and the frisky dog. I turned to look at Annie Ruth and saw she'd been watching, too, with her hands on her hips.

"Lily Rose, what are you doing with that *man*?"

"Annie Ruth, you stop it," I said. "Can't you tell he's my boyfriend?" Rather than brightening, the look on her face turned into a sour scowl.

"Isn't he handsome? He's a lawyer all settled down in Detroit."

Annie Ruth shook her head. "I don't care what he is. He's trouble. He looks just like trouble to me. And you ain't lost nothing in Detroit that you need to go find."

I clicked my tongue, and exhaled an exaggerated sigh. "He's been as sweet as anyone could possibly be, Annie Ruth. Believe me."

"He ain't *nothin'* like your daddy. I know that."

I rolled my eyes. "Oh, Annie Ruth, I know there's no one like *Daddy,* but Manny is a fine, well-educated man. He's well established in his career. Never married. We've really hit it off."

"Does he know Jesus?" She looked at me with piercing eyes. "Now, you jus' answer me that."

"Well, Annie Ruth, I'm sure he's Christian, and for that matter, he's asked me to be his wife." I held out my hand at arm's length between us.

Annie Ruth's mouth dropped open. "What are you thinking?" she asked when she recovered her voice.

With that, she wiped her hands on her apron and plopped down on the stool by the sink like all her strength had left her. She then swiped the dishcloth across her forehead. Seeing I had upset her, I went to her and draped my arm across her shoulders and gave her a little shake.

"Annie Ruth . . . it's all right . . . really."

"No child . . . that man's not right for you." She shook her head. "Not right a' tall. You must be seeing things all peachy 'cause that's how you are inside."

"Oh, Annie Ruth. I know . . . it's unexpected. It's all new to me, too. I've never had a serious boyfriend. But I think Manuel might be the one."

Her head and shoulders drooped. Then, she raised up and passionately exclaimed, "You lay down with dogs, you get up with fleas!" She said the words like she was spitting nails. Had she been a swearing woman, there's no telling what she'd have let fly in the kitchen that day.

"Annie Ruth!" I didn't know what to say. Her reaction would have been humorous, but for her obvious distress. Never in my life had I gone against her. I shifted my weight from side to side, waiting for her to recover her usual demeanor . . . waiting for the uneasiness to pass.

"Well, it's not for sure yet. I haven't said 'yes'. I'm just wearing the ring."

She looked at me and shook her head. "It ain't done like that." She sounded tired then.

Hot grease popped like a firecracker in the frying pan. I never thought that could be a welcome sound. But Annie Ruth got up then, dipped the pieces of chicken into the batter, and gently laid them one by one into the sizzling grease.

That was my cue. I wasted no time washing vegetables and getting out the cutting board. I sliced juicy red tomatoes and Vidalia onions and placed them on a plate with fresh basil.

Annie Ruth and I didn't say another word, but as we performed the familiar routine, the tension ebbed away. When Manny came back inside, the table was set, and the tall tea glasses were filled with ice.

Annie Ruth and I looked at one another. Then she glanced at Manny.

"You can step in there to wash your hands," Annie Ruth said to him.

I smiled at her. I could see love shining in her eyes.

"I'll just take this glass of sweet tea to Mama and see if she'll come in now."

The amazing spread included mashed potatoes, fried okra, butter peas, tomatoes, deviled eggs, butter pickles, fried chicken, biscuits, sour cream pound cake, fresh whipped cream, and coconut custard pie. Our dinner the night before had been delicious, but there's something extra special about a Southern home cooked meal that puts the rest to shame.

"Miss Annie Ruth, these are the best biscuits and mashed potatoes I've ever eaten."

"Help yourself to som' more. There's plenty," Annie Ruth said.

"Can you cook like this?" Manny lifted his eyebrows and smiled at me.

"Well, I've had the best teacher," I said, "but the truth is, I need practice. It takes skill to make so many dishes at once. Annie Ruth just makes it look simple, but it's not."

"Well, I don't think I've ever had such a delicious meal. You can't find food like this in Detroit."

"You sho' can't," Annie Ruth said, although she had no way of knowing. She'd never been outside of Macon County. I smiled. Manuel was laying on the charm, but Annie Ruth wasn't going to let him put anything over on her.

"Why don't ya'll sit in the living room while I fix the coffee," Annie Ruth said when she pushed back from the table.

"I'll help you clear the dishes."

"No you won't. Shoo."

So Manny and I moved into the living room and settled side by side on the sofa. We looked at the family picture album, full of smiles and memories. In its pages, I introduced him to my dear daddy and James Michael. Then we enjoyed dessert and coffee served by Annie Ruth. We agreed it was delicious and thanked her heartily, which pleased her to no end.

Then we ladies went out on the front porch, leaving Manny looking at Daddy's framed arrowhead collection. Mama barely stirred when we walked out and sat in the rocking chairs.

"You fixing flowers at the florist shop, Lily Rose?" Mama asked. "And all graduated." Her face, pale and serene, reminded me of a porcelain doll's.

"Yes, Mama, that's right." She was the same frail little woman she'd always been, just older and waiting for Daddy now instead of James Michael.

Manny's footsteps sounded on the heart pine floor of the living room, prompting Annie Ruth to speak before he joined us on the porch.

"Lily Rose," she said in a hushed voice. "Don't you get tangled up in the briers with that man."

We looked directly into each other's eyes, and an understanding passed between us. Even after such a pleasant afternoon, she hadn't changed her mind one bit. She saw in my face that I hadn't changed mine either. She let out a deflated sigh just as Manny walked out on the porch.

Chapter Seven

On the drive back to my house, Manny and I were quiet. Neither of us had much to say about the day. I was too busy thinking about Annie Ruth to wonder about what he was thinking. While the moon was still high and the diamonds still twinkled on my finger, Manny went back to Detroit.

"Come to Detroit with me," he said.

I clasped my hands together and pressed them to my lips. He gathered them into his, and drew me close, which caused my heart to race even more. I felt a little light-headed.

"Manny, I want to . . . it's just too soon." It took everything in me to say those words.

"It's okay," he said softly. "There's no hurry." And when he said that, I wondered if he was trying to reassure himself or me.

Manny took my chin in his hand and looked down into my face. "I'll come back for you. You're the only girl for me." He kissed my cheek, and when his lips, warm and enticing, touched mine, I sensed a need within us both. A sense of security overwhelmed me when he wrapped me in his arms. Those were the moments I wanted to beg him to stay. He romanced reason right out of my head. Hot tears stung my eyes.

He had to get back to Detroit, he said, but insisted I wear the ring. I didn't want to give it up any more than I wanted to let him go. Little did I realize that Manny had already decided he'd have me, so I might as well have kept it. It was one of my consolations, but in the end, it wasn't to be the most precious one.

***

By after work Monday, reality had returned. I needed to find a place to live. I stopped in the grocery store and picked up several real estate brochures, the newspaper, and a head of lettuce. I wanted to start looking immediately for a new place. And after the weekend of fine dining and champagne, fried chicken and sweet tea, I planned to eat salad and little else.

For the first time in my life I was aware of my feminine appeal, the softness of my skin, the sensuality of my curves. I felt energized. Manny brought out sensations I'd never felt before. Physical senses were heightened, but my emotional self was wavering. Being in love caused a maddening mixture of pleasure and pain.

Sitting at Daddy's desk, with a glass of iced water and carrot sticks, I spread the newspaper out in front of me. I told myself equilibrium would return as soon as I found a new place. I simply wanted to continue the delight-

ful romance, but take my time before moving on with a serious commitment. In my head and heart, I knew that was
best. I got up the gumption to tell Manny my decision—not
in person, but by phone, and when he agreed, I felt relieved. I said a silent prayer, thanking God for Manuel's
understanding.

Pen in hand, I circled several possibilities for a new
place: two bedroom stucco on Hill Street with a piazza,
large upstairs studio apartment with private entrance, a
small two bedroom cottage.

House hunting wouldn't be so bad, or so I thought.
I launched right into it. Julie, Vicky, and I had been
blessed to have had low rent for the lovely little stucco.
Everything I looked at in my price range was run-down,
even shabby. The perks my budget provided included faded paint, faulty plumbing, and cockroaches. Yuck. After
three weeks of frustrations exacerbated by time pressure, I
broke down in tears while on the phone with Manny.

"Baby, why are you putting yourself through this?"
His voice was soothing and gentle. "I want nothing as
much as I want to take care of you . . . make you my wife."

I focused on his voice and blew my nose.

"Are you listening to me, Lily?"

"Uh, huh." I nodded and sniffed.

"Lily, darling?"

"I'm listening Manny." I sniffed again. "You're so
sweet to me."

"I love you, Lily."

My stomach tightened, and a longing filled my belly
and moved up to my heart. What a twenty-two-year-old
girl in love *feels,* is more *real* than reality, stronger than
reason.

"Oh, Manny, I love you too." As soon as I said it, loneliness and loss washed over me, and I began to sob like a heart-broken child. I wanted him to hold me, I wanted his arms around me, and all those words gushed out with the tears.

"Lily, I can't take this. You've got to let me come get you. Tell me you will?"

"I will. I will." I wiped my eyes with the heels of my hand. "I'm sorry. I don't know what's wrong with me. I'm just torn up. My emotions are shot."

"You could say that, sweetheart." He sounded relieved. "But nothing at all is wrong with you. You're perfect. You can come live with me in Detroit. Stop house hunting. There's no reason we should stay apart."

And when he said it that time, I realized I had already relented. I could think of only one good reason to stay apart.

"Except, I can't live with you if we aren't married, Manny."

"I wouldn't have it any other way," he said. "I know you're old-fashioned. Take a look at the ring on your finger." He chuckled a little.

I held up my hand and gazed at the dazzling ring. I didn't want to think about it anymore. I couldn't resist Manny. But, I knew I couldn't tarnish Daddy's ideal of his little girl or tarnish his ideal of marriage either.

"Can we marry at the chapel here at my church?" I asked.

"I don't see why not."

I envisioned an intimate flower strewn ceremony before the marble altar, the sunlight shining through the stained glass windows casting rose colored light in the stone chapel. "Oh, it will be wonderful."

"I'll arrange for the movers and take care of all the expenses. You get busy planning the wedding."

That's exactly what I did. As soon as I told her the news, Miss Elaine took charge, ordering enough hydrangeas, roses, and baby's breath to fill the chapel. She and the girls from the florist shop prepared everything. I found an antique white lace tea length dress from the upscale second-hand boutique, "Something Borrowed Something Blue." I wrote invitations to a dozen friends, and called Maggie, Julie, and Vicky. Manny didn't want a full blown family affair, and would have only one of his colleagues come down for the ceremony.

Somehow I couldn't bring myself to call Annie Ruth. I convinced myself that it made perfect sense not to call her until right before we left for Detroit—that it was just too short notice to spring the news on her, that Mama would require such careful handling, and since James Michael was in France he would never make it on time. So, I didn't call. The three short weeks passed in a blur. It was easy to put Annie Ruth out of my thoughts. I was so busy making arrangements for the wedding and move there was no time to ponder that particular.

The wedding was perfect. The chapel was enchanting, and everyone said they'd never seen such a beautiful bride. My groom was magnificent with an absolute air of distinction. Not a hair was out of place on his handsome head. The wedding celebration continued at The Presidential Inn. By midnight, we'd dined and danced for as long as we could bear it. We slipped away under a shower of rose petals to the penthouse of my dreams. There we spent three days and four nights, each blending together into one breathless ecstasy.

Chapter Eight

Tuesday morning, I awoke with Manny's arm across my chest. His rhythmic breathing, soft on my face, made me smile. I was so in love with him, and in complete amazement of the man I married. The mystery of love between a man and a woman, sanctified by holy matrimony, is impossible to imagine . . . the pleasure, the passion like no other. It's no wonder it's called the "bonds" of matrimony. I was bound up tight, in more ways than I could have imagined.

He was a tender lover, and after those times of intimacy, he was as open with his heart, and as honest as it was ever possible for him to be. Those were the times I knew him best and loved him most. Those were the times we understood each other, offered tenderness, and made promises that couldn't be kept. Even now, I know he meant it when he said he loved me. He loved me as much as he was able.

On that Tuesday morning, a courtesy call woke us. The ringing jarred my waking dreams.

Manny reached for the phone. "Yes? Okay, thanks." He fell back heavily on the pillow.

"No-o," he groaned. "Not over yet." Our eyes met, and he smiled a sad smile before drawing me tight against his chest.

"I love you, Lily." His voice was hushed. "Don't ever forget it."

"I love you too, darling."

"We've got to go back to the real world," he said, his face buried in my hair. "Back to Detroit," he whispered.

"I can't believe we have to leave already."

"The movers will be there by eleven," he said, "and the phone will be disconnected this afternoon." He sat up then. "You take the first shower while I order breakfast." He brushed his lips to mine as he reached for the room service menu. All business now, but still, I didn't understand his gloomy mood.

"But, I'm not getting up Manny 'til you smile for me," I teased.

He stopped, tilted his head toward me, and smiled.

"And I'll do one better," he said. He closed the gap between us with a kiss.

***

"Come on Lily. Your breakfast is getting cold."

I slipped into my robe and joined him at the table near the balcony. He set down the newspaper and leaned close.

"Good morning, Mrs.Valenti. You're so beautiful today." His eyes sparkled and crinkled at the sides.

I reached for his hand, wanting desperately to hold onto this special time.

He took the last bite of his muffin and finished his coffee. "Getting my shower now, sweetheart," he said.

I ate in silence and said a prayer that we'd never forget those precious hours. In reality, I clung to them long after they had cooled and lost their flavor, much like the last sip of coffee in my cup.

As soon as we got to the little stucco, I walked through the house and the back yard, snapping pictures.

Manny laughed. "Lily, *what* are you doing?"

"I love this house, Manny. It's full of happy memories. I want a few more pictures."

"Well, we don't have much time for sentimentality," he said raking his fingers through his thick hair. "Didn't you have a few things to pack yourself?"

"Uh-huh, I do. I want to pack pictures and some things I don't want the packers to handle." I reached up and ran my fingers through the hair above his ear.

"Well, hurry up. They'll be here any minute. I have to make some calls, so don't mind me." He sat down behind daddy's desk and reached for the phone.

While I packed my underwear and night gowns, I could hear Manuel talking. He sounded like a different person, all business-like, stern, even harsh, dealing with his legal affairs. That man didn't sound like the one who touched me so gently and whispered words of love.

I'd just packed the last of my personal items when the movers pulled up.

"Get the door," Manny called from the desk. I hurried to open the door for the packers who swarmed in and dismantled my life in a couple of hours.

"Lily, I hate to leave you here alone, but I have to go downtown. Business." Before I could reply, he added, "And I might not be back for several hours."

"Well, okay." I blinked in surprise.

"And don't you need to make some calls?"

"Yes." I watched him stride out the door and head to his car. "Well, make them before noon," he called over his shoulder. "The telephone company will be disconnecting it."

I watched him drive away.

Gee, I thought, he's definitely in business mode. It was then that I thought of Annie Ruth. It hit me hard that I hadn't called her yet. I'd put it off as long as I could, avoided thinking about it as long as possible. There was no way I could leave Georgia without talking to her. Suddenly my stomach felt queasy, and sweat dampened my top lip.

The three workers had walked outside when Manny left. They were standing by the truck, talking. One lit up a cigarette; another took a cold drink bottle from a large cooler.

"Hey, guys," I called. "While you're taking a break, I need to make an important phone call in that front bedroom."

"No problem, ma'am," the big burly one said. "We'll save that room for last."

I took a deep breath and dialed the number. As I listened to it ring, I prayed for the right words to say because I didn't know how I was going to tell her. Had I thought I'd pull one over on her? I wasn't used to her disapproval, and I didn't want it now.

"Hello, Cates' residence," Annie Ruth answered in her proud, self-assured voice.

"Hey, Annie Ruth, it's me." I licked my lips, my mouth suddenly as dry as day old cornbread.

"Well, honey, it's 'bout time you called home. How you doing?"

"I'm fine Annie Ruth." This was going to be worse than I'd imagined. I could hardly speak. My throat seemed to have closed up.

"Well . . . are you sure? I was beginning to wonder why we hadn't heard from you." Now she sounded like a mother hen.

"I'm fine. Tell me about you and Mama."

"Well, your mama is doing good. Real good. We took a little walk yesterday, all the way down to the pond and back. And she let me take her to church with me on Sunday."

I knew Annie Ruth was pleased with that.

"Good, Annie Ruth. You can get her to do things nobody else can. And how about you and Mr. John? How y'all doing?"

"I ain't got nothing to complain about. John stays busy with odd jobs since he quit the plant, and we both healthy as two old mules." She hesitated a second. "I lost my little dog though."

"Rascal? Oh no, what happened to Rascal?"

"Well, we ain't quite sure. Now me, I have a idee . . . but we ain't quite sure."

"I'm so sorry," I said. "I know how you loved that little dog."

"She went missing the day after you visited with that man. John went looking for her the next morning after he brung me here to the house." She paused for a second. "He found her up under some bramble out by the pond. Her neck broke."

"Oh my god, Annie Ruth." I put my hand over my mouth and held it there.

"Yeah. At first we thought a snake might have got her, but John couldn't find any signs of it. We was so bothered about it, he took her up to the vet and asked him to look at her. The vet said her neck was broke."

"Oh no. That's awful."

"Lily Rose, you don't reckon that man did it, do you?"

The weirdest sensation crawled over me like spiders down my back. I could see Manny walking down to the pond and Rascal racing in barking circles, jumping up on his legs. I saw him give her a sideways kick, and then look back at me. He was smiling.

"You don't reckon do you, 'cause I declare that thought crossed my mind."

"Annie Ruth?" My throat was so dry I could hardly swallow. "I'm sure *not*." I croaked out the words. "He couldn't have."

"Humph . . . well . . . I sho' hope not . . . but I declare that thought done crossed my mind a time or two."

"Annie Ruth, we got married on Friday."

"Who got married?" Annie Ruth blurted out the words.

"Manuel and I got married." As soon as I'd said it, I burst into tears. I'm not sure why I cried, if I was crying because of Annie Ruth, or because of the dog, or because of my own guilt. Fear? I don't know, but I burst into tears, and my sobs shut out what she was saying and left me in a darkness of my own making.

"Stop crying child and talk to me," she snapped impatiently. If I'd been close, she'd have shook me.

"We got *married* Annie Ruth," I cried. Just talking to her was like a spotlight beaming full in my face. Everything looked different. She wasn't the moonlight and roses type. That was not her style at all. She had a way of parading life down the middle of the road in the broad daylight and looking it straight in the face. She never sugar-coated reality, and she never white-washed the truth. In her own dignified way, she made the best of what the good Lord gave.

"I couldn't find a house and he wanted me to come with him. I couldn't live with him without being married. I didn't know what to do. He loves me and he'll take care of me, Annie Ruth. That's the important thing.

"Oh Lily Rose, what have you done," she murmured.

"I'm sorry I didn't tell you and Mama, but there just wasn't any time. We're leaving tonight for Detroit." She gasped when I said that.

"Lily Rose, that's so far from home." I heard sadness in her voice. "If it turns out he's not the man you think he is, you know the way home?"

"Yes, I do Annie Ruth."

"You make the best of it, that's what you do, but if he's not who you think he is, you come back home. Promise me."

"Yes, Ma'am, I will."

"You promise me, Lily Rose." She desperately tried to nail me down.

"I promise."

"And as soon as you get to Detroit, you let me know how to get ahold of you. You send me an address and a phone number." She hammered harder.

"I promise I will."

"Mr. Cates would never forgive me if anything bad happened to you. And you're like my own, Lily Rose."

"I love him Annie Ruth."

"Oh child, the things people do when they think they in love." She groaned. "You knew better . . . but you ain't the first." Then she added, with as much conviction as I'd ever heard her say, "But you know the way home, if he's no good, you get on back down here."

"It'll be all right Annie Ruth. And I promise I'll write you every week."

"Lord 'a mercy. I pray the good Lord takes care of you, Lily Rose."

"He will." I struggled to hold back the tears. "I have to go now, Annie Ruth. The movers need to pack up my bedroom furniture."

"I love you child."

"I love you too. I'll write soon. I promise."

"I'll be watching for your letter."

I hung up the phone and burst into tears. I could see Annie Ruth sitting there in the kitchen with her hands balled up together in her lap. She'd be kneading them like a big ball of biscuit dough, with a heavy heart, because of me. I felt so guilty . . . guilty for getting married without really considering it all . . . guilty for getting married too soon . . . guilty about Rascal. Poor little fellow. How could Annie Ruth think such a thing? It wasn't like her to make rash statements like that. Of course it wasn't possible . . . unimaginable. I couldn't shake the horrible thought . . . like you can't shake the smell of a dead skunk on a hot summer day.

The knock at the bedroom door caused me to jump right back into the morning.

"Ma'am? We're about ready to do that room."

"Give me five minutes," I called. I stood and walked over to the bathroom sink, turned on the faucet, and looked straight into the eyes staring back at me in the mirror. Just a few hours before, those green eyes sparkled with hope. Now, besides red rims and smeared mascara, there was pain. Misgivings clouded the bright expectations.

***

The packers hauled out the last box and loaded the last piece at one o'clock. It's no wonder. After all, I didn't have much. Manny said my stuff would look out of place in his condo, but we'd take it anyway, and I could decide later what I wanted to do with it. There was no time to sort it all out before we got married.

I closed the front door of the empty house and sat on the floor in a sunny corner to wait for my husband. Since I'd sold my car at his insistence, I couldn't do anything but wait. Looking through the window into the clear sky, I watched the yellow and orange leaves sway in the gentle breeze. The squirrels dug rapidly with tiny paws beneath the curled brown leaves covering the ground under the dogwood tree. It was time to rake. I thought of raking leaves with Daddy and James Michael. We'd make huge mounds and then pile them to overflowing into the wheelbarrow. With me sitting on top, holding on for the ride, Daddy would push the wheelbarrow to the back edge of the property. I closed my eyes in order to see more clearly the memories, and I fell asleep with a smile on my lips.

"Lily?" Manny called to me as he stepped inside the front door. "Ah, look at you," he said, "sleeping there in the corner like a little kitten." He made a purring sound and nuzzled my ear and neck. "Can I join you?" he whispered against my throat.

"Oh Manny. Yes, join me." He gathered me into his arms. There we knew again the pleasure of our honeymoon, forgetting all about the time and place.

***

By the looks of the shadows in the room, it was late afternoon.

"Lily, we have to get on the road. Believe me. I wish we had more time, but we don't. I have to get back."

"I know." I put my hand on my rumbling stomach. "But I'm starving. I haven't eaten since breakfast. I don't know when I've been so hungry."

"Sorry you didn't get lunch. That was my fault." He pulled me up, set his hands on my shoulders, and rubbed them gently. "I had a working lunch while I caught up on some research for a big case I'm working on. Let's hurry, get on the road, and I'll stop and get you whatever you like. I'm driving. You can eat. Deal?"

"Deal." I smiled while lifting my face for his kiss. Revived by his love, I was ready to begin the journey to our new life.

Chapter Nine

We continued our honeymoon on the road trip which was the longest stretch of time that Manny and I had ever spent together. That fact only served to pique my sense of adventure. Conversation was agreeable, although he peppered me with questions about what I planned to do with my degree. I managed to learn about his passion for cars, and that he intended to own a plane one day. And there was laughter. When it was just the two of us together, our love seemed sufficient to sustain us, then and through the years. It was Manny's reaction to outside people and situations that first caused me pause.

"What kind of car is this, Manny?" I curled my body into the headed seat and ran my hand over the soft leather.

"A Maserati."

"I don't think I've ever heard of the model."

"Model? No, I don't imagine you have."

He laughed then. I loved his hearty laugh.

"It's beautiful and much more comfortable than my Mustang."

"I suppose it is that. I can't wait to take you to the International Car Show. There you'll see amazing cars. It's a huge event I don't miss. And this year will be even better because I get to show *you* off."

Manny didn't want to stay on the road overnight. He explained that he had to get back to work. And moreover, he didn't like the idea of parking his car in a hotel parking lot.

I'd been dozing on and off for a while when Manny decided to stop for coffee and a bite to eat. It was three in the morning. Manny needed coffee to stay awake. I was happy to stretch my legs.

"Glad you folks stopped in," said the bleached blond waitress. "It's been as dead as a grave yard around here." She laughed at her own joke as she poured steaming coffee into Manny's upturned cup. She held her pad and pencil close to her ample chest like it was a shelf. The narrow aisle between the grill and the booths seemed a rather tight fit for her girth.

"What'll it be sir?"

"I'll take a bacon and egg sandwich, no fries, hold some of the grease." Manny looked across the table at me and gave me a tight-lipped smile.

"Just iced water for me," I said with a smile.

"Coming right up," the waitress said. She brought me a glass of water. "Where you folks headed to anyway?" She looked Manuel up and down in a not so subtle manner.

Manny stared at me, rolled his eyes in apparent distain, then turned his head to peer out the window at his car, ignoring the waitress like she hadn't even spoken. I felt uncomfortable.

"We're on our way to Detroit," I said with a nervous giggle. Manny gave a slight head shake, half closed his eyes, and frowned. I got the impression he didn't want me to respond either. From her position in front of the grill, the waitress continued to talk and tried to engage us in conversation.

I looked at Manny, raised my eyebrows, and shrugged my shoulders, a bit amused at her obtuse chattiness. Manny, on the other hand, appeared agitated. His eyes narrowed to slits, and I noticed a pulse in his cheek under his cheek bone that I'd never seen before.

When she returned with Manny's plate, she leaned forward and hovered a second, then opened her mouth to say something. That's when Manny slammed his hand on the table.

"Ma'am, I didn't come into this restaurant to talk to you, would you please *shut up*."

When his hand struck the table, the waitress and I both jumped like we'd been shot. She froze in place. I held my breath. The look on Manuel's face petrified me. Dumbfounded, I stared at him, shocked at the violence in his voice.

The waitress stammered an apology and backed away. She turned and walked through a set of swinging doors and disappeared into the back. A skinny young man took her place at the grill. He glanced over his shoulder nervously at us several times, but he said nothing.

We sat in silence. I was afraid to move or do anything that might disturb Manny, who concentrated on eating every bite of the sandwich. We made no eye contact. He didn't say anything else, and I didn't dare.

When he paid the tab, he thrust an extra twenty dollar bill at the cashier.

"Give this to the woman that served us earlier," he said. "I owe her an apology."

***

The lights from the car's dash cast an eerie glow on Manuel's ridged profile. He stayed as stiff as a board for another five minutes or so. Then I noticed his shoulders soften. Out the corner of my eye, I saw him look at me.

"I'm sorry, Lily," he said in a quiet voice.

I didn't speak. I was still trying to process what had happened, where all that anger had come from. After that explosive episode, it was too soon for an apology.

"Lily?"

"Manny, you hurt that woman's feelings," I said without looking at him.

"I said I'm sorry."

I dared to state the obvious. "You scared me to death."

"I can't stand people like that." He no longer sounded apologetic.

"She wanted to talk to somebody. That's all." I glanced at him then. "Why'd you have to be so mean?"

"She should have picked up that we didn't want to talk to her. I'm not one for small talk with strangers at some greasy spoon in the middle of the night."

I watched the road up ahead. My nerves were frayed. I was even trying to control my breathing, so he wouldn't notice me.

"Let's just forget it, okay? I'm sorry it happened." He reached over and felt for my hand without taking his eyes off the road. My hand lay limp in his. He squeezed it.

"I love you," he said, a bit impatiently.

"I love you, too."

A whole minute passed before he added, "For better or worse?"

Those words offered little comfort for the confusion I felt.

"For better or worse," I replied. Of my own free will I'd gladly said those words only days before. This time, somehow, I felt like I had no choice. I escaped into a restless sleep. A rumbling jolt woke me.

"Sorry Lil. I hit those tracks too fast."

"It's all right," I murmured.

A gray mist hung over the city and streets dirty and bleak—just waking up like I was to a smell—a smell of exhaust and factory fumes so strong I could taste it. This strong odor was my first impression of Detroit, and it challenged even my powers of positive thinking. It stunk, and in the almost three years I was there, my opinion didn't improve.

Manny glanced at me a couple of times. Leaning forward, he peered around to get a better glimpse of my face.

"Don't despair, sweetheart," he said. "It gets better. Trust me."

I smiled at him. Already he read my face as well as a sworn statement. Always one of the things I hated about myself—my feelings written so clearly there.

The city seemed like New York's sleazy cousin. Its damp chill seeped into my bones. I hugged my arms tight to my chest and kneaded my upper arms. Finally, he slowed the car in an upscale neighborhood near the river and pulled into the parking garage of a high-rise. He punched in a code and we entered.

I knew Manuel had done well for himself. Anyone could see that by the way he dressed, his fine car. He'd told of his meteoric success and laughed proudly as he impressed me with tales of his uncanny savvy with investments. Still, I didn't expect what awaited me. For a man not yet thirty-five, he had a lot to show for his success. Granted, he worked like a mad man to earn his money and worked just as hard to manage his assets. But, I didn't realize he was wealthy.

While Manny unlocked the front door, I shivered, standing close to his heels. He turned abruptly and held his hands out, palms facing me. I stepped back.

"Wait here, just a second. Don't move," he said. He grabbed all the bags and set them inside the door. Then he swept me up into his arms before I realized what was happening.

"I'm carrying my wife over the threshold." He carried me inside, looking down into my face for a few seconds. Gently he touched his lips to mine as he sat me down on supple leather. He eased himself down beside me on the black sofa and pulled me tightly into his arms.

"Welcome home darling," he said, his voice a hoarse whisper.

How could I not adore the man? He said all the right words. I felt passion in his touch and saw love in his eyes. At that moment in time I didn't doubt his love for me, nor mine for him.

He drove through the night for practically fourteen hours straight. He should've been exhausted, but he eagerly showed me the place. We took a quick tour of the living room, dining area and kitchen, the master bedroom, workout room, another bedroom, and two and a half baths. Modern, luxurious furnishings, simple style, sleek design, all pricey, and a little impersonal.

"I've never seen anything like it," I said, in all sincerity. It was so sleek, lots of leather, chrome, and glass.

"You'll get used to it," he said. "And you might as well start getting used to it while I go into the office this morning."

"What?"

"I'll be dead on my feet this afternoon, but I have to go. I'll be back early, by six." With that he abruptly pulled away from me and stood.

"What? Six o'clock tonight! That's twelve hours from now. You'll fall out."

"Nonsense, Lily. I'm used to it." He touched the palms of his hands to my cheeks. His brown eyes softened. "Maybe I'll slow down a bit with you waiting here for me. That'll be one of the advantages of having a wife."

I put my arms around his neck and he wrapped his tightly around my waist. Desire kindled as we pressed our bodies together. We kissed deeply, and he moaned as I melted into him. For a moment, I thought I could keep him there with me.

He slid his hands down my sides and reached around to my behind, leaning me slightly backwards.

"Come take a shower with me darling," he whispered in my ear. "I want you there with me." He led me by the hand.

We romped like kids in the rain in a huge marble shower with multiple massaging shower jets. But then, he dressed in a charcoal gray flannel suit, a navy blue silk tie, combed back his wavy black hair, and left me curled up in his king sized bed. I wanted to beg him not to leave me, but I knew it would do no good. His focus was elsewhere.

I heard the heavy door close behind him. I listened to his footsteps growing fainter down the hall, the elevator's bell, its door closing. As long as I could hear any sound at all—I listened. And as the quiet settled around me, the strangeness began to sink in. The sounds of the awakening city drifted up to me. I felt like I was in another country. Had I needed a passport to get here? The marriage license had sufficed.

While the morning sun dried up the thick fog, I tossed in a fitful sleep.

I dreamt we were dancing in the ballroom of The Presidential Inn, and then we were dancing in the rain. Somehow, Manny slipped away, leaving me alone and lost, searching for him in a cold gray fog. He called my name in the distance, but I couldn't figure out how to find my way back to him. Then Annie Ruth spoke close beside me. I felt her presence, but I couldn't see her.

"Do you know the way home? Do you know the way home?" Her voice tugged at me.

Images swirled around me, and I tried to make sense of the muddle. Light through stained glass windows, pitch black night, warm hands and soft kisses on my face, ice on asphalt, a slam so loud glass shattered and cascaded down at my feet.

"I know the way home!"

The sound of my own voice awakened me, the sharp words echoing in the empty room. I shivered with cold, my body jerking painfully. The silk sheets were twisted around my ankles and feet. Gathering the spread around me like a heavy robe, I swung my legs over the side of the platform bed and went in search of the thermostat. I found one inside the bedroom door, set on fifty-eight degrees. After adjusting it to seventy-five, I sprinted to bed to huddle under the covers until the place warmed up.

"I hate the cold, I hate the cold," I muttered as I drew my body into a tight ball.

Blood began to circulate again through my icy feet. When a fine sweat moistened my toes, I kicked back the satin spread and reached over to the bedside table for the button that opened the wall of drapes. I looked out on a steel gray sky unlike any I'd ever seen. The digital clock read almost noon. Thoughts still swirled through my head, but gnawing hunger spoke loudest.

In a way, I was glad Manny wasn't there. I could use the solitude to find my way around the place. I got out of bed, adjusted the thermostat to seventy, and went to find something to eat.

A cup of coffee, a fried egg, that's all I wanted. Something simple. But it proved too complicated for me. I couldn't figure out the newfangled coffee contraption. Luckily I found some gourmet instant coffee and made myself a satisfying cup. I fried two eggs in a stainless steel skillet with a little olive oil and sprinkled them with sea salt.

Annie Ruth would love this stove, I thought. I liked the compact television situated under the counter.

I wondered if Manny would surprise me by coming home for lunch. The thought made me smile. But he didn't, nor did he ever.

The afternoon was long. I could almost count the minutes ticking by. How completely changeable my concept of time depending on the circumstances. I can't count the number of dreary afternoons—more than enough to last a lifetime—that I languished in that place.

I wandered through the condo several times trying to figure out where I could put my things. An extra room beside the master suite, a second bedroom of sorts, was furnished with only a loveseat. I put my cosmetics and toiletries in the connecting bathroom and unpacked my clothes on the loveseat. I figured I could put my bedroom furniture in that room and my daddy's desk in a little niche near the door.

My stuff would look out of place. Now I understood what Manny was trying to tell me. In this professionally decorated apartment, my things would look like thrift shop finds. Most of it would have to go, but I couldn't part with Daddy's desk.

Crisp stacks of shirts and sweaters neatly lined the shelves and drawers in Manny's closet. There was no clutter anywhere. On the contrary, everything was precisely placed, perfectly pressed, and organized.

In order to satisfy the bizarre thought that he didn't actually live there, I inspected further. I felt intrusive rifling through his things, still I opened every drawer. There was not an item out of place. When I came across the half empty toothpaste tube, I chuckled in relief. Had it not been for that, I would have concluded that he didn't really live there at all.

I decided it would be a good idea to have one room for my things—a comfort zone where I could close the door on my less than perfect, downright shabby stuff. Manny would appreciate that, I thought.

"Lily, we don't need to move your stuff, you know. Just pack your bags," he'd said.

"What? Leave all my things behind?"

"My condo is decorated and furnished. I'll buy you nicer things, anything you want."

"But I like my things," I whined.

"Whatever makes you happy, baby," he'd said.

We'd worry about it later, he said. My expectations had been prosaic, to say the least.

I called Julie to tell her about the trip and the pristine apartment. We laughed and commiserated about the newlywed learning curve. In spite of our lengthy conversation, the afternoon stretched on and on. I was pacing through the apartment yet again when I heard the key in the lock. My heartbeat quickened and I squealed as I rushed into his arms.

"Oh Manny, I missed you so much." I flung my arms around his neck and stood on tiptoes to kiss him. "Kiss me darling."

"Oh, baby, what a greeting." He laughed. "I'm a heck of a lucky man."

He dropped his brief case and coat on a chair and kissed me. We held each other tight as we made our way to the sofa. After an all absorbing kiss, Manny gently pulled my arms from around his neck.

"I'm exhausted, Lil."

"Oh, you poor darling." I raked my fingers through his hair while whispering *I love you*.

"I've ordered dinner for us. I hope a steak sounds good," he said.

"Certainly. You're so thoughtful." I nibbled his cheek and neck. "There's not much in your refrigerator besides eggs and beer."

"Tomorrow you can buy food. Tonight we'll relax, eat our steaks," he glanced at his watch, "which should be getting here any minute, and go to bed."

"Sounds like a plan," I said. We laughed and snuggled one another.

"I think bed is our favorite place," he said, kissing my neck.

"I think so, too." I giggled.

And to be quite honest, it was our favorite place. A sanctuary of sorts where we didn't need to think . . . where we could lose ourselves in our passion and few words were needed. At least there we spoke the same language and understood the expectations.

And so, our married life began in earnest.

Chapter Ten

Manny slipped out of bed at six o'clock and worked out for precisely an hour. I wasn't ready to give him up for the day. When I heard the shower come on, I climbed out of bed and joined him. I was marvelously in love, and the pleasure of the warm shower together with his amazing body was irresistible. He nibbled my ear and murmured, "How delicious you are." The lovemaking abruptly cut off with the shower.

"Lily, you're going to make me late." His words were punctuated by a sharp slap on my behind. "Dry yourself off, darling, and go back to bed."

I learned to wait on his call. By the time he'd stopped calling, I didn't really care to go in there with him anymore anyway.

"Manny, I need to grocery shop, but how can I do that with no checks and no car?"

He flipped through his wallet and tossed me a card.

"There. Use that for anything you want. And call a cab."

"A cab? I couldn't. It's too extravagant."

"Not at all extravagant, and it's by far the easiest thing for you to do here. You'll get used to it. I don't want you driving in the city."

At the time, that sounded reasonable. He was looking out for me. When I sold my Mustang, I expected to get something new in Detroit, but there was no real need for it. Manny said he'd rather give me the money to spend on myself than to use it buying a car I didn't need. I could think of better ways to spend my money, like visiting Maggie in New York or Julie in Canada. I didn't relish the idea of driving in the city either, even though I missed having my own car.

Manny set up a checking account for me and automatically deposited a generous monthly amount for my use. I used his credit card for anything we needed. It seemed as the days passed that he didn't care or pay any attention if or when I spent money. As long as I kept the kitchen and the bar nicely stocked, and bought the clothes he wanted me to wear, and kept the place spotless, he showed no interest whatsoever in my meager spending habits.

Winter came in earnest, so I rarely went out. I detested the ice and snow and the bitter biting wind, always slashing to the bone. I quick-froze every time I went outside. The weather was intolerable, and the winter dragged on through the dirty slush of spring. The less I went out, the less I wanted to. Manny suggested places I might like to visit, but I didn't want to go alone. I couldn't brave the wicked cold or the blank faces of strangers who didn't speak. It was my good fortune that the taxi picked me up at my entrance and dropped me off outside the grocery store, or the library, or the bookstore. I ventured out for books. Other than that, I went out only when I had to. I wrote home to family and friends every week and looked forward to their replies. I didn't realize that part of my malaise was a bad case of homesickness.

Manny worked long hours. Twelve hour days weren't uncommon—once in a blue moon he put in an eight hour day. His efforts to cut his hours to ten should've been enough to satisfy me, he said. After all his work was important to him, after all I should care about that. Thanks to Mother Church, he sacrificed going into the office on Sundays except for emergencies. But there was nothing holy about any other day. He revered law—the power, the competition, the winning. He worshipped the markets. The payoffs fed something insatiable in him, his ego maybe, and a thirst for power. I learned to accept what I couldn't understand and kept my mouth shut. It was just that I had expected more . . . for us . . . and for our marriage.

"Manny, my goodness, do you have to work like this? Can't we spend some time together? If we didn't sleep together, I wouldn't even know I have a husband."

For a minute, Manny stared blankly at me.

"Lil, I have to work, as you say, like this, for at least seven or eight more years. When I'm a full partner, I'll be able to back off a bit and work less. We'll have all the time together you want."

"Seven or eight years? Are you kidding? I never see you now. I'll be in my thirties by then. You'll be over forty. What about children?" That was the first time "children" had been mentioned. In reality, Manny and I failed to discuss critical issues during our unquestionably brief courtship.

"I'm dead serious," he said. "I'm great at what I do. Why, I'm a frickin' genius! I'm in demand. I'm powerful. And I'm making money hand over fist with my investments. How do you think I afford all this?" He threw out his arms in a grandiose gesture.

"But can't you give up a little time in the office to make time for us?" My voice softened with my last effort to persuade him.

"Be patient. It'll all be worth it." As far as he was concerned, the case was closed.

***

We had a wonderful Thanksgiving holiday. Manny stayed home for a record three days, but by Sunday afternoon he couldn't take it anymore.

"Lil, I need to go into the office for a little while," he said. "I have some important documents I want to put my hands on and read through before my briefing tomorrow."

"Must you?" I sighed.

"I want you to come too, darling. You haven't seen the office yet. Go bundle up, sweetheart. You're going with me." He smiled and waited for my reaction. He wanted me with him, and that was enough to make me happy.

The office showed his signature style—neat and spacious. A private lounging area and bathroom adjoined his office. He had a blanket and a pillow stashed in the closet.

"Manny," I commented, "you could spend the night here."

"Of course I could," he said. "And I did all the time before we got married."

"That explains it."

"What?"

"Ah, nothing," I said. He had already turned away and opened a desk drawer.

We went to New York City for Christmas like we'd talked about before we married. We spent a few days with his mother and visited his brother and his family. All of us enjoyed a festive dinner together at the family restaurant. It seemed surreal. How could it have been only five months before that I was there with Maggie? Only five months since I'd met Manuel?

We cut that visit short. I never understood exactly what happened. Manny and his brother argued. When Manny went to the restaurant early that day, he left in good spirits. I was stretched out on the bed reading when Manny returned mid-afternoon. He stormed into the room, his eyes glaring.

He plopped down on the side of the bed, thrust both hands through his hair, and then began roughly unbuttoning his shirt. He practically jerked his clothes off.

"Manny, what is it?" My chest tightened and I dropped the book I was reading.

"We're leaving in the morning." He spat out the words without turning to look at me.

"What's happened?" My voice came out in a whisper.

"I should've cut Tony's throat years ago," he growled through clenched teeth.

I instinctively drew back. Fear clutched my chest.

"He never did anything but cause trouble growing up. I was the one who cleaned up his mess. I was the one who worked the restaurant. I lived and breathed the business right along with Dad. It should be mine."

I was speechless. Why hadn't I noticed the animosity between Manny and his brother?

"Then he decided he wanted in and Dad welcomed him. With open arms! Acted like there was reason to celebrate." He huffed, then stood up and swung around. "All we did was fight after that. We didn't make it a year before one of us had to leave. That's when I made up my mind to go to law school. If I'd stayed, I would've hurt him . . . and broke my mother's heart."

"I'm sorry, Manny," I stammered.

"Don't be." He glared through half shut eyes. "The only thing I regret is not getting rid of him instead."

He stalked into the bathroom, slammed the door, and turned on the water. Like a woman turned to stone, I sat perfectly still and honed in on the sound of running water. My mind grappled with his incomprehensible words. Get rid of him, he said. My head felt like it might split in pained confusion.

When I heard him turn off the shower, I bolted upright, grabbed the book, and moved to the chair across the room. While he dressed, I quietly excused myself to help his mother in the kitchen. Manuel never mentioned that afternoon again, nor did I. It was best to let sleeping dogs lie. Annie Ruth's saying had never seemed so relevant. Besides, I told myself, he had spoken those words in anger. I was sure he could not have meant what he said.

We didn't see the play with Maggie. Manny said that we'd go the next time we came to New York, but we never did. He was always in too much of a hurry to return to his work in Detroit, or maybe it was because he couldn't stand to be around his brother, and maybe it was because his promises to me meant nothing.

***

As the weeks turned into months, he continued to spend every waking moment working. I tried to be patient. I didn't want to complain and whine about it, but I failed miserably. I begged him to spend more time with me. At first he was patient. At least he didn't overreact when I brought it up. He'd reassure me, but when he'd had enough, he was done. I'd already gotten all the compromise I'd ever get.

One evening as I was putting the finishing touches on the minestrone soup I'd learned to make from his mother's recipe, he let me know in no uncertain terms how sick he was of my nagging.

"Lil, I have told you the deal, and now I am telling you for the last time. Shut your mouth about my work. And don't bring it up again." He spat out every harsh word.

When he spoke, I'd lifted the shaker to add more pepper. I froze in place and stared at him. His eyes had narrowed. I noticed the familiar tick in his steeled jaw. He had my full attention. Suddenly he flung out his arm and pointed to the door.

"When you see me walk through that door, I'm home. And I don't want to hear another damned word of your incessant nagging!" He turned on the heels of his expensive Italian shoes and went back to stirring his drink at the bar.

For the life of me, I don't know why I uttered a word . . . why I murmured a sound. Like Annie Ruth would have said, I knew better. Maybe it was my attempt to downplay his ire, which didn't seem to match the situation. "But, but Manny . . . ." As soon as I'd spoken his name, I regretted it. He rushed at me so fast I lost my balance and stumbled a step back. Hot soup splattered on my face from the spoon in my hand. He gripped my upper arms in his hands like vice grips—so tight he shook—and held me square, inches from his face.

"Manny, you're hurting me!"

"I told you. Not another word."

So close I smelled whiskey on his breath, I could only look into those hate filled eyes for a second before turning away. My body went limp, my head dropped to my shoulder as a cry welled up from deep inside. He released my arms forcefully and stalked away. I crumpled like a rag doll, dropping to my knees. When the whimpers turned to sobs, he stormed at me again, snatched me up, and half pushed, half carried me toward the bedroom. Fear took my breath away for a moment. Then I screamed.

"Get your *ass* in there and don't come out until you can act like my wife. I won't put up with this." He shoved me into the room and slammed the door.

Darkness fell, and I didn't bother to turn on the light. At some point I went to sleep without hearing another sound from Manuel, until I heard the door slam as he left for work the next day. That horrible night had ended, but it wouldn't be the last one. The purple bruises on my arms healed quickly, but those on my heart, not so fast. That was the end of all discussions about his work. It was also the end of the sweet phase of our relationship—the end of the phase in which I could pretend that everything was fine. The honeymoon was over, so to speak.

For the rest of the winter, the atmosphere of the condo was as cold inside as the weather outside, and all attempts at warmth were but flickers with too little fuel for a decent flame. The fire of our marriage had grown cold, and it wasn't even spring yet.

Chapter Eleven

I'd entered the building after grocery shopping and stopped to adjust the weight of the bags I carried when I noticed a flyer on the community bulletin board.

"Aspiring Author's Group," I read. *Wednesdays at noon, bring a sack lunch, and your work in progress.*

Intrigued, I tore off one of the attached strips. The writers' group met in the building, so there'd be no need to go out.

I laid the paper on the counter, put away the groceries, and began preparing supper. Everything was about ready when Manny got home.

"Smells good, Lily," he said as he walked into the kitchen.

"Thanks, sweetheart. How was your day?"

"The usual. Impossible. I expect the same high level of effort as I put forth. I expect favorable results for my time and money. I'm frankly not happy with how one of my cases is playing out."

"Ah, I'm sorry." I knew he was conscientious. He thought he had to do it himself for it to be done right. I couldn't begin to understand his work, but I knew winning for his clients meant everything to him. I wanted to reach out, say something to encourage him, but I could never be sure when his temper might flare up and I'd find myself bearing the brunt of his frustrations.

He sat down heavily, put his elbows on the kitchen table, and rested his forehead on the heels of his hands. At that moment, he looked so vulnerable. Quietly I walked to his side and rubbed across the top of his back and shoulders. Tenderness welled inside me. I wanted to love him, if only he'd let me. I leaned in slowly and kissed his head. He reached for my hand.

"You're a sweet woman, Lil," he said. "I don't deserve you." He pulled me down in his lap and wrapped his arms around me. His face rested on my shoulder. We sat like that for a long time. I felt tension draining out of him. It was the first time in days he'd had his arms around me. I'd longed for his touch. I closed my eyes and sighed. Then he got up to fix a drink.

He picked up the slip of paper from the counter. "What's this Lily?"

"Oh, I got it from the bulletin board downstairs. A writers' group meets every week here in the building."

"You want to go? You should join."

"I was thinking about visiting, out of curiosity," I said casually.

"Sure. That'll be perfect for you. Maybe that's exactly what you need—make some friends, do something you enjoy."

"You think so, Manny?" I put my arms around his neck and he slipped his around me. "Since you think it's a good idea, I think I will go to the next meeting."

Then words were forgotten as we lost ourselves in each other's arms.

***

The writers' group was a compelling diversion. It was a small group, only three women and one elderly man who seemed to know everything about writing except how to finish his current novel. Every week we shared our writing, read aloud, and critiqued each other. More like a support group, it was the highlight of my week. For the ten weeks I was a part of the group, I wrote almost as many stories and outlined a novel. I would be so absorbed in my fictional worlds that I didn't care if Manny came home by seven or ten. That, in itself, made the group invaluable for a time.

On a rare Saturday outing, Manny and I were driving back from an afternoon of shopping. I felt carefree and flirtatious after modeling new outfits all afternoon for an admiring husband. I had shopping bags full of new clothes he'd wanted me to have. Soaking up much needed attention, I overflowed with excitement. As we chatted, something came up about the writers' group.

"Manny, why don't we all go out for drinks and dinner? I'd love for you to meet everyone. Or they can come over. I'll make dinner. Try one of my new recipes."

"Spend a whole evening with them? They aren't my type, are they?" he said, glancing at me. He must have seen the disappointment on my face. "Tell me about them," he conceded.

"Well, it's an eclectic group like I've said, but good people. I'm the baby of the group. Then there's Marta, the mother of two teenagers, Deanna also in her forties with no children, Lorene has a most fascinating life story, and then there's Dale—the star of the group, a published author, and the sweetest, most positive person I know, plus he has the sexiest blue eyes I've ever seen." I giggled and leaned towards my husband.

I ran my hand over the back of my neck, tossing my hair to the side. Then I flashed him a smile and reached down and rubbed my ankle, undoing the strap to one of my high heels.

"He? I didn't realize you were meeting a man in that group every week."

I paused and looked at Manny. I could see that cold severity coming over him like an icy winter blast.

"Dale is a man?" He demanded to know.

"Oh, come on, Manny, I was just teasing about his eyes. That was a silly thing for me to say. I don't even know why I said it. I've told you about him before." I spoke the words gently, but matter-of-factly.

"I thought Dale was a woman."

"Well, if you did, you weren't listening to me," I shot back, exasperated that he was complaining now about a man in the group when I'd talked about Dale several times. Manny was always so indifferent when I tried to make conversation, I could never tell if he was listening or not.

Manny didn't respond, only clenched his jaw. Then he shot a glance in the rear view mirror before pulling over sharply to the curb.

"Manny, Dale's seventy years old. I'm sure I've mentioned that before."

"Get out," he said, staring straight ahead.

"Manny, you can't be serious." But I could see he was. I tried to smile a phony smile in an attempt to hide my rising panic. "You have absolutely no sense of humor," I said nervously. My legs suddenly felt weak.

"Get your scrawny ass out of this car now or I'm going to drag you out." He looked at me through squinted eyes. His face had turned to stone.

"No, Manny, please," I begged. I put both hands over my face and rocked forward.

He jumped out of the car and rushed around to my door, jerked it open, and snatched me out. I stumbled, barely managing to stay on my feet, and dropped one of the sandals on the pavement. As he sped away, he ran over the shoe. Broke the heel clean off. I felt like the one who'd been run over.

How could he treat me like that? Bewildered, humiliated, I stood there alone, one shoe on and one shoe mashed on the road. The weather was pleasant enough, and it was only a short distance to walk barefooted to the condo, but I'd never felt so belittled in my life.

As soon as I walked in, Manny spoke an off-hand apology, laughed nervously, and excused himself for his jealousy. For his jealousy, *not* his cruelty. His insensitivity repulsed me.

I never went back to the writers' group. A crying jag reminiscent of my teenage years set in that day. A cloud of depression as thick as the morning fog engulfed me. After about three weeks of it, something inside told me to dry the tears. "Tears won't do you no good," Annie Ruth used to say. In reality, I was afraid I'd become like Mama. I prayed desperately for strength and an answer from God for my miserable marriage. What's more than that, I cried for my daddy, for the first time in years, missing him so bad, and so sorry for getting myself into a fine mess.

A few weeks after that, I missed my period—the only one I'd ever missed—and I knew instantly I was pregnant. I didn't know whether to be happy or sad, but when Manny was over the moon with excitement, showering me with attention, I began to hope. For weeks he promised good things to come, pampered me, and showed affection. My heart warmed again to my husband. We had turned a corner, I thought. My prayers had been answered.

We talked about buying a house maybe even before the baby was due. I wanted one with a fenced in backyard in a nice neighborhood where we could raise our children. The prospects of buying a home excited me to no end. We met with a realtor. Our relationship rekindled as we planned for our future as a family.

Manny had taken me to one of my doctor's visits, taking me to lunch afterwards before he'd returned to the office. It meant so much to me. But the last time he took me for an appointment, something happened that caused me to think our happiness might be just a fragile illusion.

We had driven around the parking lot several times without finding an open space within easy walking distance to the medical building. We were coming around yet again when we noticed a car pulling out of a space in the next row, but a woman was already waiting for the space with her blinker on. Manny slowed at the end of the row, and I thought he simply waited for the two cars to move on. But as soon as the car backed out of the space, he stepped on the accelerator; the car lurched forward and into the newly vacated spot. The woman who had been waiting slammed on her brakes to avoid hitting us. I saw the flash of anger on her face as she threw up her hands.

Manny saw her reaction, too, and it infuriated him. He had almost caused an accident, yet he was furious with the other driver.

"Why did you do that? We saw her waiting for the space." But he wasn't listening to me. He was already getting out of the car, cursing the unfortunate woman in terms I'd never heard in my life. She drove away with a horrified expression on her face. My skin crawled from the venomous language he'd used.

"I don't even want to get out of the car. I'm so embarrassed." I'd broken out in a sweat and my eyes stung. I felt horrible for the lady.

"Don't you dare cry," he said through clenched teeth. "Get out!" And all the anger he'd directed at the woman now turned on me.

We never saw the woman again, but I expected at any moment the cops would show up to question us regarding his abusive barrage.

I tried to shake it off . . . the feeling of waiting for the other shoe to drop, the next explosion of fury, the next humiliating scene. But I couldn't shake it after that; the feeling stayed with me like a nagging chronic ache.

***

One day in late September, I awoke to hard cramps in the bottom of my stomach. After a long shower, the pain eased off, but minutes later it returned even worse, ripping through my abdomen and my lower back. I curled up in bed with a heating pad, and along with its warmth, dread seeped through me. I felt so alone.

I called Manny's office. He would be in meetings all day. At noon, I called Julie. She advised me to call the doctor, and together we prayed.

"Mrs. Valenti, the doctor says to come on in. He needs to see you." The nurse spoke kindly.

"Thank you." I prayed on my knees in misery while I waited for the taxi. The pain—like the worst imaginable menstrual cramps stabbed through my abdomen. Almost as crippling were the waves of helplessness.

"Manny!" I cried out in desperation. I wished Annie Ruth were there.

While I sat shivering in the doctor's office, I felt fluid gush out of me. I called for help. When the nurse led me back, blood trickled down my legs. That afternoon, in the doctor's office, I lost our son. He already had fingers and toes. He would have been handsome like his father, and I could have loved that child without pain. But it wasn't to be.

The doctor explained that the miscarriage couldn't have been prevented. These things just happen sometimes, he said. Nothing had indicated a problem. I was admitted to the hospital when my blood pressure plummeted and blood continued to gush out.

Manny's sobs woke me as I slept in the hospital bed. His head rested by my thigh and his hands held them. Instinctively, I stroked his hair. We clung to each other. Our love served as a quiet balm to our sorrow. He slept on the sofa beside the bed all night. The following morning he went to the office. I slept all that day and Manny didn't come back that evening.

"Mrs. Valenti, you can go home this morning. All your vitals have returned to normal, and the blood flow is normal now too. As soon as someone comes to pick you up, we will release you."

"I'll call my husband," I said. I tried the office but Manny wasn't available. It was almost noon when he returned my call.

"Manny, I can go home as soon as you come get me," I said softly.

"I'm in the middle of something very important," he said.

"If I stay past noon, I think we'll have to pay for another day."

"What's that to me? We have the money. You rest and I'll be there before dinner."

So, I rested, alone with my grief and the overwhelming emptiness. Manny picked me up close to five. Few words were spoken on the drive home. I ate a few bites of supper, and Manny suggested I go to bed. We never again spoke about the pregnancy or about the baby I lost. It seems like it would have been the most natural thing for us to do, talk about the details until we could make sense of it, console each other in our grief. But we didn't talk about it that night, or the next, and as the days, then weeks went by and we didn't talk about it . . . to have talked about it would have seemed like the most unnatural thing.

By the time the sadness was indistinguishable from the rest of the misery in my life, our love had turned to indifference. Somehow that was preferable—it made our relationship less painful. Months went by without anything unsettling happening. There were some stretches of contentment, a few sweet Sunday mornings, but mostly, I languished alone, finding solace in fictional worlds—reading novels and dabbling with creating my own. Writing became a means of escape—a place where I had control. Like cooking—I sought ways to express my creativity and control some little part of my life.

Manny worked, obsessed with winning, on a fast track to full partner, riding waves of excitement when new challenges captivated him or venting his frustrations on me . . . more and more on me. I told myself I had no control over my life. In reality, profound disappointment paralyzed me. But I found myself becoming less patient with Manny regarding his hateful moods.

One day when Manny had just gotten in from the office, he went to the bar to prepare himself a drink. When he suddenly set the bottle down too hard on the granite, he got my attention.

"Lil, where is the soda water?" He turned around slowly and stared at me. The tone of his voice made me uneasy. For a second, my thoughts darted about.

"Manny, I'm sorry. I forgot to buy it at the grocery store today." He continued to glare at me.

"Why don't you let me make something for you? Sit down and relax." I walked toward him, but stopped when I saw his eyes.

"Lil, why can't you manage the simplest tasks?" He sneered. "I don't ask much of you, do I?" He clenched a fist in disgust and swore contemptuously.

"I'm sorry, Manny. Please don't make a big fuss about the soda water."

He cursed while plopping ice into a glass, and called me stupid under his breath.

I stood completely still, momentarily stunned, and then I went to the closet nearest the door, retrieved my windbreaker and slipped an arm into the sleeve.

"What do you think you're doing?" he protested.

"If you're going to start acting ugly, I'm not going to stay around tonight for the show," I said angrily, hardly knowing what I said. My hand was on the knob before he grabbed my wrist. In a blinding second, he twisted my arm sharply behind my back and slammed me against the door. He pushed his body against me.

"Stop it Manny!" I cried out in pain. "Let me go."

"Don't you ever walk out on me!" He spat out the words, practically touching his lips to my face. "Don't think you're ever going to walk out on me." I felt his breath and his body trembling before he released me. He spun around and stalked back to the bar.

"What is wrong with you!" I screamed and ran to the bedroom. My wrist was already swelling, and my hand felt numb and useless. I wanted to find a place, any place to hide. But I was afraid to leave the apartment. Manny must have heard me crying later in the night. He came to the door.

"Lily, I'm sorry," he said through the door. "I'm sorry." I held my breath and willed myself to calm down so he'd think I'd fallen asleep. He walked away and said nothing more.

After Manny left for work the following day, I took a cab to the hospital and made up a story about slipping in the tub. I thought my wrist was broken, but it was only badly sprained. I wore the brace for weeks. Every day it reminded me that our marriage was broken. And a new realization had entered my mind. Something was terribly wrong not only with our marriage, but also with Manny. We had a problem bigger than the both of us.

More than ever, I prayed.

God help us.

Chapter Twelve

One winter day, I received an unexpected phone call from Georgia. It was Uncle Bill, an old family friend and the executor of my daddy's estate. All through college he'd sent me quarterly distributions for my expenses. After I married, it no longer seemed particularly relevant. I had everything money could buy.

"Uncle Bill, how are you?" Suddenly I missed him. "I haven't heard from you in a long time. Is everything all right?"

"I'm fine, Lily Rose. You sound well. I can't believe I've let this much time go by without calling you. I got your number from Annie Ruth."

"It's been two years now. Manuel and I married and moved here to Detroit within the same week."

"Yes, Annie Ruth told me all about it. I hope you're happy there."

"Thank you, Uncle Bill."

"Do you want to do anything yet about your property here, Lily Rose?"

"I've practically forgotten it," I said. "It seems like such a long time ago and such a long way away."

"Impossible," he scoffed. "You couldn't forget this place. It's in your blood. You and your daddy loved it too much."

"Well, I'm not ready yet, Uncle Bill, to do anything about it." I sighed. "Let's just keep things like they've been. You manage all the particulars like you've been doing and keep the place from falling down before I decide something. I put that place out of mind years ago."

"Of course, you know I'll take care of things, but eventually you'll want to put everything in order."

"Uncle Bill, my husband doesn't know anything about the house in Wilcox Station, or the connections I have there. I'd rather it stay that way—more or less." I paused for a second to listen for his reaction. When he didn't say anything, I continued, "So, please, don't send me anything in the mail. It would be better if you didn't call here either."

"Well, I'll respect your wishes, Lily Rose, but that could put us in a bind. I might need to discuss matters with you sometime. I've been remiss as it is not keeping in touch. I hope you'll forgive me for that."

"Oh, that's all right Uncle Bill. I've been busy with my new life. But, you're right. How about I call you every month, from now on? Would that work?"

"Yes, I think it would. I'd like to hear from you every month."

"Well, let's do that," I said. "Is there anything in particular you called about today?"

"I wanted to apologize for failing to stay in touch. You are like family and I'm ashamed I let this much time go by. Also, Sugar and I were talking about the property. I'm sorry to say it's gotten run down the last few years. He wants to put down new grass and bring it back up to the standards of the other historic homes in the neighborhood. I've just had him doing the minimum to keep it from dying and looking completely deserted."

"Let him do as much as he will. Maintain the lawns and beautiful gardens." I paused for a moment as images of vibrant colors, flowering shrubs, and magnificent trees drifted across my mind's eye.

"Yes, but that costs money. Your money."

"I gave you power of attorney years ago when you read the will after Daddy died. You use whatever you need from the money to do whatever you think is right, Uncle Bill. Aside from college, I always thought that money should be for taking care of the property anyway. I trust you whatever you do."

"Well, all right, Lily Rose. I thought you'd feel that way, but I thought it best to talk to you about it. It's been awhile now, and it does belong to you."

"Okay, Uncle Bill. I want the money to be used for the place. But, remember, I don't want my husband to know anything at all about my father's house in Georgia."

"If that's what you want. But, let me remind you, young lady, the house is rightfully yours. I hope you'll enjoy it again one day."

"I'll think about that." Already memories scrolled through my mind like scenes from a movie. "It's good to hear from you." Bittersweet memories tugged at my heart.

"It's good talking to you, too," he said.

"I'll call you in a few weeks. Good-bye."

And with that call, my thoughts traveled back to Georgia, to Daddy's house in Wilcox Station. He had grown up there, and his only sister had been born, lived, and died right there in the house. Daddy and I visited several times during the year, on special weekends or holidays, but especially those two weeks every summer. I vaguely remembered the few times Mama and James Michael went with us. For years it was just my daddy and me—our special time with Aunt Martha and Miss Izzy, Sugar, and Uncle Bill, and all the friendly folks who'd known my daddy all his life. But how could any of that fit into my life now? I'd started to tell Manny about it once before, but the mention of an old abandoned house didn't interest him. Manny had gotten all he ever wanted from Georgia—and he didn't care if he ever went back.

Uncle Bill planted a seed, and that seed took root and grew until one day I realized that not only had I lost my father when he died, but I'd lost something else just as precious to me. I needed to reclaim it. Someday, I told myself, someday, I would.

***

Julie and I chatted on the phone every week carefully avoiding talking when Manny was home. I'd learned early in our marriage that he totally hated me spending time on the phone when he was around. For some reason, she called late that day. I paced back and forth talking on the kitchen phone and laughing like crazy over one of her little stories. When Manny walked in, I was so caught up in the conversation that I hardly noticed him. Normally I would have picked up on his sour mood by his staccato movements as he mixed himself a drink. When I accidentally blocked his path with the long cord, I should have seen the irritation in his eyes. I switched from speaking English to French, like Julie and I sometimes did, and continued the conversation.

"Get off that phone!" Manny exploded.

"Julie, I'll call you back tomorrow, gotta go. Manny's home."

I turned to hang up the phone and didn't see it coming. Manny slapped me across the face. My head snapped back, and pain exploded in my jaw and ear. I staggered backward and braced myself against the counter, holding on with my head bowed until the dizziness passed. I don't know how long I stood there. Tears of pain burned my eyes, but even more painful was my broken heart, shattered beyond repair.

"Don't ever do that again," Manny said.

I didn't ask him what he was talking about. I didn't even bother to look at him. When I turned to leave the room, I heard him mutter, "I know she was talking about me."

I made it to the bathroom where I splashed cold water on my face and spat out grit. It took a second to realize some back teeth had chipped. I opened my mouth slowly. My jaw locked. I manipulated it to straighten it, and even then my teeth didn't set together right. I prayed I wouldn't have to go to the doctor again, then swallowed two Tylenol and went to bed for the next two days.

When Manny left on his business trip the next morning, I mumbled that I had decided to get rid of a few things like he'd suggested.

"Good. Finally you're getting rid of that worthless junk. See you at the end of the week."

That was the week I shipped Daddy's desk to Georgia. I called Uncle Bill by pay phone to let him know to expect the delivery. I also mailed a large box of clothes, shoes, and my old typewriter. The Salvation Army picked up more things, and I made sure I left the ticket on the kitchen counter so Manny would see it. I might leave Detroit with little or nothing, I thought, but leave I would. He'd slapped me only that once, but he'd dealt the final blow against my hopes for a husband who would cherish and care for me . . . my final hopes for a marriage until death do us part. Now it was just a matter of time until I figured out how I was going to get away from him.

Manny returned from his trip, and even though my cheekbone was still plum purple, he didn't comment. Nor did I, but I could tell by his attempts at quiet conversation that he felt regret, or shame. He was more conciliatory than usual. He told me I should go visit Julie the next time he went out of town, like I'd wanted to do for so long. He said he wanted us to go on a little vacation as soon as the weather warmed up in May for some "quality time." I managed weak smiles as I listened attentively to my husband. I did nothing to let on that the idea to leave him had entered my mind. For a while, life would go on as usual, as I waited for the right opportunity to leave.

***

I had resorted to perfecting my skills in the kitchen. I knew how to make homestyle dishes. After all, Annie Ruth gave me a good foundation in culinary arts. I'd helped her make quick breads, casseroles, and desserts of all sorts. After Manny and I were married, I wanted to perfect Italian specialties to please him. I liked following the instructions— one, two, three. I'd once thought marriage would be as simple. Do my part, one, two, three, and a wonderful man would take care of me . . . happily ever after. My wonderful man wouldn't even talk to me.

I watched my favorite cooking show in the kitchen while I prepared dinner. I was in the middle of making chicken parmigiana when the doorbell rang. I wiped my hands and slid the casserole into the oven. I glanced at the clock and set the timer. Manny would be home soon.

Wiping my hands on my ruffled apron, I opened the door. A tall stylish woman in a red suit and high heels looked down at me, with a crooked smile on her heavily made up face.

"Hello, may I help you?" I held the door with one hand and swiped the other one again on the apron. Some sort of a sales call, I thought.

"Lil Valenti?" She angled her head to the side.

"Yes?" When I heard my name, I felt queasy in the pit of my stomach. Manny was the only person who ever called me Lil.

"I'm Cynthia Moore. May I come in?"

"Uh . . ."

"I need to talk to you about a mutual interest." She paused. I looked at her and said nothing.

"Your husband," she blurted out.

"Is everything all right? Is Manny all right? Certainly, come in, come in."

"Manny?" She laughed a humorless laugh. Her eyes were shrewd; her voice mocking. "Oh yes, he's fine. Just fine. I need to talk with you, woman to woman."

"I don't understand. Please sit down." I motioned to the sofa. When she sat down, I sat on the edge of the chair across from her. I couldn't take my eyes off her.

"Manuel and I work together. We move in the same circles." She waved her hand as she spoke as if to accentuate her point. "I'm an attorney as well." She paused and lifted a brow, as if to calculate her next remarks. "I'm going to cut to the chase. I don't have time for any more games. Give your husband the divorce he's requested."

"What?" I asked, incredulous. I felt a frown constrict my brows. "Who are you?" I stood up, and she did too.

"Listen, Miss Priss." She stepped closer. "I was expecting a proposal from Manuel myself, and then he came back from Georgia with *you*."

She took a step back and gave me a disdainful once-over before continuing the tirade.

"I've worked not only on this law partnership but this relationship for five years now, and my patience has reached its limit. He says he asked you for a divorce. Give it to him."

My throat constricted, but I managed to say, "I don't believe he said that." I walked to the door and swung it wide open, holding on tight to steady myself. "Leave our house, now."

"You really are stupid, aren't you?" She sneered at me then turned her head with dramatic flair and took a long stride out the door.

"What the hell?" I heard Manny's shocked voice as he must have come face to face with the woman. I stepped into the doorway.

"Manuel, I . . . I didn't expect to see you," she stammered. They stood eye to eye. He glowered at her and grabbed her upper arm.

"What do you think you're doing coming to my home?" She snatched away and ran down the hall. Not waiting for the elevator, she disappeared down the stairs.

Manny turned and took the few remaining steps into the condo. He had a ghastly look on his face, like a death mask.

"Lily, what did she say to you?"

I backed away slowly and eased myself down on the edge of the sofa. "She said she's been working on a relationship with you for five years." I ran my hands over my cheeks and they met over my lips like a prayer. "She said you asked me for a divorce."

"That . . . ," He clenched his teeth while muttering the foulest oaths.

"Five years?" My voice came out thin and weak.

"Lil, I love you. That woman has been after me for years. She's ruining my life. She's a law partner. I have to placate her as best I can, but I've never been in love with her. And I never will be. You are the only woman I've ever loved." He walked over to me, but hesitated before touching my arm. "Lily?"

"Manny, don't try to explain." I turned away, pressing my fingertips to my eyes. I felt weak and a little sick, not much else. Indignant, yes that too, but not with Manny so much as with the woman. How dare she come to my home?

"Lily, please tell me you believe me. That woman means nothing to me. She's obsessed over me for as long as I've known her. She disgusts me." He held his head in his hands for a painful minute. "It's maddening," he spat out the words, "because there's nothing I can do about it. Not a damn thing. She's a partner in the firm. I have to work with her. Do you understand that? Please tell me you believe me, Lil," he pleaded.

All at once, I realized, sadly, it didn't make any difference. Maybe some of what he said was true, but the relationship had been exposed—our marriage was a terrible lie.

"I believe you Manny. I do. I wonder if that's why it feels so tragic."

A tear slid down my cheek; he brushed it away. I looked at him. Really looked at him and felt like I was seeing him for the first time. Such a handsome man with the charm and intelligence that made it easy for women to fall in love with him, like I had done. He carried himself in such a way he seemed to have integrity. A fine facade. His eyes, which once seemed mysterious in a dreamy way, now just looked sad . . . lost . . . ruined.

Just because I'd already decided to leave, didn't mean I wasn't heart broken.

"Lily?" Manny knelt in front of me and held my shoulders gently. "Lily Rose." His voice cracked. "Please tell me you love me."

"I love you, Manny."

He hugged me then. I felt his heart pounding against mine. He held me tight against his chest, but I didn't have the strength to hold him back. God forgive me. I didn't even try.

He released me and rushed out the door. I curled up on the sofa and gave in to despair's familiar pull. I might have stayed there. I wanted to stay there, but the kitchen timer went off. I got up and removed the steaming casserole from the oven. A wave of nausea hit me.

No! I won't do this! I won't let this spoil anything. Not dinner. Not my life. Never again.

I poured myself a glass of white wine and took a bitter sip, then carefully placed a portion of tender white meat on a china plate and spooned sauce over it. The steam rose; I closed my eyes and inhaled. *Well done, Lily Rose.* But, it was impossible to swallow the lump in my throat. I spat into the sink.

When Manny returned a few hours later, he didn't eat. He drank. I heard him go back and forth to the bar, the ice clicking in the glass. I lay in bed in the dark with dry eyes wide open, planning how I would get through the next two weeks until Manny went out of town again. Planning all the things I needed to do before I left him. I'd have to think of everything, and I would. Wise as a serpent, Annie Ruth says, but harmless as a dove. Only two weeks, I thought. I can make it two more weeks.

Chapter Thirteen

I opened the window shade and looked down on patches of gray, blue, and green. From that altitude, the whole world was a patchwork puzzle. Exhilaration, like I'd accomplished a daring feat . . . like I might have actually slipped away . . . escaped Detroit, escaped Manuel, escaped the confusion and fear and the oppressive atmosphere of the last two and a half years. Freedom, like pure oxygen, expanded my lungs and gushed through my veins. I hadn't taken a deep breath in weeks. It felt good to breathe easy now on the plane to Quebec City.

Life shows us what we're made of, Lily Rose. You're made of good stuff.

Annie Ruth's words popped into my head.

I chuckled a little, remembering so clearly her saying them to me the year Daddy died—the year I crawled inside myself and hid there in a quagmire of sorrow. She'd pulled me out and set me back on life's road. She was an anchor, and said I needed a little steel in my backbone.

This time, I'd pulled myself out. And with Julie's help my backbone was strong. I'd get away from Manuel, and I'd never again let myself curl up and die. I would live the life God gave me. A confidence bound by defiance and the will to live gave me strength and a forward moving vision I didn't know I had.

The picture of that woman flashed into my mind. Missing. Cynthia Moore. Thirty-six years old. Single. Her disappearance had been reported just days after she'd stopped by the condo. I didn't want to imagine what that could mean. As soon as I heard the report on the evening news, I'd turned off the television and never turned it on again. Lord forgive me, I'd not said a word to another soul, except Julie, to whom I told everything. I'd certainly not breathed a word to Manny that I knew anything about a disappearance. I was afraid of what his reaction might be— afraid of what knowing might mean for me. I didn't want to know. I wanted to get away from Detroit and never look back.

As I walked through customs, I saw Julie waving. She held the hand of a tiny two-year-old miniature of her-self. Joy flooded my heart. I ran towards them.

"Oh, Julie." Tears stung my eyes. "What a beautiful child." We hugged, and with my arm still around her, I looked down at the child by her side.

"Hello Chloe. How are you?" I thought my heart would burst with love.

"Chloe, this is my friend Lily Rose I told you about." We both knelt down by the child.

"Hi Chloe, it's nice to meet you. What a pretty girl you are. I have something for you." I held up a little fabric doll. Chloe's big eyes sparkled. She grabbed it with her star-shaped hands and clutched it to her chest. She closed her eyes and put her face on its head. I melted.

"Julie, she's beautiful. She looks just like you." I couldn't help thinking of the baby I'd lost.

"Lily Rose, it's so good to see you. I'm so happy you're here. Thank God, you're here." Her words were soft, but serious, her eyes moist with tears.

"I know, Julie, what a mercy. You can't imagine how glad I am to be here."

"I've missed you. Let's get home. We have so much to talk about. We're going to take care of this, Lily. I'm not going to let anything happen to you. You'll see, my dear."

"I've missed you *so* much."

It was like we'd never parted. We knew each other so well—trusted each other.

Julie and Charles lived in a narrow stone condo on a winding street in historic Quebec City. The bold structure seemed a permanent part of the rock overlooking the St. Lawrence River. A sharp chill blew in the air, but the sky was crystal blue. Red tulips as bright as Cyndi Lauper's lips swayed in choreographed rows up and down the streets and around Julie's sun-lit patio. While the afternoon sun shined on us, the three of us sat in the thickly cushioned metal glider, sipping hot spiced tea, and basking in contentment.

While sitting there with Julie and her little girl, an odd sensation came over me. Like I myself, Lily Rose, was remembering me. Like I had been away for a while, wandering lost for the last three years. I had forgotten *me*. My forever friend connected me right back to myself—the real me I never should've abandoned.

"Julie, I have this awesome feeling that I'm right where I'm supposed to be."

"You are, Lily. *Bien sur*. I know you are."

Then we heard the front door open, and Charles walked in. What an event, to love and be so loved. It warmed my heart to witness the love in that home.

"Daddy's home," Julie said. Chloe ran with her arms out stretched and took a tiny leap into his arms. Julie followed. Charles balanced the toddler on the crook of his arm and put the other one around Julie. I looked on and smiled, grateful for this display of how life should be. With that simple interaction I was even surer I wasn't going back to Manuel.

After a pleasant evening and a restful night's sleep, I was eager to hear Julie's plans and ready to execute them. Julie's shop opened at nine, so we headed out the door at eight thirty. Charles walked Chloe to her nursery school just around the corner, then continued on his way to the university where he taught. Julie's shop was only five blocks away.

A brisk breeze swept strands of hair across my face. We clutched our mugs of hot coffee as we walked along the cobblestone streets. The weather was colder than I expected for May.

Along the wall of stones and glass store fronts, Julie came to a stop. The shingle above our heads read "Angelic Creations." I telescoped my hands and peered through the window.

"Julie, what a charming shop! It's lovely." Julie turned a long key in the heavy door and pushed it open. The shop bell jingled.

"It is, isn't it?" Julie smiled.

"It suits you to a T."

"I love it," she said. "And it's been such a hit. These Quebecois fell in love with my artistic flair."

"And your Southern charm.

Julie designed and created most of the artisan jewelry she sold in the shop. She also featured eclectic designer items she ordered from artists all over the world. With that, plus her winning personality, her business thrived and so did she. She showed me pair after pair of handcrafted earrings that reflected her artistic passion.

"Here, Lily, try these. They're for you. Blue amethyst waterfalls." She held up a pair of drop earrings.

"Lovely and light," I said as I turned my face from side to side. "Are they too elegant for me? I don't usually wear dangly earrings. Just these simple little hoops."

"Lily, that's the point. We're going for a different look," she said. She picked up another pair of earrings. "Blue amethyst for friendship, and citrine for good luck." She smiled.

"You're so sweet. Thank you." I accepted the two gemstone sets—necklaces, bracelets, and matching earrings. A little girl playing dress up again. Seemed like I always got around to that with my girlfriends, but this was not child's play.

"They're perfect," Julie said. "I've arranged everything, Lily. We'll leave for lunch and Monica will take care of the shop. And then we'll get down to business."

"Oh my stars, Julie. I can't believe I'm actually doing this."

"You bet you are, and I'm with you."

Those few hours in the shop that morning began the restoration of my fractured personality.

"Julie, it's so good being here with you." She gave me a quick hug. Although she smiled, she had a sad look in her eyes. We chatted up a storm, amusing Monica to no end. The Canadian was enthralled by our accents that flowed as smooth and thick as their maple syrup. Before I knew it, the morning had slipped away.

"It's been so nice meeting you, Monica."

"You as well, Lily Rose," she said. "How long will you be here?"

"Oh . . . the rest of the week." I glanced at Julie. "But I probably won't be seeing you again. I'm writing a novel. Need seclusion you know. This is a working trip for me," I lied.

"Good luck," she said.

"Monica, I'll be back around five to help close up the shop," Julie said.

We stepped out into the sunshine.

"Let's go have *le diner*." Julie slipped her arm around mine. "I know this great place. Very European. You'll love it."

Strolling down the streets of Old Quebec, I felt like I was on vacation in a colorful French provincial town. Church bells rang in an ancient cathedral which had once been the location of an old Alfred Hitchcock film. Julie enjoyed telling me all about it.

"Julie, I see why you love this town. It's perfectly charming."

We entered a wedge-shaped stone building with dark wooden floors. Jovial laughter and savory aromas filled the air.

"Umm . . . I like this place already."

"Follow me." She smiled, and then led the way to the back of the café where we ascended a narrow iron staircase to another level of the eatery. We seated ourselves at a tiny square table beside a wall of tall windows that overlooked the street below.

While we indulged ourselves with steaming bowls of bouillabaisse and rounds of warm crusty bread, I forgot about Manny. For that moment, I was a light-hearted girl again enjoying the company of my best friend.

"Julie, being here, with you, I feel . . . safe." I took a deep breath and exhaled slowly, savoring the moment. "Of course, the wine and warm soup might have something to do with this delicious feeling."

"Lily, I know you've second-guessed yourself, but you had to leave him. You had to. All the more reason this plan has to work." Julie's tense face showed concern. "Oh my gosh, I've been so worried about you. He's toxic, Lily, and possibly even lethal."

"I know." I looked down at the napkin being twisted in my lap, melancholy as my thoughts turned to him. "It's heartbreaking."

"Not as heartbreaking as it would be if you stayed with him." Julie's words conveyed the conviction she had formed months ago. "It just makes me sick when I think of what that man has put you through. I'll feel better when I know you're down in Georgia, and you'll feel much better too. You can get your life back."

"I know I can't go on any longer like I've been living. Even seeing you and Charles together confirms what I already knew in my heart." I looked up at her. "It's just not right to live the way I've been living with Manuel. Something is very wrong."

"Oh, Lily Rose," Julie whispered and shook her head. "You couldn't have known."

"Well, at this point, I don't want to think about it. It makes me sick too. What's the plan, Julie? I'm ready to do this."

"So am I!" Julie wiped her mouth, laid her cloth napkin in her lap, and then began to unfold her elaborate scheme for my disappearance. I leaned in closer so I wouldn't miss a word.

"And Lily, even if this works for only a couple of months, by the time he finds you, you'll have a safety net around you."

"A safety net?" I tucked in my chin and pursed my lips.

"Yes, your Uncle Bubba."

"Uncle *Bill*." I laughed.

"Well, whoever he is, he'll protect you. He'll have the police watching your every move. All the neighbors will keep an eye on you. You know how small towns like that are. There's nothing better to do but stay in each other's business. Manuel won't be able to get to you . . . unless he wants some kudzu growing out his ears."

"Julie!" We both laughed then. "You act like there's a bunch of vigilantes down in Georgia. Why, *my people* are law-abiding citizens." I allowed my Southern drawl to meander over those words.

"Lily, I'm serious." Julie put her hands on her cheeks for a second. "Manuel might come looking for you. In fact, he will come looking for you, it's guaranteed, but he won't be able to come down there and make you go back with him. He'd dare not come down there and hurt you."

"I understand what you're saying Julie. I can see this working. It just seems like it's too much to hope for. What if I chicken out?"

"Then you'll be eaten by the wolf." Julie snapped. "No, Lily Rose," she shook her head. "You cannot chicken out. You know you have to leave him. God is on your side. He's with you. You're going to be all right."

I looked into her eyes and thought about those words I'd heard before. *Lily Rose, you're going to be all right.* The words sounded hollow, illusory. Yet, her strong convictions bolstered mine.

"Thank you, Julie. I don't know what I'd do without you."

After lunch we went shopping nearby in a vintage clothing store. Julie picked out a long cotton skirt and a shorter floral one with scarves and blouses to match, a jean jacket, a boyfriend jacket, and gladiator sandals to suit my new persona.

"Julie, with these outfits and colors, I'll stand out like a peacock."

"That's exactly what we want you to do, but you won't be looking like Lily Rose Cates."

"Can I thank your interest in Alfred Hitchcock for this, or your hippy roots, or what?"

"Naww . . . it's just one of my hidden talents. The creative mad genius part."

Who would've thought it? We had fun. That afternoon I laughed so much my sides hurt. When Julie announced we had two more stops and then halted in front of a tattoo parlor, my mouth fell open. "Julie! No. You must be kidding."

"Brilliant, isn't it?"

"What are you talking about? My Daddy will roll over in his grave. Besides, I'm liable to fall out in a dead faint. I *hate* needles."

"It's not what you think. Henna, silly. You're going to get tattooed with henna. It will wear off in a month."

"And Manuel Valenti would never think to look for a tattooed lady." I grinned. "You are a genius."

When we walked out two hours later, reddish brown floral scrolls and curly cues encircled both my ankles. A henna cross set on my left wrist. A lace pattern with decidedly bohemia overtones started on my left shoulder and ended just above my heart. I looked exotic . . . I scandalized myself. *My faults, my faults, my most grievous faults . . .*

"All I can say is, if this *mess* doesn't come *off me*, you will owe me for the rest of your life."

"Calm down. It will. I promise. I've done my research," she said. "Now, one last stop. We have to get some hair dye."

We went into the pharmacy near her condo and picked out a shade as close to Julie's color as we could find, which ended up being several shades darker than my own.

"Here it is. *Nice & Easy*—mahogany brown. I actually tried this myself last summer. Thought I needed to spice it up for Charles." She giggled. "He didn't even notice."

We strolled back to Julie's apartment, chatting all the way.

"Make yourself at home here Lily," Julie said as she put on a pot of water for tea. "Enjoy some time alone. Use it to get your strength up. We'll all be back home before you know it. And so will you." She gave me a hug, then headed back out to the shop.

While I sipped warm tea, I wandered through Julie's home, examining the adorable framed pictures she had on display of Chloe and Charles and the three of them together. Theirs was a happy home, a blest marriage. Tears came to my eyes. Happy tears for Julie. Grateful ones, to God. Sad tears as well, due to the unexpected guilt that pricked my heart.

"Lord, I'm so sorry I ran ahead of you," I cried. "Please forgive me for marrying Manny without bothering to consult you." I covered my face with my hands and sobbed. As the tears washed down my cheeks over the next hour, I poured out my heart to God. When Julie, Charles, and Chloe arrived home at suppertime, I felt better than I'd felt in a long time. Ready for a fresh start.

***

That evening Julie cut my hair. It reminded me of all those times we'd trimmed each other's hair during our college days. But this time, instead of trimming the split ends, she cut off twelve inches. As thick clumps fell to the floor, a tight-lipped grimace stretched across my face.

"My hair hasn't been this short since I was eight years old," I said.

"Short and sassy is in style," Julie piped in.

I was speechless. I pulled sections of hair against each side of my face to check the length. This was going to be harder than I imagined.

The next morning, we were starting out for Maine. I was a bit jittery. I colored my hair before I showered, choosing to skip breakfast and get right to work completing the transformation. I heard Julie saying good-bye to Charles and Chloe as I wrapped myself in a towel. A few minutes later, I heard a knock on the door.

"Lily Rose?"

I turned off the blow dryer. "Wait just a second," I said. I quickly ran the comb through my long bangs. "Come on in."

We stared at one another for a full thirty seconds. I flipped the hair on the left side of my head; Julie flipped the hair on the right side of hers. When she did that, we

laughed. What is it about girlfriends getting together—
something about the dynamics of the relationship frees our
femininity, validates emotions. Whether it's over hairdos
and henna tattoos or jewelry and hemlines, Julie and I
laughed. With each laugh I felt like I was exhaling stress.

"It's perfect!" Julie giggled. "We have identical hair
styles."

"Yes, we do," I said. "You did it. This is either a first
rate scheme or a totally insane idea."

"Just a second," Julie said, and left the room. She
returned a minute later carrying her purse. She took out
her wallet and removed a card.

"Here, take a look at this. You will easily pass for
me." She held her ID in front of my face. Indeed, we looked
like twins.

So, with one of the new scarves wrapped around my
head to hide the new haircut from possible neighbor sight-
ings, we packed the car for the day's journey.

"Charles is totally on board. As far as he'll ever tell,
you stayed upstairs in seclusion for days writing a novel,"
Julie said. She was giddy with excitement when we got on
the road.

"You've thought of everything," I said, swallowing
hard. A sick feeling churned in the pit of my stomach. The
truth is I was getting cold feet.

"It really bothers me, Julie, that I haven't been able
to . . . fix our problems." I shuddered, and then sighed
heavily.

"You mean fix him," she said.

"Well, make him better. Daddy was a real blessing.
He made Mama better. I've failed."

"No, you haven't. Don't think like that. If your staying would make things better, you'd stay. But you can't

change the way he is. And your mama and daddy, that's totally different, Lily. Your mama wouldn't hurt a fly. Besides, she can't help how she is. It's sad to say, but back in those days, the cure for depression was sometimes worse than the illness."

"I know but . . . I expected our love to overcome any problems we might have."

"Lily, sometimes love is not enough. You can't let him continue to hurt you."

I brushed away a tear. "I know."

Julie reached over and patted my arm. I took her hand and looked out the window at the overcast sky.

The five-hour drive across country gave me time to unwind, and then wind up again. Julie talked on and on. I suspect she was trying to build my confidence and hide her own fears. We went over every detail of our stories about my week in Quebec that didn't happen. Julie even planned to take her own taxi ride to the airport disguised as me, so she could tell Manny that as far as she knew, I'd taken a taxi to the airport the morning of my pseudo departure. If anyone checked taxicab records, there'd be a record of the call to her condo. Julie prepared to fabricate as many stories as needed to baffle and confuse Manuel if ever he came looking for me.

"There's no other way, Lily," she said.

All the while she'd pretend to be as baffled and concerned as he was.

"What do you mean she didn't return home? She had a round trip ticket. Do you think something has happened to her, Manuel? Surely you don't think she ran away? Have you called the police? Might the police suspect foul play? The husband is always the main suspect, isn't he?"

"Lily Rose, he's not stupid," Julie said adamantly. "He won't go to the police. He knows they'll suspect him. And he won't find a record of you traveling anywhere but here."

"I hope you're right. I'm counting on it."

Even with my altered appearance and Julie's ID, I thought Manuel would be able to find out I bought a bus ticket. I couldn't forget how he'd tracked down my cousin Maggie. At the last minute, I came up with a different plan—I'd catch a big rig going south and stay out of public transportation all together.

Julie didn't like the idea. We drove past the mega truck stop three times before she got up the nerve to stop.

"Now, Lily, please don't hang around that place long if you don't find a ride. Promise me you'll get a cab and go to the bus stop if you don't get a ride within a couple of hours. The bus will be safe, I feel certain. You won't be recognized. I wouldn't even recognize you."

"Julie, let me give this a try. I'll call a cab if I need to. I promise." I squeezed her hand.

We'd said our good-byes in the car, but after all her bravado, Julie started crying like a baby. I was the stoic one.

"I won't stop praying. I'll pray for you night and day 'til you're safe in Georgia. I'll start praying as soon as you get out of this car." Julie was holding my hand so tight that my fingers ached. "You're my dearest friend. Be brave, Lily Rose. You can do this."

"I'll call you as soon as I can," I said. "Everything will go fine. I feel good about it. I really do."

"It has to," Julie cried. "Call me as soon as you get there."

We looked at each other for a second. Then I leaned over and kissed her cheek. "I'll call you and put your ID in the mail as soon as I can. Thank you my sweet friend. Pray."

She stopped fifty feet away from the station, and I quickly got out. I didn't look back to see her drive away. I walked away with my head held high and my shoulders back just like a scene from an old movie. Beautiful. Brave. Confident. But it was all a lie.

Icy rain pricked my skin as I made my way across the wide parking lot.

"Oh God, what have I gotten myself into?"

Annie Ruth's words drifted through my mind.

"Don't get tangled in the briers with that man, Lily Rose."

That's exactly what I've done, I thought. And it hurt. It really hurt. I just hoped it wouldn't draw blood.

Chapter Fourteen

Rain pooled in wide muddy puddles. Another eighteen-wheel behemoth pulled into the truck stop, causing me to jump to avoid the muddy spray. Julie was gone, and I felt alone all the way down to my wet toes.

I mentally ran through the plan we'd made. Scope out the place and listen for a mild mannered person who looked harmless, not too outlandish, to ask if he knew anyone headed down south.

But, hey, I look pretty outlandish myself, I thought. Act like you know what you're doing, Julie had said. Easier said, than done. I looked for the restroom.

As I walked by, a rugged looking man with a barrel chest was exiting the men's room. He stopped, lifted his chest, and adjusted his belt with his thumbs at his waist. He raised his eyebrows and turned his head to look at me.

When I came out of the restroom, he stood only a few feet away. His eyes followed me. Was he waiting for me? Probably not, but that's all it took. So much for acting like I knew what I was doing. I was totally spooked. It was all I could do not to run like a scared rabbit.

A row of booths lined the wall beside the windows. I slipped into the one across from the grill and nearest the door, rummaged through the floral tapestry bag Julie had gotten for me at Goodwill, pulled out a notebook and pen and proceeded to write in an attempt to calm my nerves.

Oh Lord, help me. My heart was racing. I felt so out of place, but since my outfit belied my true state of mind, I tried to appear confident.

A parade of folks flowed in and out of the truck stop, and as long as they didn't notice me, I felt fine. After what seemed like an eternity, I knew I had to speak to someone if my plan was going to work. The operator of the grill seemed like a reasonable source.

But, when I approached the counter, I barely managed to order a coffee. My mouth felt stuffed with cotton. I returned to the booth with the coffee, picked up a greasy Enquirer magazine someone had left there, and started turning the pages.

Oh, my God, what am I going to do? Driven by fear, I couldn't get my thoughts together. I reasoned that I might have to call the taxi and head to the bus station after all. But I wanted to try to make the trip this way if possible because it would be harder for Manny to pick up my trail.

About that time, a couple in their late fifties or early sixties walked into the station, and fortunately, stood close enough to me that I heard their conversation. I feigned interest in the tabloid's bizarre pictures while I eavesdropped.

"What I'd give for some grits and red-eye gravy," said the jean-clad man. He pulled a baseball cap off his bald head and then smoothed down some strands of gray on the back of his head.

"Honey, you jus' gonna have to wait 'til we git home," said the woman. She had a head-full of teased red hair.

Hearing the familiar accent coming from this mom and pop ignited a spark of hope.

"Ma'am, excuse me please, where're y'all from?"

"Alabama, sugar. Near Birmingham." She smiled. "How 'bout yourself?"

I gazed at her, hesitating so long, the smile disappeared from her face.

"Well?" she asked.

"Me, too. The South. I need to catch a ride down south," I stammered.

The man at the grill heard the exchange and came over to the table. He appeared to know the couple. He looked closely at me, frowned as he leaned toward me, and then spoke in a low warning voice.

"Listen, lady, I don't allow prostitutes—at least none that I know about—to bother my customers in here."

For a second I was confused, and then I was mortified. My voice stalled out for a moment. "Oh no sir, I'm not a prostitute. I just need to get a ride. I'll pay for it."

Warmth spread up my chest and neck. I could imagine the red blotches popping out on my burning cheeks.

"Well, you look like you're up to something," said the skeptical fry cook.

"I'm just trying to get home." My voice cracked and my eyes stung.

The red-haired woman suddenly waved her hand out by her side like she was shooing him away. "Russ," she said in a reassuring voice, "I think she's okay. We'll take care of this."

My panic subsided somewhat when she came to my rescue, but tears had already welled up in my eyes. I saw kindness in hers.

"Can I get a ride with y'all? I can pay you. A hundred dollars." I cleared my throat and licked my dry lips.

"Um . . . now . . . well . . . ." She looked at the old guy who at that moment was reading the posted menu. She looked back at me. "Honey, there ain't room but for one woman in his truck, and that's me. I'm sorry." She lowered her eyes, then looked up at me.

Bless her heart, was she threatened by me? I was embarrassed again, but what could I say. My confidence sank like a rock. Still, she showed a flicker of compassion.

"You'll need to be careful who you climb in with, that's for sure. And don't be telling nobody you got money." Her tone softened.

"I understand." I rubbed my hands over the sides of my dyed hair.

"I don't think you do," she said, shaking her head. She ordered her food and cut her eyes back at me. "You can't be too careful."

The man at the grill had heard everything. He shook his head without looking at either of us, as if to say, he had little hope for me. *Lord have mercy.* I looked away to gaze out the window. *Christ have mercy.* I watched the rain, falling harder, ping-ponging in widening puddles. *Lord have mercy.*

Suddenly the woman exclaimed, "Well, I declare. Look who just walked in."

Her partner swiped the back of his hand across his mouth. For the first time, he spoke to me.

"Girl," he said, looking directly at me, "you must have an angel looking out for you."

They grinned and flagged down the man who had just walked in. He walked over to their table, and they all shook hands.

"How ya' doing Earl?" the woman asked.

"Ain't seen you in a month of Sundays," said Pops.

"Yeah, my route changed for a while. I'm back running Florida to Canada. Headed down thata way today. Y'all doing all right? You lookin' good."

When I heard him say "Florida" my heart beat quickened, I sat up a little straighter, and stiffened.

Then the woman said, "Earl, you got room for a passenger? That little woman over yonder," she pointed to me, "needs a ride down the country. Says she can pay you a hundred dollars for it."

Earl, a Willy Nelson looking character, turned his gaze on me. Wiry salt and pepper hair curled out the top of his plaid shirt. He crossed his arms over his chest for a moment before reaching up to rub his bearded face, and then swiped his hand down his neck. He then took off his brimmed felt hat.

"You don't talk too much, do yah?" He looked at me with a solemn expression on his face.

I shook my head, a definite denial.

"Any bad habits I need know about?" He looked at me quizzically.

"No, sir," I said, frowning.

He threw back his head and laughed. Mom and Pops laughed right along with him. I swallowed hard, unable to grasp the humor in the situation.

"I'm jus' playing wid you," he said, chuckling a little. "Sure you can ride wid me. But don't call me sir. The name's Earl."

He stuck out his hand, and I grabbed it. "And who might you be?"

"Julie. I'm Julie Combier."

"Uh, huh, I see." And I knew he had caught the lie. "Well, I'm going all the way down to Tallahassee," he continued. "It's a right far piece but you can ride all the way if it suits yah."

"Thank you, sir. I mean, Earl. Thank you very much."

"Don't go too far, little lady. I'll be ready to go in less than an hour." He turned back to mom and pop. They swapped more stories and laughs. Then he shook the man's hand again and wished them well before walking in the direction of the restrooms.

I closed my eyes and said a silent prayer. Then, I stepped over to the couple.

"Thank you so much. I'm forever grateful."

"Hope you make it home," she said, her eyes smiling.

"Reckon I got time to run to the restroom?" I asked.

"Yeah, go on. Earl won't leave you. He'll grab a shower first and a bite to eat. We've known him for ten years. He's as good as an old hound dog."

The man I'd come to think of as her husband chuckled and then resumed picking his teeth.

I breathed a sigh of relief as I walked quickly to the restroom.

***

After two hours on the road, Earl hadn't so much as cleared his throat. Hadn't even turned any music on the radio. His question about whether I talked too much or not made perfect sense now. Silence suited me too. I was relieved there was no barrage of questions, especially since he seemed to have detected the lie about my name. I hate lies, and I'd told enough of them. I didn't want to tell any more.

I was beginning to think that Pops back at the station had been right. An angel *was* watching out for me.

Thank you, Julie, for your prayers. And thank you, Lord.

The hum of the big rig beneath me lulled me into a hyper relaxed state. As the miles rolled by, I felt like I was floating on a raft in the river. When Earl started talking, it took a second for his words to register.

"Look at that sky," he said. "Beautiful, jus' beautiful. It's the best thing about being out here—the changing sky." He talked without glancing in my direction. I sat up a little straighter and focused my attention on the sky.

"People say to me, 'You must like the open road, the changing scenery.' And I say, 'Yeah, I do.' Don't even bother explaining that what I like most is the open sky and how it changes. Why it's a landscape in itself, as scenic as the country side."

He looked at me then. "More scenic." He paused a minute. "You doing all right? Settling in?"

"Yeah, just fine, thank you." I managed to stifle a yawn while saying it.

"You trying to get home." He didn't say it like a question.

"I am." I nodded.

"You running away from something?" I felt like he was reading my mind.

I started to lie, but it stuck in my throat. When he looked at me, I knew he saw the truth.

"Yeah, someone," I said.

He nodded.

"Life's tough. There's some mean folks out there don't make it no easier."

A crucifix dangling from the rear view mirror caught my eye. I assumed it was little more than a good luck charm to Earl. His deep voice broke into my thoughts.

"Yeah," he continued talking. "Being out here like this, all by myself and all, gives a man a lot of time to think about life. Jus' like that road up there, just keeps on going. You know, life keeps right on going on . . . forever."

I raised my eyebrows and nodded at the unexpected nugget of wisdom. A joyless tight-lipped smile froze on my face, and I looked straight ahead out the wide window. I didn't know whether to offer a response or not.

"I realized one day I'd been talking to God without even knowing how I got around to it." His voice lilted upward as he spoke, looking straight ahead. "Then some time later, I realized he was talking back to me." He gave a little incredulous laugh.

"He sho' did," he said in a hushed voice. "He was talking right back to me. That was twenty years ago." He looked at me again, and for the first time I noticed his eyes. Deep set in his tanned wrinkled face, they were as sincere and honest as a child's. A spark of understanding passed between us. My heart warmed, and a smile slowly spread across my face.

"I don't go nowhere without him." He smiled and twisted his shoulders from side to side in a stretch. "You should do that more often," he said.

I wasn't sure what he was talking about.

"You were looking kinda peaked before. Smile like that lights up your face."

I smiled. He laughed. I breathed deep, surprised to realize that all the tension I had held in my body was gone. I couldn't have been any more relaxed if I'd been sitting in a rocking chair watching the sun go down. I marveled at how that had happened. A little honest communication and empathy go a long way.

"Glad you're satisfied over there 'cause I won't be stopping for another couple of hours."

"That's fine," I said. "I'm fine."

The hours rolled by. Looking back, it astounds me how well that trip went. After a few hours sitting in that truck with Earl, I was stronger. I thought about what the lady in the truck stop had said, and I had to agree with her. He was as meek and trustworthy as an old hound dog.

I sat up high and watched the changing colors of the sky. They were glimmers of hope confirming a new tomorrow. Coming into cities as darkness fell, then in the twilight, watching the light chase the dark away—it was promising. Just like Earl said, I had lots of time to think, talk to God, and listen for God to talk back. Earl was right about the sky. It just keeps right on going. Earl was right about a lot of things.

Chapter Fifteen

We stopped at a pancake house in the morning—but it was nothing like the other time I'd stopped at one. Earl was a regular the servers were glad to see. While I ate my grits I intended to ask him which way we were going through Georgia. I wanted to get off as close to Wilcox Station as possible, without telling Earl my final destination. He'd made it easy to stick to the plan of secrecy. He didn't ask questions, just seemed to say enough to get me talking. He respected the gravity of my situation.

"I'll be going through Macon this afternoon to see my daughter and her young'uns," he said. "I usually stay for supper, might even spend the night with 'em. You'd be welcome to stay. I'll get right back on the road in the morning."

"Thank you, Earl. I appreciate it. But the truth is I need to be getting out before Macon."

"Okay then," Earl said. "You just let me know when and where." When we got back in the truck, I pulled a hundred dollar bill out my jacket pocket and handed it to him.

"Thank you, Earl," I said. "This is yours."

"No," he waved his hand, "keep your money. I can't take pay for helping a little lady get home where she belongs. I'd want somebody to do it for me or mine."

Tears pooled in my eyes and one spilled onto my cheek.

"You're a good man, Earl," I said. "God bless you."

"He already has. Now, dry your eyes."

I wiped the palm of my hand across my cheeks. He gave me a nod, and we chuckled a little. Then we gazed out at the road ahead and the clear blue sky.

"WELCOME TO GEORGIA." When I saw the sign, happiness bubbled up inside me, causing me to get misty-eyed again. Images of home—Daddy sitting in his chair, reading and smoking his pipe, Annie Ruth slicing peaches in the kitchen. The happy glow turned into exhilaration. I'll never forget that feeling for as long as I live. I was on the home stretch. Back in my own stomping ground. Almost home free.

"I'm from Georgia," I blurted out, sounding more like an excited ten-year-old than a twenty-five-year-old woman.

Earl cut his eyes at me and smiled. "Yeah, I figured as much."

"I'm almost home," I said.

***

We stopped at a large service station at the intersection of the interstate and a historic highway. The crossroads was a familiar one. My daddy used to stop for gas and Co-Colas there on our way to Aunt Martha's.

Earl climbed out the truck and proceeded around and under the vehicle, inspecting each set of tires. For a few minutes I sat there, working up the will power to strike out on my own. This was the right place.

"I'm going on, Earl," I called when I climbed out of the truck. I tugged at the gaudy tote which fell on my head, almost knocking me down. I trudged across the parking lot and into the station. Even though it wasn't summer yet, it was still eighty-five degrees that afternoon. I bought a cold bottle of water.

When I came out the station, Earl was walking toward me.

"Are you sure you won't let me take you all the way?" he asked. "I don't mind a' tall."

"I know you don't, Earl, but I can do this. I need to do this," I said. Even though I'd met him hardly more than a day earlier, it seemed like I'd known him a long time. I never expected to tell him anything about my situation. But since I had, I didn't want to get him any more involved than he already was.

"I won't forget you. Thanks so much." I couldn't resist giving him a hug. He patted my back and stood watching me as I walked off.

***

I started walking along the edge of the two-lane highway, fully intending to walk all the way to Wilcox Station. With any luck, I'd be there before supper time. In my mind, it should have been only ten miles or so. Not that I'd ever walked ten miles. I think the longest distance I'd ever walked was the four miles I hiked on a Sunday school picnic. In reality, I discovered later that it was closer to twenty miles to Wilcox Station. Julie and I had checked every particular. We had no need to check the number of miles from the highway to the town because we thought the Greyhound bus would be taking me as far as I needed to go. Nonetheless, I struck out quite confident I'd make it on my own. Proving again that ignorance might be bliss, but it's short-lived, and on the downside it invariably bites you in the butt and scares the living hades out of you.

A white wood frame church sat at a fork in the road, marking the half-way point between the interstate and Wilcox Station. I remembered the stained glass window of Jesus holding the little lamb in his arms. He wore sandals and a long robe. Here again my childhood perspective was off. I'd walk ten miles that afternoon before I'd get to that church. As I walked along the highway, I kept expecting to see the steeple at any minute, but that was a long weary while coming.

Few cars or trucks passed on that stretch of highway that day. The bag I carried seemed to get heavier with each step. I'd been sweating for some time when I decided to walk through the ditch and up the other side to rest under some low hanging branches of a cedar tree. There I could rest as long as I wanted without anyone seeing me. The air felt soft and sultry on the edge of the woods.

I sat on the cool ground under the bough and pulled my skirt up to my thighs. The open gladiator sandals weren't fit for walking. I took them off and brushed off my sandy feet, using the hem of the skirt to wipe between my toes. The cedar scented the air with Christmas memories.

When I was a child, every Christmas we'd go out into the woods behind the house, chop down a fat cedar tree, haul it inside, and decorate it with bubble lights and tinsel. I rested in my scented daydreams, drank the cool bottled water, and then peed in the woods. I laughed out loud at myself. You see, Lily Rose Cates, a well brought up Southern girl, would never have peed in the woods. But, *I* had. For some reason, that elemental act emboldened me. It said to me that I could do whatever I needed to do in order to regain my life, in order to move ahead with it. It said to me that at the end of the road today, I could start a new life. I was woefully naïve. I picked up my bag and ran down the side of the ditch and up the other side to the edge of the road.

Time passed but I didn't seem to make much headway. All I could see were more cedars, tall pines, and oaks creating hazy edges along the two lane road that went on and on. As I got hotter and more tired, my pace slowed to barely more than a crawl. I had walked for hours and I still hadn't seen the church steeple.

"Oh Lord. Am I lost?" I looked up into the cloudless blue sky. A hawk suddenly swooped down over the road ahead and flew upward toward the top of the trees. *Thud.* I heard a noise like a rock hitting a watermelon as the bird's talons grabbed a squirrel out of the top of a tall pine tree. A cry of pain escaped me, whereas the helpless creature hung silently in the deadly grasp. My stomach cramped. Why did it seem so tragic? Fears and fatigue cast a dark shadow on my journey.

Lord help me, I was ready to drop by the time the church steeple pierced the horizon. It was still a long way off, but at least I could see it.

About that time a scruffy little animal came running out the woods, startling the daylights out of me. My heart lurched into my chest and my hand flew over it.

"Go away!" I shouted. A small half grown dog with curly matted fur and a tail that waved like a flag over his back ran up to me. "Go back," I said. "I don't want a dirty mutt following me. Besides that, you scared the heebie-jeebies out of me." I stomped my foot in front of him and scowled.

He paid no attention and showed exuberance at making my acquaintance. He continued to follow me, no matter how much I stomped my feet and fussed. Changing my strategy, I ignored him, pretending not to see him while my thoughts wandered to the church that was slowly growing larger on the horizon. With the church beckoning me, and the little dog skipping beside me, I trudged on.

So many thoughts scrolled through my head. By the looks of the sky it was late afternoon. At that rate, I was going to be walking into Wilcox Station way after dark.

About that time a battered pick-up truck full of farm workers drove by. Three men crowded together in the front, and two more sat in the open back. Without a second thought, I waved to them . . . as is customary in rural Georgia. I regretted it immediately.

"*Mamasita, senorita bonita!*" The grinning men called. "Hey pretty lady!"

That almost threw me for a loop. When they sped up and drove on ahead, I sighed with relief. Then, to my dismay, the truck turned around in the church's parking lot. They drove back toward me. My uneasiness turned to fear.

Oh my God! Help me. All I could do was pray and keep walking. The church was the only building in sight. The truck passed me.

Every one of the men waved or hollered something, most of which I couldn't understand. I looked straight ahead and pretended not to hear. Then they turned around on the road behind me. I wanted to flee from the menacing hum of the approaching engine and the jeers of the grinning crew, but something held me back.

Act like you know what you're doing, Julie had said.

I walked as fast as I could and tried to look as unruffled as any woman could tramping along the highway with a satchel. "Come on dog."

They drove beside me, keeping pace with my steps. If they'd stretched out their arms, they could've touched me.

"*Mamasita*, where are you going? Need a ride?" The man on the passenger side hung out the window as he called to me. "We give you a ride." They howled with laughter. I swerved out of reach and walked further off the road on the edge of the ditch.

"Leave me alone. My friends are meeting me at the church up there." I hardly recognized the sound of my own voice. Out the corner of my eye, I watched them, praying that no one jumped out of the truck.

The fiesty dog ran between me and the truck, barking tirelessly in a salvo of support. Although he scared no one, he played his part well. He looked like a crazed toy bouncing up and down. When the church was within a hundred yards, it was all I could do not to break into a run.

At the same time, up ahead on the left, a blue Oldsmobile sedan stopped at the stop sign.

Oh Lord let it turn this way.

It didn't. It turned left onto the highway ahead of us. It had barely pulled onto the road when its driver put on the brakes and threw the car into reverse. It sped backward to the stop sign where it had just been. Then the car pulled straight ahead to the edge of the church property.

Gravel grated beneath its tires and flew out as it jolted to a sudden stop, rocking in place. At the same time, the driver laid on the horn. That's when I broke into a run, and the truck's driver floored it.

I fell against the car as the truck sped away.

"Oh my!" I struggled to catch my breath. A wrinkled old woman with a long cigarette dangling from her lips gaped at me as if she were trying to figure out what had just happened.

Casually, like she had not a care in the world, she scissored the cigarette between her boney fingers, squinted one eye, and blew smoke out the corner of her mouth.

"You looked like you needed some help." She spoke in a gravelly drawl.

Still propping myself against the car, I panted. "Those men scared me. Thank God you came along."

"You look terrible. White as a sheet. What are you doing anyway? Do you need me to take you somewhere?" She frowned.

"Thank you. I certainly could use a ride. I'm going to Wilcox Station."

"Get in," she said. "My name's Wanda."

"Nice to meet you Miss Wanda. Mine's Julie."

"Wilcox Station? I'm going right through there. Put your bag in the backseat. The dog, too."

When I opened the car door, the dog jumped in before I could protest. It wasn't worth the trouble to explain he wasn't mine. The little mutt had raised a fuss on my behalf. I reckoned I owed him something. I set the bag, now as heavy as a sack of rocks, on the floor. Strength sometimes has a funny way of hanging on no longer than it has to.

"Those men scared me so bad I'm as weak as water."

"I'm sorry," she said. "Y'all are okay now. They were jus' having some fun at your expense. I doubt they'd have hurt you, but you never know." She patted something in her lap—something heavy, metal.

"That's why I always take Willy with me," she said.

"Willy?" My mind must have been pretty addled. I looked over my shoulder for the man, Willy.

"Yeah." She pulled a long barrel pistol out of the folds of her skirt and held it out between the two of us. "A woman can't be too careful these days."

"Good gracious," I said with a start, leaning sideways up against the door. "You must be right. I keep hearing that. Personally, I'd be afraid to pick up that thing."

She laughed hoarsely provoking a coughing fit. Then she looked into the backseat. I looked too. The dog, standing alert, stared out the window. I thought of how he'd thrown himself between me and those devilish farmworkers. His tail swished left, then right. *Is it helping him keep his balance? Useful gadget. I could use something to help me keep mine. Not a long barrel pistol either.*

"I have to go right through Wilcox Station. Lucky for you I wuz passing by. I'm on my way up the country to help my daughter. She's just had a baby, and she's got three other young'uns and a husband as sorry as the day is long. I'm going up to help her out a while. We'll be there in ten, fifteen minutes. Where'd you walk from anyways?"

"From the interstate."

"Gracious sakes alive! No wonder you look like something the cat drug up. You must've walked three hours or more." She looked at me like I'd lost my mind.

I ran my fingers through the sides of my chopped hair, brushing it back from my face, and picked some dried grass off my shirt. I said nothing. What could I say? I imagined I did look frightful. To make things worse, the heat and sweat had brought out the scent of hair dye, and it made me nauseous.

I found myself watching the sky—*the changing sky*. Soft shades of tangerine, pink, and lemon fanned out from the horizon. I thought of Earl. It seemed like a long time since I'd left Earl. He would be looking at the same sky, the same setting sun. Contentment came over me when I felt that connection.

Wanda pointed out to my right a green pasture surrounded by a white roughhewn fence that seemed to amble on for miles across the fields. A long dirt road ran perpendicular to the highway and ended at a large two-story house. Pecan and oak trees shaded the place.

"Ain't that just the prettiest piece of property you ever did see," Wanda said. "Belongs to Doc Watson."

"It's beautiful. Nice looking horses, too," I said. Several chestnut brown horses meandered toward a small wet weather pond. In the distance, a man sitting tall in the saddle moved at a slow gait toward the other horses.

"There's some cows too. But not like it used to be when old man Watson was alive."

"It's a nice place." I sighed, too tired to talk.

"Doc Watson and his sister own it now. And I hear he's a fine looking man," she said. "Just like his daddy was. Yeah, some people have it all."

Some seem to, I thought, but you can never really tell by what things look like on the outside. After all, how had Manny and I looked . . . on the outside . . . like we had it all.

We rode on in silence. Wanda lit another cigarette. She blew out the smoke with a soft lazy whistle. I watched it curl upward where it joined with Daddy's cigar smoke drifting above where he stood talking politics under the oak trees at the American Legion. I tried to grasp my drifting thoughts but they slipped away. I had dozed off good when I heard Wanda's voice calling me.

"Julie, we're almost there. We're about to the main square. Ain't that where you wanted to get out?"

"Yes, ma'am," I said. "That'll be just fine."

The big clock on the courthouse still kept time. A quick scan of the square told me that nothing much had changed in the last ten years.

"Thank you, Miss Wanda. I appreciate it so much. I hope you enjoy your visit with your daughter and grand-children."

"You're welcome. No problem at all."

I grabbed my bag from the backseat, and the dog jumped out at my heels. We stood at the end of the alley behind the courthouse. I watched her car's tail lights disappear around the corner.

Thank God for that ride. It was a godsend. I don't think I could've made it if Miss Wanda and Willy hadn't shown up when they did.

Chapter Sixteen

I can't imagine what a sight we must have made that day—me dressed like a gypsified hippy, lugging a carpetbag, and that dirty little dog prancing beside me. It's a merciful fact that there's not much action in downtown Wilcox Station on a normal Tuesday evening in May. It allowed me to come into town unnoticed and make my way to Daddy's house only six blocks away from the center of town.

As I walked I prayed no one would notice me, prayed no one would notice me walking down the dirt driveway beside the house, that no one would see me pushing the gate open and going into the back yard. Even the dog stifled his sharp bark and behaved as if he knew I counted on him not to draw attention to us. Although I could have explained and rightfully gone on the property, I didn't want to face anyone that night.

Yet, if my feet had not hurt so bad, I would have danced like a fairy in the moonlight amongst the cascading sprays of tiny flowers on the white spirea bushes. Instead, I sat in the swing under the arbor and rested. Rested my weary bones, like Annie Ruth would have said. Rested, and thought about Manny.

I thought about what he'd be doing. He wouldn't have given me a thought yet. He'd be doing whatever it was he always did when he went out of town. It would be another week before he'd return to our condo in Detroit. Then another two days before he'd expect me to return home from Quebec. Julie would let me know if, or rather, *when* he came looking for me there. I had earned myself a little time. Time. It gave me an amazing sense of freedom and peace.

Manny, I'll probably love you my whole life, but I won't live with you. I won't let you destroy me. I want my life back.

Tears ran down my dirty cheeks, but they weren't all tears of sorrow. More like tears of relief brought on by exhaustion. I thought of Julie, my true friend. She'd given me courage because of her confidence in me. I thought of those I'd met who had helped me get home—the red haired woman, Earl, and Wanda.

I pushed back in the swing, lifted my feet, and swung forward. Relief bubbled up inside me. I laughed out loud, and then the dog barked, and the fact that I couldn't get him to stop yapping made me laugh more. I bent down and rubbed his back briskly, and he rolled over in delight.

"That's better," I said. "Now you be quiet. We still have to get in the house."

The last time I'd called Uncle Bill, I told him I'd be coming soon, and asked him to leave a key for me. He said he'd put it under a cement block beside the back door. I searched all around the back door. There was no cement block, thus no key.

A spare house key used to be hidden behind the birdhouse on the tree behind the carport. I wondered if I could find it in the fading light and considered giving it a try. After I walked around to the side of the carport, I decided not to try after all. It was too overgrown for me to go clawing my way through that bramble to the tree and with the weather warming, there might be snakes. I shuddered.

"Okay, pooch. What should we do?"

I went up the back steps and tried the door. Locked tight. I walked back into the yard and scanned the back of the house. I caught sight of a half opened upstairs window. It was open a good ten inches or more.

An arbor with a trellis covered with dainty pink roses jutted out into the yard perpendicular to the house, right under the window. Aunt Martha used to have a table and chairs set in its shade. Cheerful clusters of pink roses flourished and glowed in the fading light. I grabbed a section of the trellis. It seemed too lightweight to support even my one hundred pounds. The corner post of the arbor, however, was strong and solid. I could hang onto the trellis and climb up the arbor, then stand on the frame to reach the window ledge.

Quickly I stripped off my skirt and pulled a pair of jeans from the bag. I took off the sandals and put on some boots. The possibility that I might fall and knock my brains out didn't cross my mind, but I would protect myself from the thorns.

The dog stayed at my heels, sniffing as if he were trying to figure out what we should do next.

"You stay right there," I said. I grabbed hold of the trellis and the post and began the precarious climb to the top. Don't ask me how I made it. I still can't believe I did. The hardest part was getting the window up enough and working my way through. I had to keep stopping to catch my breath and regain my grip. The faint fragrance of roses trailed behind me. Finally I fell into the house and tumbled onto the floor of a room as dark and musty as a tomb. For a somber moment, I was afraid. But within a few seconds, my eyes adjusted to the gray speckled gloom.

If only I had a candle, I thought. And then I remembered the matches were in the medicine cabinet. Aunt Martha always kept matches in the cabinet near the toilet. Moonlight reflected on the mirror and I got a glimpse of my wide eyes and disheveled hair. I opened the metal cabinet and found matches on the bottom shelf. I lit one. A dusty candle on a crystal saucer sat on the vanity.

I've never been so grateful for a candle in my life. By its soft yellow light, I made my way into the stair landing and down the creaky stairs. I felt my way down the wide hall to the kitchen and the back door. I unlocked and opened the heavy door to fresh air, moonlight, and the dog. Leaving the wooden door open, I latched the screen and looked around the familiar room. I pushed open the swinging door that led to the dining room, but there was nothing but pitch black. Not a glimmer of light came through the boarded up windows.

I was worn out, but I didn't want to share a bed with the mice I was sure were lurking in the shadows. Carefully I set the candle on the kitchen table. I retrieved a broom and swept the area that fell within the candle's glow. I didn't dare go find a blanket. After I made it into the kitchen, I couldn't make myself go back up those creepy stairs.

I opened my bag and made a pallet with the clothes on the floor. I used the bag for a pillow. I lay there gazing out the back door into the sky. As more stars came out, my body and mind quieted down, like the pendulum of the old kitchen clock in need of rewinding. The candle flickered soft light on the ceiling. I was vaguely aware that a warm smelly creature burrowed against my back, and I fell fast asleep.

***

The dog pranced all around me and pulled at the clothes. He must have been trying to wake me for a while when I finally awoke. The daylight was bright in the backyard, but inside was dim.

"Okay, okay," I grumbled. "Give me a minute." My body ached.

"Dog, you stink! Phew!" I cleared my throat. "Yuck!" Then I started to chuckle.

"Dang that know-it-all Annie Ruth. She said if I laid down with dogs I'd get fleas. Well, she failed to mention I'd stink."

I turned my face away from the scruffy animal that was now licking my chin.

"I think I should call you Pépé le Pew, like the little cartoon skunk."

He barked, ran to the door, and scratched.

"Okay," I said as I stood up and crept over to open the screen door. "Go on out Mr. Le Pew, but as soon as you're done with your business we have to get cleaned up."

I stepped outside into the fresh morning air and smiled at the birds' delightful chorus. I'd missed their song in Detroit. As I looked around, I remembered the yard and how it had looked in years past—well-tended with lush flowering borders all around the fence. Irises were blooming in a large center bed—the vibrant blossoms looked healthy. A brick privacy fence went all around the sides and back of the property. The yard furniture was gone, but I could still see Aunt Martha and Daddy sitting out back—Daddy smoking his cigar, and Aunt Martha smoking a cigarette. Mama hated that about her. My aunt smoked as much as any man and didn't care what anyone thought about it.

Peppy skipped back to me. We went inside, and I found a metal cake pan and turned the handle on the water faucet at the kitchen sink. The pipes knocked and howled, then water gushed out. Uncle Bill had turned on the water after all. Peppy noisily lapped up every drop.

I pushed open the door to the dining room. Even in daylight, it was still dim. When I hesitated for a moment in the doorway, my hand inadvertently brushed over the light switch. The chandelier lit up. In my exhaustion the previous night, I had assumed that since Uncle Bill hadn't left the key, he'd also failed to turn on the electricity and water. But, it was probably a good thing after all that I hadn't turned on the lights the night before. I might not have slept so soundly if I had seen the cobwebs that hung like weeping garlands from the chandelier.

"Ewww . . . " I said aloud.

Furniture still sat where it had sat for ages. Daddy and I made a trip to Wilcox Station to sort out Aunt Martha's things after she died. No one had ever finished the task. Uncle Bill had had the place boarded up after Daddy died.

Besides cobwebs, a thick coat of dust blanketed the rooms, which were otherwise basically in order. The living room wasn't too bad, and neither was the kitchen. But mercy, what a mess I found upstairs. Books, and more books overflowed the built-in shelves. They were stacked on the sides of the stairs and around the furniture, and a mountainous pile covered the floor beside Aunt Martha's bed. Crammed in every nook, not only books, but also magazines and law journals. I wondered, had she kept every printed word she'd ever read?

A little hook near the top latched the door of one of the bedrooms. I hammered it off with an iron door stopper, pushed open the door, and took one step before my breath caught and chills ran through me. Eyes, dozens of glassy eyes stared back at me. Life-sized dolls, boy dolls and girl dolls, black ones and white ones, stood in boxes around the room, sat in the chair and lay on the bed. A crib was full of more dolls. I knew Aunt Martha loved dolls. She'd bring several for me to choose from when I came to visit. But I'd never seen all these. I'd never been in that room either. It had been Miss Izzy's and she kept the door shut.

The other two bedrooms were familiar ones. The one I used to stay in had only a high ornate iron bed, a mirrored wardrobe piled high with patchwork quilts, a square bedside table with spindle legs, a reading lamp, and a cozy chair. The fringed wool rug on the heart pine floor softened the setting. The bedroom Daddy stayed in was as simply furnished. These also housed lots of books, but there was still room to walk through in them. What was I going to do with all the books? And how could I begin to clean up with them in the way?

With Peppy at my heels, we went into the bathroom. A deep claw foot tub sat in the center of the large room. *Folies Bergère* and Avon dusting powder, Evening in Paris cologne, and ornate perfume bottles, hair pins, combs, and a brush full of long gray hair adorned the vanity. Rummaging through the drawers, I found a pair of scissors.

"Come here Peppy. Let's get some of those tangles and grass spurs out of that matted fur."

I laughed at the resulting cut, but after I bathed him in baby shampoo and washed his pointed ears, he looked cute. Without the grime, his legs and beard were golden tan, and his back was black and shiny.

I scrubbed the tub, filled it with warm water, and stripped off my dirty clothes. It felt good to be out of them. I lathered my hair and let it float around me as I soaked in the deep tub. I might have stayed there for hours had I not been so hungry. When I stepped out the tub, I realized I had not brought my clothes upstairs. I towel dried my hair lightly with the rough towel, and then draped it around my breasts. I ran downstairs to pick up my clothes from the kitchen floor.

Peppy started raising Cain and pounced on the screen door just as I walked into the kitchen.

"Hey in there," a man called out as he abruptly shoved open the backdoor.

I gasped, standing in a policeman's line of sight.

And then, I screamed, scrunched up, and clutched the towel tightly around my body.

"Sorry, ma'am." He jolted and turned aside. "I didn't mean to scare you. But the neighbor reported that she heard somebody over here. What are you doing in this house?"

"I own it!" I shouted. "Call Mr. Hollister. And if you'll excuse me I'll go get dressed before we continue this conversation."

I snatched up several items of clothing and exited like a crab scampering across the hardwood floor. I turned and fled up the stairs. My heart was pounding so hard I had to sit on the commode for a minute to catch my breath. I pulled on jeans and a t-shirt and combed my wet hair. I stared at myself in the hazy mirror—green eyes wide, wet wavy hair tamer than the night before. I heard the officer on his phone.

I reentered the kitchen a bit more gracefully than I'd left it.

"Sorry, ma'am," said the officer. "I just spoke to Bill Hollister. How was I supposed to know? He failed to let me in on your arrival. Are you all right? I'm sorry I scared you." He looked at me then, like he was seeing me for the first time.

"It's okay. I'm fine."

The dog was sniffing the officer's pant legs and wagging his tail.

"Peppy, you could have warned me a little sooner." The man chuckled.

"I'm Jeff Barkley," he said and smiled. He was a clean-cut man, probably no older than I was.

"I'm Julie Combier." I held out my hand to him. He frowned and narrowed his eyes inquisitively.

"No, you must already know. I'm Lily Rose Cates."

"Nice to meet you," he said, giving my hand a firm shake. We stepped out onto the terrace.

"I wonder which neighbor called. With the high fence and the trees, looks like nobody could see in the yard," I observed.

He pointed up to a small square window barely visible through a pecan tree's branches. "Consider those windows eyes," he said, twisting his mouth into a sly smile. "Is there anything I can do for you before I leave?"

"Well, since you asked, how about a ride to Mr. Hollister's office?"

"Under the circumstances, I think I can manage that." His eyes roved over me in a studied manner.

I put my hand to my chest to hide the lace tattoo, which only made more visible the tattooed bracelet on my wrist.

"So, you're Miss Martha Cates' niece?" He looked skeptical that I was related in any way, shape, or form to anyone in town. Like maybe I was guilty of breaking and entering after all. He probably would have agreed with Miss Wanda—maybe a cat had drug me into town.

***

When Peppy and I got out of the patrol car, the officer still looked me over, but not in a disapproving way.

I waited in front of a receptionist's desk while she talked on the phone. Through the louvered shades, I saw the police car drive slowly away.

"May I help you?" The receptionist spoke in a poised voice, more capricious than professional.

"Good morning. I'd like to speak to Mr. Hollister, if possible."

"He's with a client right now," she said. "Would you like to make an appointment?"

"Could I wait until he's free?" Peppy squirmed in my arms and licked my neck and ear. "Stop, Peppy."

"I don't think you'll want to do that. He's going to be tied up for some time."

"I see. Does he have any time free later today? I can come back."

"Well, his next appointment isn't until four. He'll probably have a few minutes before that appointment, but I can't guarantee he'll see you."

"Okay. I'll come back later," I said. "Without the dog."

"Who should I tell him came by?" Her chin dropped and both brows rose.

"Tell him his niece has arrived, and that I need to speak with him as soon as possible."

"Oh," she said. Her lips formed the word and lingered there in an oddly amusing way.

"See you later." I smiled.

In a matter of steps, I remembered the layout of the town square. An old Piggly Wiggly store hid three blocks away around a corner if my memory served me correctly. That would be my next stop. Peppy followed close on my heels. I knew I couldn't take him into the store. I stood gazing down at him for a couple of minutes before I decided to pick him up and head inside anyway.

I got no further than the checkout register before I came under the stern scrutiny of an elderly man. He gave me a look a tad more inquisitive than the police officer's had been.

"Sir, would you mind if I hold him just long enough to buy a leash? Then I can tie him outside while I shop."

"Can't see why not," he said, leaning his head to the side to follow my movements.

I tied Peppy to the cart rack along the front wall and hurried in to purchase a few things. Bread, apples, peanut butter, tea, coffee, sugar, milk, scrub pads, Ajax, and two cans of dog food. I couldn't carry any more than that. Near the checkout, a shiny bag of Hershey's chocolate kisses caught my eye and I remembered Daddy buying them whenever we came into the store. I could see him unwrapping one while keeping his eyes on the book he read, then he'd pop it into his mouth to let it melt slowly as he read. He loved the little chocolate drops. I grabbed a bag.

"Could I have plastic bags, please, so I can hold them easier?" I asked the old man at the register.

"Sorry, little lady," he said. "We only have paper sacks."

"Okay, that's fine. Thank you."

"Settle down, Peppy, so I can get you loose. We've got one more stop."

Now that I had a chance, I called Julie on the pay phone outside the building. I dialed the number with shaky fingers and deposited the change when prompted.

"Hello, may I speak to Mrs. Combier?" I tried to disguise my accent.

"Hold a second, she's with a customer." I hoped Monica had not recognized my voice.

"Certainly," I said. Lord, make her hurry, I don't have much change.

"Hello, this is Julie speaking," Julie's voice brought joy to my heart.

"Julie, it's me."

"Oh, thank God. Are you there? Are you safe?"

"I'm here. I'm in the house, and everything's fine."

"Praise God." Julie sounded breathless and on the verge of tears. "I'm so happy to hear your voice."

"I'm happy to hear yours, Julie. It's amazing how well everything went. I know you were praying for me."

"*Please deposit two dollars and twenty cents.*" The automated voice sounded obtusely.

"Julie, I don't have much change; I have to hang up, but I'll call you again in a couple days."

"I love you Lily."

I deposited the change with only a few cents to spare, but I felt practically triumphant and greatly relieved having made that call. I walked the few blocks back to the house with a definite spring in my step.

"How about lunch, little fellow?" I scraped half the contents of a can into a bowl and set it down for him. Then I made myself the most delicious peanut butter sandwich in the world.

As soon as I had eaten, I got the broom. Cleaning the house would take weeks, maybe months. I made a mental note to ask Uncle Bill if he could find me some help. I started in the kitchen. I found some rubber gloves and ammonia under the sink, along with roach droppings and evidence that mice had taken up residence. Then I scrubbed the sink and washed off the counters and the stove. The refrigerator had been emptied and cleaned years before, but I cleaned it as well to get rid of the stale odor.

Before I knew it, it was time to go back to Uncle Bill's office. I brushed my teeth and bobbed hair and put on a clean blouse, the cute floral skirt, and the sandals, all the while hoping I wouldn't cause him too much of a shock. I certainly looked different from the girl he'd known.

After securing all three doors to the kitchen and putting everything out of reach, I left with Peppy inside.

"Sorry, fellow," I said. "But I'll be back before you know it."

As I rounded the corner to the square, I couldn't resist peering in the window of the old hardware store where Daddy had spent many an afternoon chatting. The antique schoolhouse clock still hung on the wall. It was already mid-afternoon.

When I walked into the law office, the receptionist picked up the phone.

"Mr. Hollister, she's here," she said softly.

Before I'd spoken a word, Uncle Bill opened the door and came out to greet me. I'd forgotten what a big man he was—tall and broad. With his arms open wide, he walked up to me and about smothered me in a bear hug. I was a little girl again.

"Why, if it isn't little Lily Rose Cates?" He looked glad to see me and he didn't seem at all put off by my tatted appearance.

"I'm surprised you recognized me."

"Of course, how could I forget your pretty face? Come on into the office. There's a lot we need to talk about."

"Thank you, Uncle Bill. Thank you for turning on the water and the electricity, too." Mr. Hollister wasn't really my uncle, but that's what I'd always called him.

He pulled a set of keys from his pocket and handed them to me. "I'm sorry I didn't put the key out for you like we'd discussed. Quite frankly, I didn't expect you so soon."

"I'm ready for the help you offered, Uncle Bill. Tackling that house will be a chore. Can you send Mr. Burns over as soon as possible to help me make the place livable? And could you contact the phone company for me?"

"Yes, yes, definitely. I'll have my secretary call the telephone company today. Sugar Burns will be over first thing in the morning and you can count on him to do anything you ask him to do. He took care of that place for a long time. He'll be glad to do more than the minimum for a change. In fact, he'll be tickled to death to see you."

"That's great. I'll be glad to see him too."

Uncle Bill thumbed through a stack of papers on his glossy mahogany desk and pulled out a folder.

"My appointment calendar is full, but I have to talk to you about your inheritance. I've been waiting for this a long time. Could you make an appointment and come back on Monday morning?"

"Yes, of course, I will."

"In the meantime, let me give you this." Uncle Bill handed me a roll of what looked like several hundred dollars in twenties.

"Oh, that's not necessary, Uncle Bill. I have some money."

"Nonsense," he said. "It's yours anyway."

He noticed the question on my face.

"Your father's estate has over $80,000 in it for you. That's all that's left after your schooling. Your mother's and Annie Ruth's needs will always be provided for. There's a comfortable portion from your aunt's estate as well remaining after her donations to several churches and charities."

"I have to admit, I didn't expect there'd be that much."

"Your aunt worked practically her entire life and never went anywhere. She was frugal, but also very generous." His phone rang. "Yes, yes, thank you. I'll just be a minute."

"Lily Rose, I'll come by and see you before Monday. Is there anything else you can think of that I can do now?"

"Would you please tell Officer Barkley to keep an eye out for me . . . at least until I get settled in and make friends around here."

"I'd do anything for Mike Cates' daughter." He stood up and walked around the desk. "You know, he was my first friend and the best one I ever had. It's mighty nice you've come back home, Lily Rose."

He put his hand on my shoulder. "Your father was one of the best men I've ever known. We'll be blessed to have his daughter here. You better believe we'll look out for you."

"Thank you Uncle Bill." I smiled. We walked out together. After speaking to the receptionist, he called in his next client.

"When would you like to come on Monday?" asked the receptionist. She was friendlier than before. I had the odd feeling that she'd heard the conversation with Uncle Bill. We scheduled a morning appointment.

With money in my pocket, I headed over to the drug store. I bought a blanket and a small dog bed that would make do as a pillow until I could get something better. One more run on the Piggly Wiggly for eggs, oil, lemons, toilet paper, and paper towels. I figured it might be days before I cleaned everything in that kitchen.

Peppy's yapping welcomed me home. His body shivered in delight like he greeted a long lost friend. I declare that dog could smile.

"I won't feel lonely with you around, little fellow." I put down the bags and stroked his back. As I petted him, I looked around the dingy kitchen. I couldn't wait to get back to cleaning, but after only a couple more hours of scrubbing, I was exhausted. Peppy and I shared scrambled eggs for supper.

The new blanket made a more comfortable pallet on the floor where we slept another night. As far as I could tell, it might be days before I could sleep in a bed. The thought of critters and spiders gave me the creeps, but strangely enough it didn't seem so bad. I could stand that better than I could the conflict and uncertainty of life with Manny. I couldn't believe the change in my expectations. I'd never known anyone to act like Manny—he was practically a Dr. Jekyll and Mr. Hyde—which I suppose added to my anxiety and heartache. All I wanted now was peace.

In spite of the Spartan conditions, I slept soundly. In that state between sleep and wakefulness, I lingered listening to a growling dog and the hum of a mower before I realized morning had come bringing a buzz of activity. The irregular rhythm of hammers pounding on the house, rattling the windows, pulled me up from my make shift bed. Peppy's sharp yapping added to the racket. He could hardly wait for me to open the door before he darted out.

After a sprint to the bathroom, I pulled on my clothes and joined him outside to see what was going on. The morning sun cast a corridor of light across the backyard.

"Morning, Miss Lily."

"Sugar? Is that you?"

"It sure is."

A medium height, slightly built, black man stood with his hand on his hip and a big smile pulling at the corners of his mouth. He was dressed in worn out jeans and work boots. "You sure have grown up, Miss Lily."

"And you haven't changed a bit." I shook my head slightly perceiving a flash of déjà vu. Every single time we'd come to Aunt Martha's house, Sugar was there. When he was only a boy, he had started taking care of the yards, running errands, and doing odd jobs for Aunt Martha. He was the nephew of her best friend Miss Izzy, a black woman who worked for her for years, then lived with Aunt Martha as her companion during the last few years of their lives. Those two ladies loved Sugar like a son.

"I can't say I'm not surprised to see you. Are you here to stay?" Sugar asked that question in a way that made it seem like he'd much anticipated asking it. "Mr. Hollister said you might be here to stay."

"I might be, Sugar," I said with a grin. "We'll just have to wait and see."

"Well, that's what I wanted to hear. I'll take care of things for you. I've got two of my nephews working with me today. They're taking the boards off the windows, and we'll be washing down the house and the porches, and getting started in the yard. Tomorrow I'll help out in the house, if you want."

"That's wonderful. I'm going to work in the house today myself. But, Sugar, why don't you just call me Lily from now on." I held my hands out, palms up. "Gimme a hug."

"Oh, well, 'Lily' might take some gettin' used to." He grinned. "And I'm already too sweaty for hugs." He reluctantly gave me a sideways half hug with a pat on the back. "It's so *good* to see you, you just don't know."

A few minutes later, I watched Sugar from the kitchen window. He looked exactly the way I remembered him except a bit more angular. It seems unconscionable to me now how I'd never thought about how he must have felt when Daddy died, and we never came back to this place. First Miss Izzy died, then Aunt Martha two years later, then Daddy the next year, and I never came back. His whole world must have changed overnight with Aunt Martha's death. Aunt Martha and Miss Izzy were like mothers to him. How could I have been so insensitive not to think of him? Seeing him now made me feel good. His presence made it seem even more like home.

I made myself a cup of instant coffee and sliced an apple to eat with peanut butter. I filled the sink with hot soapy water and put some dishes in to soak. I opened the doors to the other rooms downstairs and began sweeping down cobwebs. I gathered up several armloads of books and took them upstairs. I'd decided to stack as many books as possible under the center front upstairs windows. Open and spacious, I could pile mountains of books there until I could go through them and decide their fate.

I gathered the books from along the stairs. Mice or rats had gnawed a few and left their telltale droppings. I collected books from mine and Daddy's old bedrooms. I couldn't think of tackling the doll room or Aunt Martha's room yet. They seemed a bit smothering and creepy. Even though more than a decade had passed since anyone had occupied those rooms, I had the uncanny urge to knock before entering. As it was, the mountain of books grew taller and taller.

My grumbling stomach called for lunch, but first, I went outside to see how the men were progressing. Besides hosing down the house, they'd neatly mowed and raked. One of the young men was putting the last piece of yard furniture in place. It was dripping with soapy water. The white round iron table and two chairs, and a green and white medal glider and two matching spring chairs brought back memories.

"Sugar, where did you find those?" I hollered to him across the yard.

"In the shelter," he said, pointing toward the door on the back side of the car port. "I put them in there after Miss Martha passed." We smiled at each other, remembering.

"What else is in there?" I walked over to see for myself. Stacks of red clay pots in varying sizes lined the walls. A couple of large urns, a wheel barrow, and yard tools filled the majority of the space, but the real hidden treasure was Aunt Martha's old blue bicycle.

"Oh my goodness," I said. "It reminds me of my brother's bike, the one we rode all over tarnation." I rolled it out, swiped off the seat, and climbed on. Shaky at first, I managed to steady the bike, and took off pedaling around the backyard. My jaunty ride slowed to a crawl. Sugar laughed, and I laughed at him laughing at me.

"Looks like the tires have dry rotted."

"Oh, is that what it is?" I stopped and looked at the tires that had now gone flat.

"I can fix 'em, no trouble at all," he said, brushing his hands on his pant legs.

"I know you can, thanks, but first . . . " I skipped back towards the backdoor. "How about some lunch?"

"Yeah, we could use something to eat," he said, "and something cold to drink."

"I wish Miss Molly's Fried Chicken was still in business. Yum."

"Miss Molly's Fried Chicken is still in business." He nodded and grinned.

"Does she still make fried catfish?" I remembered the crisp moist delicacy.

"She *sho'* does. Why don't I ride over there and get us some?"

"And a gallon of sweet tea?"

"You bet," he said.

"Let me get you some money."

"No need. I can take care of it."

"Well, all right then," I said. "I'll go inside and make sure we'll have a clean place to sit down when y'all get back."

In no time, Sugar was back, and I was washing up in the kitchen. I'd cleaned off the dining room table and pulled back the dusty drapes. Sugar and his nephews came in and washed up in the big kitchen sink.

"Would you please push up the window, Sugar? I couldn't get it opened. We could use some fresh air in here."

With a warm breeze drifting in, we sat around the dining room table and enjoyed our country fried dinner and conversation. For a little bit it seemed like no time at all had passed since I last sat at that table. I almost expected Aunt Martha to walk into the room and to hear Daddy say, "Pass the hushpuppies please."

Chapter Seventeen

Peppy and I slept on the kitchen floor yet another night. Until the beds and linens were clean, I could not bring myself to sleep on one of them. The likelihood of sharing it with critters was too great. One scruffy dog was enough of a strange bedfellow for me.

Bright and early on Friday morning, not long after I'd let Peppy out, Sugar tapped on the door. I was making coffee.

"Come on in," I called. "How are you this morning?"

"Just fine, thank you."

"You sure worked hard yesterday. I can't get over how much better the house looks already."

"It's a show place, Miss Lily. It always was a show place. You're going to make it come alive again."

"Do you really think so?" I searched his face.

"I do." He was as sincere as he could be.

"Okay, what should we do today?"

"I've got a vacuum cleaner, which might help cut down on the dust, and I could wash the windows so you could see out of 'em," he said. "And this afternoon I have a big surprise."

"What?"

"No, can't tell, we got to get some work done first, 'cause after I tell you what I've got to tell you, you won't want to work no more."

"Oh, you gotta be kidding me!" I put my hands on my hips. "Well, as soon as I finish my toast and coffee, you can count on me to do my share."

For the next several hours, we worked. I cleaned the bathroom upstairs and dusted a large section of book-shelves and books. I gathered all the throw rugs and took them out back, then took the sheets and quilts off two of the beds. It was time to see how well the washing machine worked.

Sugar had made his way upstairs to clean cloudy windows. The ones downstairs sparkled. It had taken him all morning to clean the tall windows.

"Sugar, how about a fried egg sandwich for lunch?"

"Sounds good to me," he said, coming down the stairs.

I poured two glasses of sweet tea and then fried four eggs for the sandwiches.

"Sorry I don't have much to offer. I'm limited to what I can tote home in a grocery sack." I chuckled.

"It's good," he said.

"Are there any furniture stores around here that might carry mattresses? After I took the sheets off those beds upstairs, I got a good look at the mattresses." I made a face. "WWII era, I think."

Sugar feigned a cough, stifling a laugh. "It's very well possible, but I'm sure they haven't been slept on that much."

"Too dusty for me. Maybe even dry rotted like those old bike tires."

A few minutes later I poured myself another glass of tea and washed my hands in the sink.

"You want anything else?" I asked.

"No, that's a' plenty."

"Well?" I looked at Sugar with my eyes all round and jutted out my chin.

"What?" He chuckled.

"You know what. Don't play games with me. The surprise you promised?" I held out my hand to him like I was waiting for him to hand me something.

"Okay, okay. Actually . . . I was wondering what you might do for a car around here." He looked at me and searched my face for clues of understanding. I scrunched up my face and put my hands on my hips again.

"I don't want to think about buying a car right now. The bicycle will do fine. And what does that have to do with anything? Get on with it."

"Uh, well, I was kinda thinking about Sophie." Nonchalantly he scratched his head.

"Sophie? Stop it, Sugar, don't kid me like that. Sophie?" He was grinning now. "Mr. Hollister sold it, didn't he?"

Sugar turned his head slowly from side to side while still keeping his eyes on me. Then he jumped up from the kitchen table and took off running out the back door. I squealed and ran out behind him, both of us headed for the carport. A large padlock secured the doors. Sugar pulled a key out of his pocket and fitted it into the lock.

"Mr. Hollister let it be known he planned to sell Sophie. I think he might've even told folks he sold her. He told me I could tinker with it and keep it running, but not to get any wild ideas about it. He said if anything happened to it that he'd see to it I went to jail."

"He said that?" I bounced up and down in place. "No."

"I swear on a stack of Holy Bibles he did. Miss Martha loved it so much, he just couldn't bring hisself to sell it."

As the wide doors swung open I saw Aunt Martha's smoky blue DeSoto—her only indulgence. She lovingly called it Sophie, pampered it, took it for more check-ups than most children have doctor visits, saved every record regarding it, and drove it as little as possible. The farthest she'd ever driven it was when she and Miss Izzy went to Warm Springs one year.

"Sugar, does it still run?"

"You bet it does."

"Let's go for a ride." I ran around to the passenger side and hopped in.

"That's what I've been waiting on all day." He slid into the driver's seat and started the engine. With it idling, we rolled down the windows.

For us, it was a joy ride *par excellence*. For the town, it was a spectacle. When we drove through the town square in that mint condition 1950 DeSoto, there could be no doubt that Miss Lily Rose Cates had come to town to claim her inheritance.

Chapter Eighteen

Sugar couldn't come to the house on Saturday because he had his own lawn care and handy man business to tend to. So when Peppy started barking, and I heard knocking on the front door, I wondered who it could be. I swung open the wide door and faced three women standing on the porch, with brooms, buckets, and mops in their hands.

"Hey there, Lily Rose," said the heavy-set woman. "Mr. Hollister sent us over to clean your house."

"Oh, my gosh. That's so nice of him. And you as well. Come on in."

"We work for him and Miz Hollister. Worked for 'em for years. You can just turn us loose to do what we do best. I'm Renee Hill, and these are my oldest daughters, Ruth and Rebecca. The twins," she added with pride.

"It's nice to meet y'all. Thank you so much for coming."

She was already directing orders to her grown girls. They began an energetic and systematic cleaning spree. When they finished about seven hours later, the house had been thoroughly dusted, and the entire house had been mopped, not once but twice.

I left them working and drove over to the Family Furniture Store, where I purchased a set of mattresses for my bed. Since I paid cash, they threw in a set of sheets and pillows and promised to bring it all over and set it up before evening. I couldn't have been happier.

When I walked back into the house, ammonia and Pine Sol never smelled so fresh.

"It sure smells clean in here," I hollered up the stairs. Renee was coming down, carrying a sheet tied up like a giant hobo sack.

"I don't mess around," she said. "I like me a clean house. I'm taking your dusty linens home to wash. I'll bring them by one afternoon next week."

"That'll be great. I can't thank you enough."

"No need to," she said. "I like my job and Mr. Hollister pays us good. We'll be back next Saturday, too. After that, you might be able to manage. We'll come back whenever you need us."

They left as quickly as they had come. I was amazed at all they'd accomplished. With their help, the place would be in great shape in no time. When the mattresses were delivered a little later, I made the bed with the smooth white sheets and fluffy new pillows.

"Peppy, here's your bed." I placed the corduroy pet bed against the wall. "You get your own bed now. No more using it as my pillow, no more sleeping on the floor. We've moved up in the world."

***

I slept late on Sunday morning. Peppy didn't even bark to go out. When I opened my eyes, his nose rested politely on the edge of the bed, his little black eyes patiently watching. When I took him out, I heard church bells and music playing. I'd forgotten those bells. I picked up the tune to the old hymn and was humming "Whispering Hope" by the time I walked back inside. Sunshine and a soft breeze drifted through my bedroom window. Had I already been there five days? Five days, and still Manny wouldn't have missed me.

Thank you, God. Thank you so much. I knelt beside the bed, rested my forehead against the mattress and prayed. When I stood up to go downstairs for coffee, I felt as fresh as the morning.

Peppy and I wandered around the back yard while I sipped my coffee. A huge magnolia tree shaded one part of the yard. An oak dominated another. Only one set of windows was close enough for anyone to see us there.

Those windows have eyes, the police officer had said. I looked up at the window which peeked through the pecan tree, smiled my most winning smile, and waved like Miss America. I giggled, prompting Peppy to prance beside me. I'm going to have to meet my neighbors soon, I thought, but today, I'm going to read.

With the morning sun shining through the wide windows, I sorted through books. *The Complete Works of William Shakespeare*, Franz Kafka's *The Trial*, Kennedy's *Profiles in Courage* and *A Nation of Immigrants*—Daddy loved those. Carnegie's *How to Win Friends and Influence People*—Manny could use that one. I chuckled. *Gideon's Trumpet,* never heard of it, *Clarence Darrow,* and *The Scopes Monkey Trial*, Milton's *Paradise Lost, Invisible Man, Decline and Fall of the Roman Empire, In Cold*

Blood, Steinbeck's *Grapes of Wrath*. Ah, of course, the one and only *To Kill a Mockingbird*, by Harper Lee, 1960. I wondered how many people that book had influenced to go into the practice of law.

I sorted the volumes into three stacks. Stack number one—throw away. Time or the mice had gotten the best of them. Stack number two—donate to the library. Others should have the opportunity to enjoy them, since they didn't interest me. *Friends of the Library, you're going to love me.* Stack number three—keep for my own. There'd never be enough time to read all of them, but I would try. I settled back with an original copy of *To Kill a Mocking-bird*.

For a moment, I was Scout. I read several pages aloud to hear the sound of my own voice.

"When he was nearly thirteen, my brother Jem got his arm badly broken at the elbow . . . ."

Lyrical, I thought, and chuckled to myself. Rather brilliant, I thought, how Miss Lee launched into her story that has never grown old.

Peppy barked.

"Good dog, Peppy. You're getting to be a good watchdog." I looked out the window to see Uncle Bill emerging one limb at a time from a long shiny car. I ran downstairs to greet him.

"Hey there, Lily Rose, how are you?" He stuck out a beefy hand, which soon smothered mine.

"I'm doing great, Uncle Bill, thanks to you."

He and my daddy had both grown up in Wilcox Station. They'd gone to grade school and high school together, and then gone on to UGA. Even though I'd never spent much time with him, because of Daddy's stories, and our summer visits here, I was fond of him.

"Well, it looks like Renee and her daughters did a good job."

"Oh, yes they did, a very good job."

"Don't know what we'd do without them." He sank down into a sage green leather recliner and stretched out his legs. "Now, tell me, Lily Rose, what's going on? What made you finally come back home? Why all the secrecy?"

"Uncle Bill," I said, lowering my face. "I've left my husband." I held my breath for a second awaiting his response. When it didn't come, I raised my eyes and looked into his thoughtful ones.

"I'm sorry to admit it. I can't bring myself to talk about it, but . . . I will say, I felt I had no choice." He watched me without expression and waited for me to go on.

"I'm afraid of him sometimes. That's why I left the way I did. That's why I don't want him to know about this place. The dyed hair and these ugly tattoos were all part of the scheme to put off his finding me." I scrunched handfuls of hair with both hands and turned my gaze to the ceiling. Still, Uncle Bill said nothing.

"As it's turned out, I don't think I needed to do all this after all." I held out my wrist and examined the lingering tattoos.

"Well," he said, slowly rubbing the palms of his hands together and stretching out his legs. "These things happen. I'm just real sorry to hear that they've happened to you. How can I help?"

"If he comes, I don't want to go back with him," I said, shaking my head. "There's a possibility," I stopped and swallowed the lump in my throat. "There's a possibility he's in trouble, but I don't want to speculate. Maybe it's just my fears deceiving me. But I couldn't risk it. I just couldn't stay with him any longer."

"I'm sure you have good judgment, Lily Rose. It runs in the family." Uncle Bill was unperturbed.

"Please have the police keep an eye out for him." My throat tightened and my eyes burned. Tears threatened to spill out. "I wish I never had to think about this again."

"Well, Lily Rose, you're going to be fine. I'll tell Jeff Barkley to drive down this street several times a day. We'll keep a watch out for any out of state license plates."

"And I don't want Mama or Annie Ruth to know I'm here yet, in case he calls them looking for me," I interjected. "I'll just let them think . . . " I paused, thinking to myself. "I'll figure something out so they won't know. I need to give it some time to see if he's coming for me or not. I haven't figured it all out yet."

"You will. I believe you will. You'll figure out exactly what you need to do." He hoisted himself out of the chair, walked over to me and laid his hand on my shoulder. "There are a lot of folks who love you and will watch out for you here. When the time comes, as it will, for you to deal with your marriage, I'm sure you'll do what you need to. I'm here to help."

"Thank you Uncle Bill."

"Welcome home, Lily Rose, and come see me in the morning for us to go over the will."

Chapter Nineteen

Monday morning I walked the long way around to Uncle Bill's office. I couldn't resist strolling through the neighborhood. The sky was blue, the weather about perfect, and spring flowers were in full bloom. Several elderly ladies worked in their flowers and some sat on their front porches. They smiled and waved at me as I passed by. I felt my hair bouncing with each step. It seemed just like the first day of summer vacation.

The most surprising thing about the will was that I had forgotten there was one. I couldn't remember much about the time right after Daddy died. His death blasted a gaping hole in my soul and I lost a span of time. Uncle Bill had my power of attorney and he took care of everything. I knew the property existed, but as part of my avoidance of any and all reminders of Daddy's death, I had put it out of my mind. I didn't want to be reminded of it. And for some reason, I'd never explained it to Manny. I tried to tell him about it once, but he wasn't interested. I suppose I didn't want his insensitivity or indifference to sully my memories. I suppose I did want to keep it to myself, so I never mentioned it again. I'm sure providence had something to do with that and with Uncle Bill's phone call that day in Detroit. His call brought it back into my frame of reference.

Aunt Martha left everything to Daddy, but in the event that he'd passed, then everything was passed to me, that is, with the condition that I kept ownership of the house. In the event that I sold the place, then the money would be divided equally three ways, amongst me, James Michael, and Sugar. Uncle Bill laid out all the conditions for me.

"I'm staying here . . . at least for now . . . and I won't sell it."

"I hoped you'd say that," he said. "And there's no need to mention any of these particulars to anyone. It's already been read once."

"I understand."

"All the money that was left in her estate, along with the interest accrued, has been in my firm's trust account, as your trust. We will transfer that to you." He handed me a slim folder.

"As I always did for your Daddy, I will continue to take care of any legal matters that you have, at no charge." He touched his fingers to his forehead like he was tipping his hat to me.

"You might not be aware of this, Lily Rose, but it's because of your aunt that I practice law here. Before your granddaddy passed away, she learned everything he could teach her and read the law with him. As long as he was alive, no one questioned her. When he passed away, she faced a lot of challenges as a woman. She wanted a man to practice with her because of the obstacles she faced in this profession. I didn't have any money to set up a practice. She gave me my start."

"Thanks for telling me that, Uncle Bill. I appreciate that."

"Oh, and I have the shipment that you sent here. I'll have Sugar bring it over one afternoon this week."

"That's great."

On the way home, I stopped at a little church. A black iron gate standing ajar drew my gaze to the path leading to the door of a white-shingled church. The heavy wooden doors opened with a creak when I gently pushed the handle. The tiny sanctuary couldn't have been any bigger than eight hundred square feet. Rows of stained glass windows along each side made it seem like a jeweled box. The brilliant cobalt blues and reds sharply contrasted with the dim interior. The holy place filled me with awe.

I remembered sitting near the front beside Daddy. I slowly make my way to the altar. "Daddy, I've missed you," I whispered.

Peace surrounded me, soothing my loneliness and pain. I gazed up at Jesus on the cross. Then I knelt in the silence and prayed.

Our Father who art in heaven, hallowed be thy name . . . .

I don't know how long I stayed there, but when I finally emerged into the daylight, I knew that not only had I reconnected with my home and family, but I had reconnected with my heavenly Father. I'd found a place of healing and hope.

I continued my stroll down the shady street. Old oaks grew all along the edge of the sidewalks. A curious neighbor peeked out her front window. Lace priscilla curtains drew back and a face appeared. I couldn't help my-self. I waved. But the face had disappeared.

Every neighborhood has one, I thought, the nosy neighbor that watches all the others. The neighbor right next door to my house was sitting on her front porch.

"Good morning," I called out cheerfully.

"Good morning. I don't think I know you. Why don't you come sit up here on the porch and talk to me a while?"

"Thank you, I will," I said. "Your Shasta daisies are lovely."

"My husband and I planted them. They were always his favorites. I'm Mrs. Walker and I've lived in Wilcox Station since 1949," she said. "We came here right after the war."

"Oh. I've just moved here, right next door." I point-ed to the house. "The house was my Daddy's family home. My Aunt Martha lived there all her life."

"Lands sake alive, you're Mike Cates' little girl." She laughed and clasped her hands together. "I do declare. I was just wondering how it was possible that someone be-sides a Cates could move into that house. Well, I declare."

"It's nice to meet you, Miz Walker. My name's Lily Rose."

"Yes, I remember now. Lily Rose. You don't re-member me. You were just a teeninny thing. Your Daddy's pride and joy. We were so sorry about his passing. My hus-band passed too since him."

"I'm sorry."

"Yes, now I'm a widow lady. Our young'uns grew up, and they both live in Atlanta and they got grown chil-dren, too, but I just can't leave this place. My heart belongs here where I raised my babies and made a life with my husband. I'm too old to start over someplace else. But nothing is the same here for me since he went to be with the Lord."

"Yes, ma'am, I understand."

"I hope you'll come see me sometime." She smiled and her face crinkled. "I'd love to fix you some supper. It's hardly worth the effort cooking for just me."

"Well, thank you, Miz Walker. I'd like that. It's a pleasure to meet you."

She held my hand in her cool bony fingers when I said goodbye.

"It will be nice having you here," she said. By the twinkle in her eyes, I knew she meant it.

It was only a hop and a skip to the house. As soon as I walked up on the front porch, I saw an aluminum bucket of daylilies and several pots of Gerber daisies. Someone had brought flowers.

I read the attached card:

Good morning, I am the neighbor who lives right straight out across the road from you. I'm Grace Wayne. My husband Ralph will be glad to help you with anything that needs fixing around that house. And I can help you sew anything. You're probably going to be needing some new curtains. I can't wait for us to sit and talk a spell. We don't get new neighbors on this street because it's all us old folks who've lived here forever. I thought you might like some of my plants for your garden. I'd be glad to give you more. Warm regards, Grace

P.S. I am on the welcoming committee for our church, Providence Methodist. Welcome to Wilcox Station.

I turned around and looked across the street at the grand white Victorian. Rocking chairs welcomed visitors to sit a spell, while Boston ferns shaded and softened the edges. Sweet peas and daisies grew in bright beds around the porch.

"Hey, Peppy."

He braced his paws on my thigh, and I rubbed the top of his head and behind his floppy ears. "We've got neighbors, Peppy," I said, a bit breathlessly. "And just look at these friendly flowers."

Later in the afternoon, I thought, I'd decide where to plant them and get them in the ground. In the meantime, I went inside, made lunch, grabbed my book, and sat down to enjoy both.

When I tired of reading my novel, I returned to the task of sorting through the pile of books. I stayed at it for hours because I couldn't resist leafing through the pages and reading snippets or long passages from one book after another.

In late afternoon the sound of trucks in the driveway roused me from my book lover's paradise. Peppy ran barking downstairs, and I looked out the window. Sugar was getting out his truck while another one pulled in behind his. When I saw the large crate in the back of the truck, I ran downstairs.

"Hey, Miss Lily, we have a shipment for you from Mr. Hollister."

"Bring it in, Sugar. I need y'all to carry it upstairs. I have the perfect place for it." I buzzed around the men like bees around a honeysuckle vine.

Sugar and the other man carried the carton to the upstairs landing and placed it against the wall between my room and the one Daddy used to stay in. I'd already gotten the furniture polish and a rag. I waited for them to remove the carton. I smiled, pressing my hands to my cheeks.

"There you go," Sugar said. "Looks like you're mighty happy to have it."

"I saw my daddy sit at this desk every day of my life up until he died," I said, rubbing my hand slowly over its surface. "To me, it's a part of him."

Sugar nodded. "I know what you mean. 'Bout the same as this house is to me."

"Yeah, I guess so," I said as I sprayed polish on the rag and began wiping down the side of the oak desk.

"Thank y'all so much." I lovingly polished the desk.

I heard a truck leave, and then Sugar hollered up the stairs.

"Miss Lily, I'm taking these plants around to the backyard."

When I went outside a little while later, Sugar was hoeing in a large flowerbed. He'd pulled some weeds and was digging a spot for the lilies.

"Aren't those pretty," I said. "Mrs. Wayne from across the street brought them over."

"Yeah, I know. They're some of her show lilies."

"Sugar, I bet your wife has the prettiest flowers on the block."

"My wife? No, Miss Lily, you know better." He stopped and cut his eyes at me. "Well, maybe you don't."

"What?"

"You know how I got the name Sugar?" he raised his eyebrows. I frowned and shook my head.

"My daddy said I was sweet, and he didn't mean nice. Well, I ain't that."

"Oh, I didn't realize." I felt a little awkward and hoped my face didn't flush to make matters worse.

"It's true. I don't care a thing about a woman," he said. "But I don't care a thing about men either. Now, some folks have tried to make me fit one way or the other, and I used to stay worried up about it, but not no more. I finally accepted that Aunt Izzy was right."

"Those old folks were right as rain most of the time. We just don't realize it until we've matured a little."

"You know what she told me?" I shook my head. "She said it was a gift from God, His mercy on me to save me from a heap of heartache. I'm almost forty now, and I know it's true."

"Well, that's one way to look at it," I said.

"Yep." He chopped several times in the dark dirt. "I thought *you* was married?"

"Uh . . ." I looked away and wrinkled my nose. "I don't really . . ." I sighed.

Sugar stared at me for a minute.

"That's my point exactly," he said solemnly, and went back to breaking up the soil. "We'll talk about you another day. Now, take this flowerbed. I get real excited working in the dirt. I just love to get my hands in it."

For some reason his serious tone and facial expression tickled me. A giggle bubbled up in me, and though I tried hard to hold it back, I just couldn't. I dropped to the ground and laughed. "Oh, Sugar. You're a hoot and a holler." Bless his heart, he looked at me like I'd lost my mind.

"Miss Lily, don't you make me throw this dirt at you." Then he chuckled too and lightly kicked my foot with the toe of his boot.

We planted the flowers amongst the daylilies and irises and pulled weeds. We watered the plants, slowly soaking the dirt around the roots while talking about what we wanted to do next to make the yard as beautiful as it used to be. He held the hose for me to wash my hands and then washed his off. When he walked around the house to his truck, I followed behind him.

"Take care, Miss Lily. When I come back, I'll bring a load of manure to fertilize the flower beds, and after that we'll go get a truck load of plants from the nursery."

I don't know who was happier. Me or Sugar. Over the next few weeks, we worked in the yard, planting Shasta daisies, black-eyed Susans, and phlox—a kaleidoscope of color and a butterfly's delight.

I talked to my neighbors Miz Walker and Miss Grace every day and got acquainted with others while walking around the neighborhood, visiting the shops on the town square, and shopping in the grocery store. Being out amongst familiar faces, getting acquainted chatting about our day, I felt like I was a part of it all, and with each passing day I felt more and more like I belonged in Wilcox Station.

Manny was no longer the first thing I thought of when I opened my eyes in the morning. In fact, I could go almost all day without thinking of him. I didn't like thinking of him. Memories of our life together made my insides jittery. But, when I climbed into bed at night, I couldn't help myself. I thought of him and so much that had happened. I was relieved there'd been no word from him. I never thought he'd let me get away so easily. I'd expected a dreadful scene. I felt grateful nothing bad had come of my leaving. But was it too early to believe?

Hope grew with each passing day. Hope that I'd be able to start over and lead a happy life. And, as much as I hated to think of it, I knew the time would come when I'd have to talk to Uncle Bill about a divorce.

Chapter Twenty

While I swept off the front walkway, Miss Grace watered the ferns on her front porch. I dropped the broom and walked over to her yard.

"Good morning, Miss Grace. How you doing this morning?"

"Just fine, Lily Rose," she said. "Come sit for a while and let me fix us some tea."

"I think I will." I eased myself down in one of the big white rockers and immediately started a deep slow rock. "You get a nice view from your front porch," I called to her as the screen door slammed. She was back in no time with two glasses of sweet iced tea. She sat in the rocker next to me.

"It's so nice to see you out every day. You brought life back to that house. This neighborhood, too." She looked at me and smiled. "I remember when you and your daddy came every summer."

"Those were happy times." I smiled wistfully.

"Yes. You must miss him."

I nodded slightly. We were silent, and I listened to the creak of the rockers on the wide planks. Then, she said, "Now, tell me Lily Rose, what did you study in college?"

"Journalism, creative writing, and French."

"Is that right? Well, now, that's interesting." She nodded her head. "You know we have a county paper and a magazine right up the road?"

"Yes, ma'am, I picked up a magazine in Uncle Bill's office."

"Have you gone down there and talked to them? Told them about your qualifications?"

"I haven't, no ma'am." I shook my head and looked down at my sneakers, in no hurry to go talk to anybody about my qualifications.

"The magazine is very nice, pretty pictures, mostly local interest stories of course, essays, and sometimes they have a short story. I got a bunch of saved ones if you want to look at 'em."

"Oh, no need for that. Aunt Martha saved them, too." I smiled. "But about going down there. I worked at a newspaper before, but I haven't written anything like that in a while."

"Lily Rose, you'd probably write better than ever now that you're older and more experienced. I mean, you have been out in the world. I bet you write well. You're probably just as good as any of them down there."

"I don't know," I said. I felt sadness drift over me when I thought about the last few years since my newspaper job. Had it only been three years? Those days seemed light years away.

"Sure," she continued. "Don't you have confidence in yourself?" She waited for my answer. She actually seemed to expect one, which forced me to look inside.

"Uh . . . I used to . . . seems I've struggled to hold on to confidence in myself ever since Daddy died."

"You are who you always were, Lily Rose," she said softly. "I see you coming and going, working around that beautiful house, practically skipping up the street, and you're just the same sweet girl you've always been. Full of life and smart as a whip."

"Miss Grace, nobody's talked to me like that in a long time. You sound like Daddy and Annie Ruth."

"Now, your daddy, he was a man who could tell a good story."

"Yes, he could that," I said with a sigh. Then we rocked without talking, each of us remembering our own memories and listening to the creek of the rockers.

"Thank you, Miss Grace, and thanks for the glass of tea." I rose from the chair and handed her my empty glass. "I can't stay. I need to be going. I'm going up to the library this afternoon. I have hundreds of my aunt's books I want to donate."

"Is that right? Did you know I'm on the Friends of the Library committee?" She stood as well.

"No, I didn't know that." I had already walked down the steps.

"Come to think of it, I got a book needs returning. Would you take it for me? I don't feel like walking up there, and since you're going . . . well, would you take it?"

"Sure." I stepped forward to get the sun out of my eyes. She opened the scrolled screen door, stepped inside, and promptly retrieved the book from the hall tree.

"I'll be sure to return it for you this afternoon. See you later, Miss Grace."

I'm just the same person I always was. Miss Grace couldn't have realized how her words had spoken to my heart. *I'm just the same person I always was.* How often I felt diminished because of what I'd gone through over the last three years. The disappointment and heartbreak from my marriage. The lingering sadness and vulnerability over the loss of our child. No less painful was the sense of my own inadequacy, my own stupidity. The events of those years had cut away a part of me, wounded my personality. How could I not feel less than I used to be before it all happened?

"I'm just the same person I always was," I said aloud. That should be my new mantra I thought.

After lunch, with Miss Grace's book, *God and Vitamins* in hand, I walked to the library. I'd forgotten what an impressive historical building it was. The afternoon sun shone through a large floor to ceiling stained glass window—a spectacular Tiffany glass window commissioned by the library's benefactor. For several minutes, I stood still and admired it. The vibrant colors of the glass bathed in the sun's rays cast a magical glow over the dark wood furnishings.

"What a treasure," I said quietly to no one in particular.

I heard someone talking with the librarian at the circulation desk, but I continued to look at the spectacular window.

"*God and Vitamins.* Aunt Mae said be sure to give her a call as soon as it comes in." When I heard that, I looked at the book in my hand, and then turned around.

"Excuse me. I'm returning the book you requested." At the sound of my voice, he turned toward me. I had turned from one spectacular view to another. He was tall and tanned, with sandy blond hair curling behind his ears, and a five o'clock shadow that had never looked so good. Our eyes met, and he smiled. I'm not sure if I smiled back or not. Sound faded into silence while seconds passed before either of us moved. Then I handed the book to him without a word.

"Thanks," he said, and turned back to the circulation desk. He glanced back at me like he wanted to say something, but I turned back to the stained glass window. When I heard him say 'good-bye' and the door close behind him, I took a deep breath. The librarian joined me to look at the window.

"It's beautiful, isn't it," she said. "We're very proud of it. Would you like to know its history?" She turned her gaze toward me.

"Yes. But first, let me ask . . . I'd like to donate some books to the library. I have hundreds of my Aunt Martha Cates' books that I'd like to donate."

"Is that right? Miss Cates' books? We'd be grateful to have them. The ones we don't add to our collection, we'll sell at the annual book sale."

"So, you'll take them?" I asked matter-of-factly.

"Of course. It's not often that we get a collection like she must have had. I'll even send someone to get them tomorrow if that's convenient for you."

"Yes," I said, "that would be great. Thank you."

I forgot my manners. I didn't stay and chat with the lady so eager to tell me the history of the Tiffany window. I didn't even introduce myself.

"Let me give you this brochure before you go so you can read about it." She hurried over to the display rack near the door, pulled out a brochure, and handed it to me.

"Thanks again," I said as I headed out the door. Distracted, definitely, and baffled. I had stumbled upon more than one masterpiece, and my unexpected reaction to him was completely unwelcome. Only once before had I had a visceral reaction to a strange man. Only once, and it had not ended well. Not well at all. Now I just wanted to get back to the house as quickly as possible, where no one would trouble my thoughts, where I could curl up with a book and a glass of sweet tea and hide away for a while in solitude.

I walked briskly, more than a little annoyed with myself. Just as I approached the house with the peek-a-boo curtains, I noticed long jean-clad legs striding down the front steps, heading towards the pickup truck parked on the street.

"Oh my goodness," I gasped. "It's *him*." I hesitated, stopping momentarily in my tracks. There was nothing I could do to avoid him. The distance between us had closed to speaking range. When you're already face to face, it's too late to turn around and go the other way. My manners hadn't gotten that bad.

He halted, put one hand on his hip, the other braced on the hood of the truck. A wide disarming grin spread across his sun-tanned face. He looked like a modern day cowboy in boots and faded blue jeans.

"You aren't following me are you?" He spoke in a deep resonant voice. His blue-green eyes sparkled and humor crinkled the corners.

When I didn't say anything in response, his playful cockiness subsided.

"Okay," he said as he stuck out his hand. "I guess you're not. I'm Sam Watson."

"The veterinarian," I whispered, my eyes widening.

"Yes."

He seemed puzzled. Instead of a grin, he smiled a crooked smile and cocked his head slightly. His forehead wrinkled as his eyes scanned me head to toe.

"I'm Lily Rose Cates," I said, grabbing his hand, now paused in mid-air. By then he seemed to be struggling with the moment as much as I was.

"It's nice to meet you," he said.

A nervous giggle erupted like a hiccup. "I've just moved into my daddy's family home." I pointed down the street in the direction of the house. "My Aunt Martha lived there all her life."

"Oh, yeah. I did hear that Miss Martha's niece had moved to town."

"That would be me," I said, and felt my face flush.

"Welcome to Wilcox Station."

"Thank you."

"I hope we'll see each other around."

"That would be nice," I said, feeling foolish.

He opened the door to the truck and then hesitated. "By the way, my Aunt Mae lives here." He nodded toward the house. "She and your aunt were good friends. I'm sure she'd like to meet you. Stop by when you have time. She's confined to a wheelchair. I come see her as much as I can."

"Oh." I glanced at the window just in time to see the curtain flutter. "I'd like to meet her. I'll do that."

"It's nice to meet you," he said again.

"Nice to meet you, too."

"See you around." Then, he climbed in and started the loud engine. I walked as fast I could without looking back.

By the time I got home, my forehead was damp with sweat. I made a mental note to apologize to the librarian for my behavior and to go by to visit Sam Watson's aunt. That explained why she was always sitting near the window. I had assumed she was the proverbial nosy neighbor peeking from behind the curtains. In reality, she sat at the window and watched the world go by.

I'll go visit her . . . I should do that, I thought, but I'll definitely steer clear of that big green truck and its owner.

Chapter Twenty-One

The morning sun cast a soft golden light across my bedroom. From my window I looked at the cloudless blue sky and let my eyes travel over the yard and those of the neighbors. I watched the birds flying in and out of the oak trees. It was a spectacular spring day. I was expecting Sugar with a truckload of plants. Over the last six weeks, I'd spent as much time working in the yard as I'd spent cleaning the house. I wanted to bring the flower, herb, and vegetable gardens back to the way Aunt Martha had them—gardens that complement a one-hundred-year-old house. Another call to Julie the previous day had me humming ever since and fit to tackle any task. She'd still not heard a word from Manuel. Nothing at all.

Was it possible that he was going to let me go without a fight? It didn't seem like him. Maybe he did have something more serious to worry about, like Julie had said. With that missing woman, he couldn't afford to call attention to a missing wife as well. I closed my eyes tightly and shuddered. I'd certainly not thought all that through when I left. I just knew I had to get away.

As soon as I'd had some coffee, I walked outside. I understood what Sugar meant about loving to get his hands in the dirt. My mind would move along on auto-pilot while I worked in the flowerbeds. Maybe truck driving was like that for Earl. Lots of time for him to think and talk to God. The sound of the breeze rustling through the trees, birds chirping, the fresh fragrance of air and earth, and the warm sun on my skin and hair created a healing atmosphere for my body and soul. My thoughts glided along like a swing . . . calming, healing my frayed nerves. A brown thrasher flew low across the yard to the magnolia tree. I smelled the sweet, subtle scent of its blossoms from where I sat on the grass.

Through the years, Uncle Bill hired Sugar to do upkeep of the yards, preventing them from totally dying. Yet Sugar loved it so much he'd slip over in his spare time and work in the backyard behind the tall fence. Fortunately, he had fertilized the lawns and beds and mulched before I'd come. I had missed the crocus and daffodils this year, along with the golden forsythia, the camellias, and a variety of vibrant pink azaleas. Next year, maybe, I'd see the entire magnificent display.

I worked in the yard all morning until hunger forced me to break for lunch, but before going in I picked some magnolia blossoms to float in a bowl. A sandwich and sweet iced tea didn't quite satisfy me. My search for something more yielded the bag of chocolate candies. Peppy watched me intently—his wet little nose quivering as I opened the bag and unwrapped a chocolate. I'd just popped one into my mouth when the doorbell rang.

"Peppy," I scolded, "you're falling down on the job. You're supposed to bark?" And then he did bark, so vigorously he bounced.

A couple of young people from the library had arrived. I showed them upstairs to the appropriate pile of books. They looked at each other for several seconds before packing the cardboard boxes. Then, they hauled away a substantial collection; floor space cleared—a mutually satisfying exchange.

I spent the remainder of the day working in the yard. By the time I climbed out of my warm soaking bath and slipped into silky pajamas, I was ready for bed, bone tired from a full day of working in the sun. I quickly fell asleep.

In the middle of the night, I was startled awake. What woke me, I wasn't sure, or if anything in particular had, I didn't know, but I lay there paralyzed with fear and stared straight ahead into the eerie moonlight. After a long minute, I was able to exhale the breath I'd been holding.

Manny? Could it be Manny? Fear shot through me like a jolt of electricity. Then I heard a distinct whimper and scuttling noises on the hardwood floor. The noise was coming from the kitchen. It took a few seconds for my hazy thoughts to clear, but then I sat up and looked at Peppy's bed. Empty. I jumped out of bed and ran downstairs.

The scene in the kitchen made my stomach lurch. Peppy lay on his side, twitching all over as cocoa colored saliva drooled from his mouth. His legs shook so hard they lifted off the floor.

"Peppy!" I shrieked. I knelt beside him and put my hand on his side. The muscles under his skin were rigid and jumping. I felt his heart pounding. Wild eyes pleaded for help. An agonizing fear stabbed my heart.

"Oh no, Peppy." I ran to get my purse and grabbed a towel. I shoved my feet into flip flops, picked up Peppy in the towel, and hurried out the back door. It seemed to take forever to open the door of the carport. Putting the car's gear in reverse, I stomped the accelerator and spun out the carport in an arc, facing the back gate. More agonizing seconds passed while I opened the gate. I had to get Peppy to the farm I'd seen weeks ago on the drive into town. We had to get to Doc Watson's before it was too late.

My heart threatened to burst during the drive through town and out to the vet's. My poor Peppy was suffering horribly, and I suffered right along with him. Aunt Martha surely rolled over in her grave the way I drove Sophie that night. I made a heart-stopping turn onto the fence-lined dirt road. The pecan trees blocked the moonlight. I pulled up to the house, wildly honking the horn. The headlights glared off the windows. Leaving the motor running, I jumped out the car and ran to the front door. Dogs barked as I pounded frantically. I heard a man's voice and footsteps approaching.

I was hollering for help when the front door swung open.

"Please, I need your help. My dog is dying. He's having a seizure or a stroke or something awful. Please help me." I grabbed his arm.

For a moment our eyes met—his full of compassion. Then he yelled at the dogs behind him and hurried to the car. He felt Peppy's chest, then held his head and looked into his eyes and mouth. Gathering up the dog, he motioned for me to go to the small building attached to the house by a breezeway. He went inside the house, carrying my puppy. Within seconds, he opened the door of the clinic, and I followed him back to an open room with a long metal table. Together we held Peppy so he could examine him.

"I'm going to have to pump his stomach." He was pulling out gadgets that I'd never seen before. "Can you help me hold him? From the looks of it, he has chocolate poisoning."

"Oh no," I whimpered, with tears running down my cheeks. "He won't die, will he?"

"I'll do the best I can. You can help by holding him as still as you can. I have to do this," he said.

"There was a bag of Hershey's chocolate kisses."

"He probably ate it all."

"Poor little fellow. I'm so sorry, Peppy."

I held the quivering body and prayed through my sniffles. The fear-induced adrenaline fired courage in me I didn't normally have and gave me the strength to stand there. Tears trickled down my face.

The vet moved efficiently, plunging a hypodermic needle into Peppy's hip, stopping the tremors. I held on to Peppy and shut my eyes. After pumping out the contents of his stomach, he said he had to pump charcoal in to absorb the toxins. The rhythmic sound of the machine washed waves of nausea over me. After what seemed like hours, the veterinarian had done all he could, and Peppy lay still, hooked up to an IV.

I glanced at the wall clock. It was three in the morning.

"You don't need to hold him now," Sam said gently. "Let me slip this around you." He took off the unbuttoned lab jacket he was wearing and helped me into it.

I pulled it around me tightly and shivered. Then I sat down cross-legged on the floor beside Peppy's cage.

The IV needle was secured to his shaved leg with surgical tape. The sedation was working. He slept.

The vet opened a closet and pulled out a folded cot, like one used for camping. "Here, why don't you lay on this. It's the best I can do."

He led me to it, holding my forearm with one hand, the other draped around my shoulder. I lay down and he covered me with a quilt. Before I shut my eyes, I noticed he was wearing a pair of jeans and nothing else. We must have made a funny sight—he dressed only in jeans, and me in my skimpy pajamas.

"I'm going over to the house," he said, "but I'll be right back. You rest."

"Thank you," I whispered, already falling asleep as he walked out the door.

***

A ringing telephone woke me, but I didn't move. My body ached. My eyes scanned about for clues to my whereabouts. Then I heard a woman in an adjoining room say, "Doc Watson's Veterinary Clinic", and it all came rushing back. I sat up in a sudden panic.

A woman wearing scrubs was closing the door of a cage.

"Hi, I'm Lisa," she said, as she walked over to stand with me beside Peppy's cage. She looked to be in her mid-thirties. "He's doing well."

"Is he?" I turned and searched her vaguely familiar face. "Is he going to be all right?"

"Sure, full recovery," she said. She pushed a clump of dark blond hair from her eyes. "Your dog is fine. We have to keep him sedated, of course. You can talk more with Sam about him this afternoon. I'm his sister."

"He's not here? I would like to talk to him."

"He had to go pull a calf." When she saw the look on my face, she laughed a little half-laugh. "Don't worry. He'll be back after lunch. He told me to tell you to go home, get some sleep, and come back at five."

"Oh," I sighed, greatly relieved, and then I remembered my manners. "Thank you." I held out my hand. "I'm Lily."

"Nice to meet you." She smiled. "By the way, cute pajamas, but you might want to change those before you come back."

I looked down at my pink taffeta pajama pants. The skimpy white tank with rosebuds and spaghetti straps covered little of the faded tattoo.

"Yeah, Victoria's Secret." I laughed. "And the tattoo is another story."

"I can't imagine," she chuckled. "But I'm sure my brother didn't mind."

I stroked Peppy's fur a few minutes more, then drove home. After a long nap and a hot shower to ease my sore muscles, I returned to the vet's at five.

"I really can't thank you enough for saving my dog." I said. "He's become very important to me."

"I can see that. I'm glad he pulled through." He smiled. "You have a nice little Norfolk terrier mix. Where did you find him?"

"I didn't. He found me. He just took up with me on my way here."

"Well, he's lucky to have found you." He smiled just enough to reveal a dimple in his cheek.

"As if you haven't already done enough . . . I need to ask another favor." I glanced at Peppy sleeping in the cage. "I don't think I can sleep a wink if I go home without him.

Would you mind very much if I slept over?" I looked around for the cot and lifted my eyebrows.

His brows arched as well, and he studied me for a second.

"It's in the closet. You won't be very comfortable, I'm afraid," he said. He rubbed his hand across the stubble on his chin. "But, okay. It's been done before. I keep it here for emergencies. I'll get blankets and a pillow from the house."

"There's no need," I said. "I packed a bag."

"In that case," he said, shrugging his shoulders, "make yourself at home. But you're going to be very bored."

"Not at all. I've brought a book." I pulled it out of my purse and held it up for him to see. "And a notebook for writing."

"Oh, the scholarly type." He leaned toward me to read the title. "*Wuthering Heights*. Humm . . . " He chuckled a little. "Don't mind me. I have some work to do before I call it a day. You go escape to the moors."

I giggled, surprised he knew anything about the story. I was a bit intrigued as well. He didn't look like the type to read romances. Larry McMurtry's, maybe.

I brought in my bag, then sat in the only chair available—a metal one. I watched the vet as he moved around the room caring for the animals. He glanced shyly at me a couple of times, so I opened the novel and read. In reality, I read very little. I kept glancing at the vet. He seemed to fill up the whole room. I couldn't help watching him, but I held on to the book as if I were absorbed in it.

"I'll be back in a couple of hours to check on my patients," he said, glancing at the book in my hands. "Can I bring you anything?"

"No, I'm fine. Thank you for letting me stay."

"How could I say no to my best assistant?" He winked as he walked out the door.

I relaxed then, opened the cot, and stretched out as best I could. There was a quiet hum about the place. Peppy slept soundly nearby, and it was comforting in a cozy sort of way to know that Sam Watson was nearby too.

I think he came back in during the night, but I didn't hear him. I slept, waking only when the first rays of morning's light shined through the windows.

Doc Watson released Peppy and wished us a good day.

"Call me if you have any questions, or if he fails to behave like his normal self." He gently stroked Peppy's back while he kept his eyes on me. I felt a bit self-conscious when his fingers touched mine.

"Thank you," I said.

"You're very welcome." He turned to focus on another furry patient that awaited his care.

On the way out, I spoke to Lisa, who sat at the front desk.

"Thank you for everything."

"He looks fine now," she said, and reached out to rub his paw with her index finger. "Glad everything turned out well."

"So am I. By the way, does your brother have a favorite food?" I paused to wait for her response.

"A favorite food? What's not his favorite? That boy loves to eat." She laughed. "I can say that. I'm his big sister."

"How about a favorite dessert?"

"Well, he likes cobblers, peach and blackberry . . . but his favorite is banana pudding. The old-fashioned kind with real meringue," she added. "Mama used to make it for us. Nobody makes it as good as she did."

"Okay." I grinned. "I have to do something special for him." Peppy squirmed a bit in my arms and licked my chin. "After all, he saved my little friend. Bye-bye," I said as I hurried out the door.

There was not a doubt Peppy was as good as new. On the way home, he barked in the car and jumped out as soon as we got there. He ran around the backyard and half-heartedly chased a squirrel. I smiled or laughed out loud the entire time I watched him play.

"My goodness, Peppy, if I love you this much, I can't imagine how much I'll love my children." I held the back door open for him. Unexpected sadness touched my heart when I thought of my baby. How precious he would have been.

***

Early the next morning, Peppy and I headed out to the Piggly Wiggly. I was on a mission with a list in my hand—bananas, milk, and vanilla wafers. I intended to have that pudding made by mid-morning. Annie Ruth's banana pudding could rival the best in the South. I prayed I'd remember how she'd taught me.

Peppy had gotten used to my hitching him outside the store. He laid down and waited for me without pulling against the tether. On the way back home, I noticed the open curtains at the vet's aunt's house. I decided to stop just long enough to introduce myself.

I heard some commotion as she made her way to the door. A lady with black hair touched with silver opened the door. She looked younger than I expected. Her skin was creamy and fair, and her violet blue eyes sparkled.

"Hello," I said. "I hope I'm not disturbing you."

"No, not at all," she said in a timid sounding voice.

"I just wanted to introduce myself. I've met your nephew, Sam, and your niece. And I heard you were friends with my Aunt Martha." I smiled. She listened intently. "I'm Lily Rose Cates, Michael Cates' daughter." I saw an immediate spark of affection in her eyes.

"Martha and Michael Cates. Two of the nicest people I've ever known. They were older than me. Their kindness encouraged me after my accident. Martha became a special friend."

"I'm living in my father's house now."

"I've seen you walking by, and I saw you talking to Sam a few days ago." She smiled.

"He saved my puppy who ate a bag of silver tips, paper and all. Chocolate poisoning. I'd left the bag on the table. I never thought that he might climb up on the chair."

"Oh my. Well, I'm glad Sam could help. He's always been good with animals. He's a smart boy. So much like my brother."

"Well, I can't stay, just wanted to introduce myself. I'm going home now to make a banana pudding. It's a surprise for the vet."

"He'll love that." Her eyes sparkled. "Please come back and visit."

"I'd like that. What time is best?"

"Anytime. In the morning, or late afternoon. Right after lunch, I usually watch my shows and do my sewing. But I always like company."

"I look forward to visiting soon," I said. "Have a nice day."

"Bye now. Hope that banana pudding turns out good."

"Me, too. Good-bye."

As soon as I got back in the kitchen, I began making the pudding. Eggs were already out on the counter so they'd be at room temperature. Annie Ruth always said room temperature eggs make the best meringue. I remembered all the cooking tips she'd taught me. I decided then it was about time I called her. I'd call her as soon as I talked to Uncle Bill about Manny and our marriage. I needed to tell him about the incident with that woman, too. I wondered if she was still missing, and I felt guilty about having pushed it out of my mind for so long. Missing Annie Ruth might give me the nudge I needed to go ahead and deal with the unpleasant details. I couldn't put it off forever, and maybe Manny would be reasonable after all.

When I pulled the pudding out of the oven, the peaks of meringue were perfectly golden. *Annie Ruth, you would be proud.* Then I set the entire dish in a basket and draped a large cloth napkin over the top.

"Sorry, Peppy, you have to stay home. I can't risk you stepping in the pudding."

When I presented it to Doc Watson a few minutes later, his mouth fell open.

"Wow! Is that banana pudding? For me?"

"It certainly is. I hope you enjoy it."

"I'm sure I will." A wide grin spread across his handsome face.

"Well, I declare," Lisa said, "it looks just like the ones Mama used to make. Now, Sam, don't you eat that whole thing by yourself. Save some for me." She nudged him with her elbow.

"Why don't I man the front desk, while your sister takes the pudding over to your house?"

"Go right ahead." He smiled down at me. "Lisa, stay out of that pudding," he said. "I get the first bowl."

On the way home, I passed Officer Barkley making one of his neighborhood drive-bys on my behalf. I smiled and waved. When I got home, still smiling, it occurred to me that I had smiled more in the last seven weeks than I had in all the two and half years in Detroit. If smiles were any indication, this was the place I needed to be.

Chapter Twenty-Two

If I were going to stay in Wilcox Station, I needed to find a job. The inheritance wouldn't last forever. With that in mind, I gathered up some typing paper and slipped it into the pages of a notebook, and then headed to the library in the hopes of preparing a resume and cover letters.

"Good morning," I said to the librarian. "What did you think of the books?"

"Wonderful. It's a fine collection. Thank you so much." She seemed genuinely pleased.

"It was my pleasure. By the way, I'm Lily Rose Cates. I'm sorry I failed to introduce myself the other day. I don't know what I was thinking. I realized it as soon as I got home."

"Don't worry about it," she said, with a flutter of her hand. "Those things happen to all of us sometimes. Why, I failed to wave to the preacher when I drove passed him on the street the other day. I was trying to remember whether

or not I'd turned off the iron. I looked right through him."
We laughed.

"Thanks for putting me at ease," I said, and glanced around the library. "I need to use a nice typewriter. Mine's not quite up to standard. Do you have one for patron use?"

"Yes, as a matter of fact, we do. Come with me. You're going to love this."

She led the way through the reading room. "We have a brand new electric typewriter. Just sign your name and the time in the log book. It's yours for an hour. If no one else needs it, it's yours for the duration."

"Great."

"I'll just leave you to it," she said.

I sat down, inserted the paper, and got to work. Before long I had made three sets, one for the magazine, another for the newspaper, and one set for myself. The pages practically flew out the sleek machine. The finished products looked so clean and crisp, I decided to go on over to the county magazine office, introduce myself, and leave the paperwork.

Their office was the last one on the street, right next to Uncle Bill's law office. Glass display windows facing the street showcased art from local artists. So many plants and vines filled the space it looked like an atrium. I liked the atmosphere as soon as I entered the open office space where several people typed and worked intently at their desks. When I gave my resume to the receptionist, she said they weren't advertising any openings at the time, but she would give my resume to the editor who would get back with me.

When I left, I decided to stop at Miss Mae's on the way home. I munched an apple as I walked.

Miss Mae welcomed me with a smile and directed me to an armchair across from her.

"I've missed your Aunt Martha," she said. "I'll never forget her because of what she did for me."

"Is that right," I said. "She must have been a good friend."

"Yes, she was. Nobody knows how much she meant to me." Miss Mae closed her eyes for a minute. When she opened them she gazed out the window. I sat with my hands folded in my lap, mirroring hers.

"Since you're the closest to a daughter she had, I want to tell you about it." She looked at me then. "I'd like you to know."

I could tell by the tone of her voice that it was important to her. I nodded, and after a brief silence, she began.

"Your Aunt Martha and I shared a secret." She paused and took a deep breath. "When I had the accident, it was the first of March. The fields were wet, and I rode that horse hard across the pasture. When we ran through the ditch, he stumbled. It was a freak accident. But I should have been more careful." I heard her sigh as she looked toward the window again. "I was twenty-four and engaged to be married in two weeks. I was three months pregnant, too, but nobody knew about the baby but Jake and me. We knew we were going to get married someday, so I didn't think of it as a shot-gun wedding. We'd been seeing each other for several years. Nobody suspected anything when we announced we were getting married."

I nodded slightly, at a complete loss for words.

"When I had the accident, I lost the baby. Doctor Baker—he was a saint—promised he'd never tell a soul, and to the best of my knowledge he never did."

Miss Mae spoke as if she was revealing an event of sacred proportions. I alternately squeezed and then released my fingers. "I'm sorry," I said.

"When Jake and I heard Doctor Baker tell Mama and Daddy that no medicine or man, nor miracle of our gracious God could help the harm done to my back, I lost Jake, too. He left my bedside that night and didn't come back. I never saw him again."

"Oh, no," I whispered. My throat hurt. I covered my mouth with my hand.

"So, I lost my baby and the man I loved and the use of my legs all at the same time."

Miss Mae's face looked serene. I tried, but failed to stifle a sniffle.

"Oh goodness, don't cry," she said softly. "It's all right. And I need to tell you about your aunt."

"Yes, ma'am, go on."

"Well, Mama died three years after my accident and it like to have killed me. Daddy tried, but he couldn't take her place. For some reason that I can't explain, with Mama gone, I started thinking about the baby again. My thoughts were consumed by all I'd lost." She paused for a long moment, a picture of grace and serenity. Her eyes smiled then.

"Your aunt came to see me one day. Daddy had told her how bad off I was. In my distress I poured it all out to her. I told her what I couldn't tell my own Mama. We sat back there in my bedroom and talked for hours. Martha held my hand while I cried about losing the baby and Jake and Mama and how my life might as well have ended too. The next afternoon, she came back. Every day she came and sat with me in my room. After about a week, she came with two naked baby dolls and said, 'Mae, could you make some clothes for these dolls? I want to give them to the children over at the hospital.' Everybody knew I could sew like a top, but after the accident I wouldn't even try to sew. But, those little pieces I could make by hand. I took an interest in that for Martha and the children. She'd come to visit, like clockwork, and bring dolls in nothing but their underpants. We'd sit and talk and hold the dolls and she'd leave them with me so I could make the clothes. A few days later, she'd be back."

At that point, I could see tears glistening on her cheeks, but her expression was not one of sorrow.

I wiped a tear from my face, and tried not to cry, although my heart was breaking a little. Then she laughed, really hard, startling me. It sounded like pure joy. When she composed herself she said, "I asked her one day, 'Martha, haven't you given enough baby dolls to the hospital?' And she said, 'Oh, I'm giving them to Children's Services, too. There are foster children who need them.'"

"That was sweet," I said quietly.

"But you see, we rocked those baby dolls, and I made doll clothes for about five years. Five years!" She laughed again. "One day I said to her, 'Martha, I don't need to make any more baby doll clothes', and she said, 'Good, I ran out of children to give them to a long time ago.'" Then Miss Mae and I both laughed, with tears streaming down our cheeks.

"You see, she helped me work it through and got me out of myself. I don't know how she thought of such a peculiar thing, but somehow she knew just what to do for me. After that, I started sewing for the ladies' missionary society, making baby blankets, aprons, tablecloths, and napkins. Embroidering most everything I made, too. I've been doing it ever since. Every year we sell the things I've made at the church bazaar and send the money to missionaries."

"Miss Mae, that's wonderful."

"Look right over yonder," she said, pointing to the dining room table. "Go look at the tablecloth." There was pride and a spark of joy in her voice.

"It's beautiful," I said.

"And open the buffet drawer. Look at the napkins."

"They're so pretty. You're very talented."

"It's been a real blessing. I can't believe how much people pay for those things, and it all goes to the missionaries. I've helped hundreds of children that way."

"Yes, I imagine you have."

"Here's a little something I made for you," she said. She held out a small bundle wrapped in tissue paper. I unfolded it slowly to reveal a white lace-edged handkerchief. "Lily Rose" was embroidered in a beautiful cursive script. Tiny pink and blue flowers with yellow dot centers and delicate green leaves encircled my name.

"Oh, how delicate," I whispered. "Thank you Miss Mae. You're so kind."

"You might want to carry it on your wedding day," she said softly.

For a long moment, I stood still as if I was studying the handkerchief in my hand, but in reality I was thinking of my wedding day. I didn't have the heart to tell Miss Mae that I was already married and that I was here because I'd deserted my husband. She'd know eventually, but I couldn't tell her then.

I'll never forget that afternoon. That graceful lady treated me like family by taking me into her confidence. The clock chimed, reminding me it was time for Peppy's supper.

"Miss Mae, I've got to be going. I've sat here all afternoon. I appreciate you telling me your story. And thank you for this beautiful gift."

"I've enjoyed myself," she said. "Felt good to remember and talk about it."

"Now, I'd like to do something special for you. What can I do for you?"

"Oh, my." She clasped her hands together and blinked her eyes. "Well, since you offered, let me think." She pursed her lips while she thought. "I'd like some blackberry cobbler. Do you know how to make one?"

"I do," I said. "But first I'll have to find out where blackberries grow around here."

"Oh, I know just the place," she said. "There's a big patch of 'em on the property along the fence near the back pasture. At least, there used to be. Ask Sam and he'll show you."

"The property? You mean the blackberries are on Doc Watson's place?"

"Yes, that's right. We all used to pick them when I was growing up. That's where Mama always picked them."

"Okay then. I'll see what I can do."

Before I knew it, I was walking down my drive. Without realizing it, I'd paid no attention to the shady street with its lovely gardens and historical homes of which I was so fond. I thought about Miss Mae's remarkable story. I couldn't imagine the grief and disappointment she had suffered, and yet she'd moved past it, made something beautiful of her life, and gave to others. No bitterness poisoned her days. Was it because she had "gotten out of herself," as she said?

Her story touched me deeply and I've often thought of it through the years.

I noticed Sugar's truck when I got home, so I walked around back. When I went through the gate, Peppy raced towards me, leaping and running in circles around my legs.

"Stop, Peppy, before you trip me." I giggled. I leaned down and scratched behind his ears. He fell over in ecstasy.

"I'm finishing up here, Miss Lily," Sugar said. "Put in a few more impatiens and begonias over here under the oak tree."

I plopped down in the glider and looked at the silky scarlet petals set amongst the ivy blanketing the ground at the base of the tree.

"Thank you Sugar. Those are so perky." I stretched back in the glider. The metal lawn furniture had set there as long as I could remember. Daddy and Aunt Martha loved to come outside after supper, sit with their glasses of iced tea, and talk while I caught lightening bugs in a Mason jar, or laid on the grass and looked at the stars. Our world seemed as big as the sky.

"I love this yard," I said with a sigh. "It's the kind of place makes me remember everything sweet about my childhood, and why I loved coming here so much."

"I know, Miss Lily, I'm right there with you," he said as he walked toward the gate.

"Hey, Sugar, wait a second."

"Yeah?" He paused and looked back at me.

"Would you build a wheelchair ramp along the side of the front porch?" He stood there looking at me for a second. "I want to have Miss Mae Watson come over for dinner."

He smiled and nodded. "I can do that. I certainly can. I'll see what my nephews and I can do this Saturday."

"Thank you." I waved good-bye.

"Supper time, little boy," I said to Peppy and we headed inside. I filled his food dish and set it down for him, then ran clean water into his bowl. While he ate, I ran upstairs. There was a special place I wanted to see.

I opened the door of the doll room, walked over to the window, and lifted the shade. The afternoon sun cast a golden glow on the faces of the dolls. I looked around the room, amazed at the transformation brought about by my change in perspective. It didn't seem creepy anymore. I picked up a doll and gently fingered the delicate dress, decorated with lace and tiny buttons. I sensed the love that had gone into each stitch. Now I knew what I needed to do. I'd wash the dolls and their clothes and find children to give them to. A few could be taken to the antique shop in town. The others I'd keep, for me . . . and mine . . . and some I'd give to Miss Mae. Won't she be surprised? Life does have some delightful surprises. More than outweighs the bad ones, I thought.

I glanced at the clock. Past supper time, but I wondered if I might catch Doc Watson at the clinic still. I decided to give it a try. I pulled the card from under the magnet on the refrigerator and dialed the number. Just as I was about to hang up, he answered.

"Hello."

"Doc Watson," I said.

"Hey, Lily, how are you? Is Peppy doing okay?"

"Yes, we're fine, thanks. I need to talk to you. It seems I have another favor to ask."

"Don't tell me you want to sleep on my cot again," he said, laughing.

"No, not that." I giggled. "I went to see Miss Mae."

"Wonderful."

"We had a great visit. She's a special lady."

"I knew you would like her," he said.

"Well, the thing is, I'm going to make a blackberry cobbler for her, by special request, and I need to find a good blackberry patch."

"Oh, ho ho ho." He pretended to laugh. "I know exactly where this is going. Let me guess. You want to ravage the sacred blackberry patch."

I laughed in earnest. His ability to make me laugh rivaled my brother's.

"She said the best blackberries were on your property," I said with my voice lilting upward.

"Well, I'll reveal to you the secret location and let you have all you want, under one condition."

"And what might that be?" I asked, intrigued. "Are you going to lead me there blindfolded?"

"Not a bad idea. But I was thinking more like I come pick you up, and we can pick them together." His voice softened. He no longer sounded playful. I don't think he was sure how I'd respond.

"That sounds like a good idea."

"How about Saturday morning at nine?"

"That's perfect." I felt a tinge of excitement.

"Why not plan on me providing lunch too?"

"Okay. Another good idea. I'm making out like a bandit on this deal," I teased.

"And, Lily Rose, for Pete's sake, call me Sam. Peppy can call me Doc Watson."

I chuckled. "Sure, Sam."

We said good-bye and I stood there a moment, picturing him. He looked so boyishly handsome. He made me smile. Maybe that's why I felt like giving him a big hug, with his good-natured self.

Sure enough, Saturday morning brought visitors and lots of excitement. Sugar and his nephews were cutting boards and nailing them in place by eight o'clock. By nine, Sam was knocking at my front door. I opened the door to blue skies and sunshine framing *a fine looking man*, like Miss Wanda had said. Sam reached down and petted Peppy.

"Hey. You want to come in for a cup of coffee?" I asked as I swung open the door.

"Sure," he said. "I'll have some." He was smiling from ear to ear.

I poured him a cup, and while he drank it, I looked for a container for the berries.

"How about this?" I held up a rectangular straw basket.

"Not big enough," he said, shaking his head. I continued rifling through Aunt Martha's baskets stacked in the pantry.

"I've found a perfect one," I said, holding up a straw bucket with a substantial handle.

"Yeah, I think that will do. Looks like one for peach picking."

"And *this*," I grinned, stretching out the word. I pulled the brim of a large straw hat over one eye. "Now I look like all the other old ladies on the street."

"Not possible," he said. "Actually, you'll need it. It's going to be a hot one today. We don't want your nose to burn. Which if you don't mind, let's discuss your outfit."

"My outfit?" I postured with phony indignation. With my hands on my hips, I stuck out a foot, pretending to admire my boot. My legs were the color of coffee with cream, but they needed some sun, I thought.

"The boots . . . good idea. But, what about those cut-off jeans? There might be chiggers, and you could get scratched up in the briers."

"What is it about getting scratched in the briers? Geez."

"Just saying." He smiled. "I'd hate for you to scratch those nice legs."

"Okay, I guess you're right. I'll go put on some jeans." I started to go upstairs.

"Lily, if you like you could bring the cut-offs too. You can change before lunch."

The men were making good progress on the ramp when we said good-bye. I told Sam the plan to bring Miss Mae to the house for lunch.

"That's nice. You're becoming a part of the community."

"Yeah, I guess I am."

I climbed up into Sam's big truck, and we headed for his place. Country music played on the radio as we turned onto the familiar pecan tree lined road leading to his house. Then we followed it on around the house and back through the pastures. After bouncing along the dirt road, we drove down a hill. A few scrubby trees dotted the hollow, and then I saw a long stretch of barbed wire fence smothered in blackberry brambles.

"Well, here it is." He smiled. "My coveted blackberry patch."

"Wow," I said. "There must be enough blackberries here to feed a multitude."

"And the birds of the air too," he said. We looked at each other, our eyes wide, and burst out laughing.

"God bless Sunday School," I said.

"Yeah, who could forget all those Bible verses we had to memorize." He shook his head and grinned.

As I picked berries, I popped plump juicy ones into my mouth.

"Yummy."

"Sweet," he said.

We talked. Mostly, he talked.

"This patch of blackberries has been here since I was a little boy. Of course, there's more of them now. Daddy planted some amongst the wild ones that grew here. Mama used to make blackberry jelly. Lisa and Mama would pick them by the bucket. I mostly played, ate berries until my stomach hurt, and poked around hoping to come across a snake. Which I did more than a few times."

I gasped and stopped dead in my tracks.

"Keep using that stick I gave you," he said. "You got on your snake boots." He nodded at my boots. From then on I poked around several times in a spot before I reached in.

He seemed a bit shy at the clinic, but he wasn't shy that day. He talked on and on. I never expected it, and as I listened, I felt perfectly content, as contented as the cows mooing in the pasture. He reminded me of Daddy, the way he told stories.

He talked about his memories of growing up on that big country place, about his love for animals, and his happy childhood.

"I'll bet I haven't picked blackberries in fifteen years," he said. "I remember the summer before I went off to UGA. I picked some for Mama. Connie was with me. I think that was the last time."

"Who's Connie?" I asked. "Is she your sister?"

"Connie is like a sister . . . now," he smiled, "but, no, she's not my sister. Connie was my girlfriend for about eight years."

"Eight years?"

"Yep. A pretty long time, huh? Part of that time she was my fiancé," he said. "We more or less grew up together. We started liking each other when I was in eleventh grade; she was a sophomore. I graduated and went to Georgia, and she followed right along behind me. After she got her degree, she starting teaching over in Macon. I stayed on to finish my degree. We were engaged by then."

"What happened?"

"She fell in love with someone else," he said nonchalantly.

"That must have been devastating."

"The initial shock was pretty bad, but sooner than you might think, it was okay," he said. "It shook her up even more than it did me. She's happily married to the guy now with two little children."

"Oh my."

"My mother said that it was for the best." He stopped and looked at me. "She said she'd always thought there was something missing between us. She didn't explain what she meant by that. I probably wouldn't have bought it at the time anyway."

"And now?"

"And now, I'd say she was right." He smiled a tight lipped smile. "She should have known. I've never seen two people as in love as my mama and daddy." He nodded, and took a deep breath. "They were mated for life, like geese."

"Ah, that's wonderful," I said.

He was momentarily silent, lost in thought.

"I think we have enough, don't you?" I held up the bucket over half full of berries.

He nodded. "Yeah, more than enough."

He sat down on the tailgate of the truck in the shade of a little tree. He reached out to help me up.

"And your parents?" I asked.

"They died in a car accident five years ago. An oncoming driver had a heart attack behind the wheel. Hit 'em head on. Mom died instantly. Daddy was transported to Grady Memorial, but died a few hours later."

"Oh, Sam." I gently gasped his forearm, and he slipped his arm around my back.

"My sister and I agree that it was better that way. He wouldn't have wanted to live without her. I've never seen anyone so devoted to a woman as he was to my mother."

"I'm so sorry."

"They had been up at the cabin in the North Georgia mountains celebrating their thirty-fifth wedding anniversary. They called me that morning before they got on the road. They were happy." His voice was soft and deep.

We hugged each other then. He wrapped his arms around me, completely enfolding my body. At some point, he slipped off the tailgate and stood there in front of me, still holding on.

I thought I was comforting him, but his arms around me were more comforting than I could have imagined. We must have held on to each other for five minutes or more.

"Hey," he said. Pulling back, he searched my face. "It's getting hot out here. You hot?"

"Yeah." We both laughed. The sadness was gone.

"Let's go up to the house and get something cold to drink." He put his strong hands around my waist and lifted me off the tailgate.

Sam's sister and her husband and children had gone off for the weekend. They all lived together in the family home. Sam said it felt better that way after his parents died, and they'd never seen the need to make different arrangements.

I changed into my cutoffs, and Sam changed his T-shirt for a short sleeved shirt. When I came out of the bathroom, Sam had already poured two glasses of tea.

"Okay," he said, like he was about to make an announcement. "What will it be? My sister's delicious homemade chicken salad, left over spaghetti, also delicious. We could make ham sandwiches, or . . . well, it looks like that's about it. Oh yeah, and chocolate chip cookies." He stared at me, awaiting my response. "It's not too late to change your mind. We can go to the diner in town?"

After a few moments of grinning at him, I said, "I'll have the chicken salad, please, and a slice of that ripe tomato there on the window sill."

"I think I'll have the same," he said. We ate at the kitchen table. For a few minutes, we were silent. He seemed shy again.

"I can't believe I've talked so much. I've hardly let you get a word in edgewise," he said.

"That's all right. I enjoyed hearing about your childhood."

"Well, now, it's your turn. And to be fair, you have to talk as much as I did." He finished eating, put more ice in the glasses, and poured more tea.

I'd just told him about my family and Julie and Vicky and the wonderful time I had at the university, when the phone rang.

"Hello, yes, oh hey, John," he said. As he listened intently, his eyebrows knit into a frown. "Yeah, yeah, I understand. I can be there in about an hour. You try to keep her calm." He hung up the phone and turned towards me. His face showed no expression, and then he scowled.

"I have an emergency, Lily."

"I thought so. I'll clear the table and grab my bag."

"It's a friend. He needs my help with one of his horses. I'm going to get some things from the clinic. You come on out to the truck when you're done here."

I could tell Sam was worried, but he also seemed reluctant to leave. I was sorry to go too. I could have listened to him talk all day. On the drive home a thought occurred to me.

"Sam, could you come over for dinner Wednesday? I'd like to invite you and several of my neighbors and Uncle Bill. The ramp will be finished by then, and I can bring Miss Mae up to the house to join us. I'll make a big dinner with blackberry cobbler for dessert. Can you come?" The idea of cooking for my new friends delighted me.

A slow smile lit up his face. "I wouldn't miss it for the world," he said. I was surprised at what a simple little trip to the blackberry patch had done for our relationship. We'd become friends. We exchanged a quick hug before I jumped out the truck. For the rest of the afternoon memories of warm hugs and laughter kept me company.

For the next three days, I planned and prepared for the luncheon like I was expecting the Junior League. And I had so much fun doing it. I hadn't felt so carefree in months . . . maybe in years.

***

The house looked magnificent for my guests. An amazing transformation had been wrought in the weeks since I'd come to my daddy's house. No dust or cobwebs, nothing moth eaten or moldy marred the beauty of the stately home. Sparkling windows, polished floors, crystal chandeliers, and flowers adorned the rooms. Matching pairs of overstuffed chairs with side tables and large stained glass lamps sat by the windows in the living room, and a comfortable sofa anchored the room for conversation. Watercolors painted by local artists depicting area historic homes graced the walls, and a few treasures from an antique shop gave the rooms a style all my own. All the unnecessary pieces had been carted away, making the spacious rooms even more open. One of the first things to go had been the heavy drapes. With light filtering in through the tall windows, which looked out on flowering shrubs and trees, the house had a fresh airy feel. I was proud to show it off. That, along with my cooking skills.

The menu consisted of typical Southern dishes— fried chicken and buttermilk biscuits, snap beans and tiny red potatoes, macaroni and cheese, creamed field corn, sliced tomatoes, pickling cucumbers in vinegar, deviled eggs, pound cake, ice cream and blackberry cobbler, and lots of sweet tea. Officer Barkley and Sugar would have to drop in when their jobs allowed, but Sam, Uncle Bill, Miss Grace and Mr. Ralph, Mrs. Walker, and Miss Mae would gather around the table with me at noon.

Miss Grace and Mr. Ralph came early. While Miss Grace set the table, Mr. Ralph walked out into the backyard. He wanted to see what Sugar and I had done with the gardens.

"I want to see for myself those legendary flower-beds," he said. So he wandered on back and smoked a cigarette under the trees and judged our green thumbs for himself.

While Miss Grace fixed the tea in the glasses, I walked down to Miss Mae's to bring her up to the house.

"I'm ready," she said when I stepped in the front door. "I'm so excited. Mostly I go to church and missionary meetings. I don't usually get invited to dinner in the middle of the week."

"Wait 'til you see the entrance ramp Sugar built for you."

By the time we walked in, Miz Walker was there with her homemade fig preserves and butter pickles, Uncle Bill was there with muscadine wine, and Sam brought a bag of peaches and a chew bone for Peppy. We sat down to dinner, and at two o'clock when Officer Barkley got there, we were still sitting around the table, laughing and talking. I poured a glass of tea for Jeff, while he piled his plate high. Miss Grace and Miz Walker excused themselves from the table and started cleaning up the kitchen.

"Now, Lily Rose, you sit there and visit with your company," Miz Walker said.

Sugar stopped in only long enough to say he'd have to come back later. He was short-handed, he said, plus he didn't want to offend anybody with his "sweaty old self."

"Sugar, you come back later now," I hollered after him. "I cooked plenty for you too you know."

"If there's any way possible," he said as he waved good-bye. "I can't pass up blackberry cobbler."

Uncle Bill pushed back from the table and sighed. "Goodness, that was a fine meal." He rubbed his big hands across his belly. "I've enjoyed it. Thank you, Lily Rose."

"You're very welcome."

"I'll see you at the barbeque on Saturday, I hope," he said as he gave me a hug. "I know you want to come out and see the family, as well as the house."

"You know I do," I said.

"Now, who all's coming to the house on Saturday?" Uncle Bill asked. "Everyone is invited. The children and grandkids are coming in, and we got started on the preparations days ago."

The Hollister's annual 4th of July barbeque was a much anticipated event. Uncle Bill and about a dozen other men barbequed the pigs and made the Brunswick stew, but the guests brought cakes, pies, and enough casseroles to feed a drove of folks.

"See you Saturday," I said and waved good-bye.

Sam lingered in the kitchen long after he said he needed to be going. The look on his face defies description. He looked like the cat that swallowed the canary. At the time, it didn't dawn on me what might be going on inside him. I was struck with the urge to grab his cheeks, ask "what?", and give him a kiss right on the mouth.

"I'll see you Lily," he said sheepishly. "You're a great cook. Anytime you want to pick blackberries, let me know." He winked. I walked with him to the front door and paused a moment after saying goodbye. A few minutes later with my hands in soapy water up to my elbows, I wondered what it would be like to touch my lips to his.

Miss Grace brushed beside me, bringing me back to reality and out of my illicit daydream.

"This kitchen is a mess," I said. "It looks like I used every pot and big spoon in the house, and I dirtied a dozen dish rags."

"Don't you worry. We'll get it done in no time," said Miss Grace, taking over at the sink.

"It's the least we can do," said Miz Walker. "You've been cooking for two days."

When I came back from taking Miss Mae home, the ladies had dried and put away every dish. The dishcloths and aprons were in the washer machine. After refilling our glasses with sweet tea, we moved out to the veranda, settled in the rockers, and visited for a while. After they left, I went upstairs and curled up on my bed with a book. I fell asleep on the first page. It was dusk when Peppy woke me.

He sprang to his feet beside me on the bed. His ears perked up and a tiny low growl caused his throat to tremble. He took a flying leap to the floor. About the time he barked, I heard footsteps in the kitchen. I smiled to myself. Sugar has come back to get a dish of that cobbler, I thought. Peppy ran down the stairs with me in my bare feet following behind him.

"Who's sneaking into my house," I teased, speaking in a gruff voice.

"Backdoor guests are best."

I stopped dead still, the joy draining out of me like dirty dishwater down the drain.

"That's what the sign says." He pointed to the plaque by the backdoor. "Is that right, Lil?"

"Why sure," I replied. My voice was calm and steady. Not like my heart which pounded wildly. Not like my thoughts which darted about like scared rabbits. But I couldn't run. My legs trembled while I watched him light a cigarette. He inhaled deeply and smiled a tight-lipped smile while his eyes roved over my body.

"Well, aren't you something with your new hair style," he said. He reached forward and brushed his fingers through my hair. "You're still as pretty as ever, even without the long hair." His hand dropped to my chest where he traced the rusty scrolls with the tip of his finger. I shivered.

"I never thought I'd see something like this on you," he said, still looking at the tattoo. "You were trying to disguise yourself." He looked into my eyes then, like he was seeing something for the first time.

"Hi Manny," I whispered. My lips smiled a bit, my eyes not so much. My heart . . . his fingerprints were all over it.

He continued to look at me without responding, and his eyes narrowed.

"By the way, All State Freight left a message on the answering machine. They appreciate your business and trust the desk was delivered as promised to Georgia." I could hear my heart beating as I stared into his eyes.

Then, the frown on his face relaxed. "I've missed you, Lil." His voice softened. "I wish you hadn't left without talking to me."

"We haven't talked much, Manny, over the last two years." I lowered my eyes.

"I know I worked too much. I've thought about all that. I'm going to change. When you come home, we'll spend time together. It will be like it was when we first got married."

"Manny," I sighed. "Even when we first married, we didn't spend time together." I forced myself to swallow the lump in my throat. "I'm happy here."

"You look beautiful." He reached for me with one hand still holding the cigarette in the other. He would've taken me in his arms, but I took a step back.

"No, Manny," I said, surprised by the sadness in my voice. "It's too late."

"It's not too late. You love me. I know you do." He moved closer. I sidestepped and walked over to the refrigerator.

"Can I get you something to drink? Some iced tea, a Coke?"

He chuckled and shook his head. "Your sultry accent has returned, thicker than ever."

I didn't respond.

"Lily, I know you love me." He stepped towards me again and I sidestepped again. A rush of warring emotions caused my eyes to sting and my throat to tighten. I started to walk away from him then turned back.

"So? I love you. I won't deny that. But I can't live with you anymore. Sometimes love is not enough." My flippant tone sounded strange to me.

"Who have you been talking to?" he asked, sneering. He reached over and crushed the butt of his cigarette in the sink. "Give me a Coke."

He took it before I could pour it into a glass, popped the top, and walked around the kitchen and through the swinging door into the dining room. My hands shook as I poured myself a glass of tea.

"Nice," he said. Then he walked into the wide central foyer and looked up the elegant staircase. He rubbed his hand slowly up and down the heavy banister. I watched him standing in the foyer, eyeing the decorative woodwork and the tall ceilings. My eyes followed his to the wavy panes of glass in the windows. He turned to look at me.

"Nice place here, Lil. I cannot believe you never told me about it." He looked bewildered, and then he cut his eyes at me again. "You are full of surprises."

He continued to walk slowly through the gracious rooms, looking up at the ceiling and the ornate crystal chandelier. He ran his hand over the mantel above the open fireplace. "You know how much this place would bring in today's market?" His question was more a statement of his appraisal.

"You know I don't. And I don't care. I could never sell this place."

He went on as if he hadn't heard me, turning from side to side as he gazed at the wide planks of the aged pine floor. "We could sell this place and buy something spectacular in Detroit."

A blank faraway look came into his eyes, and I knew, he had left for a moment. I was used to it. He would focus on something with such intensity, he'd be gone. I knew he was calculating the potential property value. I could have gone off and hidden then in that sprawling old house and he couldn't have found me.

"Lil, we would get a fortune for this place." He snapped out of his calculations, turned, and stared hard at me. In spite of my nervousness, I returned his gaze, oddly protective of the house.

"I'd never sell this place, Manuel," I said. "Never. It's my home now." A strange look came over him and it unnerved me. I realized I'd spoken to him without sugarcoating the words with kindness. He liked me accommodating, not assertive.

"You enjoy the place. Okay then. Stay for a while. When you tire of playing the Southern belle, you can come home."

"I am home, Manny. As it is, if the house were sold, the money wouldn't belong to me alone. It would be divided three ways. My aunt was a lawyer. She knew what she was doing when she wrote the will. She intended for the house to stay in the family. It's my heritage."

"Do you think I care about a will or your heritage?" His face contorted into a sneer. "We *will* sell this house. You can't count me out."

I sucked in a breath. When I spoke, my voice trembled. "Manny, please understand. I'm happier here than I've been in a long time. This place has made me remember why family and home are important to me. I need to stay here. I belong here." Much more than the heavy silence separated us. Tension hung like a palpable force in the air. My heart thumped faster causing the blood to throb in my ears. I'd said too much.

He swore. Then he grabbed my forearm and pulled me into his arms. His mouth was on mine, harder and more insistent the more I struggled to pull away. His fingers wound around my hair and tightened into a fist, pulling the hair on the back of my head as he forced my mouth to his. "You belong with me. I want you. And I'll have you."

"Stop, Manny," I pleaded. "You're hurting me." I tried to push him with the heels of my hands. I hit his back with my fist. Peppy barked, sharp piercing barks, like he'd lost his mind. In a frenzy, he jumped up again and again on Manny's legs. Peppy yelped when Manny kicked him aside, but he sprang right back.

"Stop you blasted dog! I'll break your neck." His words struck blows to my chest. The fight went out of me.

"Manny! No! Oh no, you killed Annie Ruth's dog." I crumpled to the floor, shielding Peppy in my arms.

"What are you talking about? I only kicked that mutt. Now make him shut up."

"Let me hold him," I whined. "He'll calm down." A surge of fear made talking and breathing painful. "It's okay Peppy. It's okay, boy," I said with phony calmness. "Hush, boy, hush." *Annie Ruth knew. All along she knew.*

Manny picked me up then, carried me through the foyer and up the stairs.

"I haven't stopped aching for you since you've been gone," he said with a throaty groan. "I'm going to remind you where you belong."

My protests meant nothing to him. Conscious only of his desire, he satisfied his craving, fully having his way with me, oblivious to the fact that I wasn't a participant in his cruel lust. Did it even matter to him? How had our love come to this? Tears streamed down my cheeks, soaking into my hair. I didn't cry out . . . I dared not . . . for Peppy's sake . . . for my own. But inside I cried. Inside I screamed.

***

My mind searched for explanations as I gazed into the void. Rascal . . . it had been unthinkable to me that he had killed Annie Ruth's little dog. Now, without a shadow of doubt, I knew he had. The knowledge of it sickened me. If Rascal, then maybe Cynthia Moore. I listened to Manny breathing beside me. I felt his heat and his heart beat so close to mine, yet a great unsurpassable gulf separated us. Despair washed over me.

Sleep finally came near dawn. Light was shining through the window when I realized Manuel was whispering to me. He brushed his lips across mine.

"Goodbye, darling Lil." He kissed my forehead. "I love you. Come home soon. I need you in my bed."

My eyes flew open, but I didn't move or speak. He'd already dressed, and then he was gone as abruptly as he'd come. I lay there dazed, unable to move. I felt like I was in a time warp. Was it possible that Manny was not aware of what had happened between us? His bizarre behavior made no sense. The fact that his voice sounded sweet that morning, his touch gentle. The incongruence of it all only made me more determined to stay away from this inexplicable man. Forever. I cringed and pulled the covers tight.

Peppy put his paws on the side of the bed, and then touched the edge of it with his nose. His eyes were full of compassion.

"Oh, Peppy, come here boy." I helped him jump on the bed and hugged him and scratched his ears. His unconditional love and acceptance melted my heart. I held him and cried, sobbing so hard I had to run to the bathroom to throw up. Anger, pain, resentment, a volley of emotions pummeled my heart. Not only was I devastated by Manny, I was mad at myself. Finally, when I was all wrung out, I stumbled downstairs to take care of Peppy.

I left the back door open and went back upstairs where I curled up in bed. I wanted to hide. I felt lost, cast into a sea of confusion. For those hours, I drifted, my world nothing but darkness and grief.

Insistent knocking at the back door woke me. Someone called my name, again and again. Finally, the voice registered. It was Sam. Hope touched my heart.

"Coming," I said, and sat up dangling my feet over the side of the bed. He called again. I cleared my throat. "Coming," I said louder. I grabbed a robe and pulled it around me.

When I saw him standing in the doorway, I wanted to fall into his arms and cling to him while he held me close, saying nothing. He seemed so tall standing there at the kitchen door. His dark blonde hair fell over his forehead. He was holding a large bouquet of yellow daylilies and pink roses.

I stared at the pretty flowers. The significance of his choices, the sweetness of it, touched me. "Oh, Sam," I said in a weepy voice.

"Lily, you're still in bed?" he asked tentatively, his smile vanishing. "Are you all right? Your eyes. You're crying. Lily?" Concern knitted his brow and he stepped towards me.

I felt my weak smile turn upside down, and my lips quiver in a childish pout. Tears filled my eyes.

"My husband was here," I said, in a raspy whisper.

"Your husband?" He squinted thoughtfully. A frown clouded his blue-green eyes.

"He just left."

"Your husband? I'm sorry for the intrusion." He laid the bouquet on the kitchen table. "Those are for you, for the nice dinner yesterday. I wanted to . . . to thank you." For the second his eyes met mine, a thin smile pulled at his lips. Then a conflicted look overshadowed his face, he turned away, and walked out.

He was gone. I could hardly breathe. Another piece of my heart crumbled. How could it break any more? I'd been humiliated enough. How was it possible to feel even more humiliation? I leaned back on the kitchen wall and gave in to the weight of misery. I slid down and sat on the floor. Eventually I got up the strength to go back to bed where I stayed for the next few days.

Chapter Twenty-Three

I sat in Uncle Bill's office with my legs crossed, foot bobbing, waiting for him to call me back for my appointment. Rather than wring my hands, I pulled a book out of my bag to have something to hold. Mostly I hoped to hold onto some dignity during this painfully necessary meeting. How much did I need to tell him? No matter how many times I went over it in my mind, I knew I had to tell him everything, no matter the shame. After what had happened, Manny coming, Sam seeing me a slobbering, crying mess, a little dignity might be too much to hope for. Four days had passed since that awful night. I couldn't let another one go by without doing something.

The receptionist, more animated that usual, started making small talk.

"I didn't see you at your uncle's barbeque on Saturday. We expected you'd be there," she said. "By the way, I'm Sherry. I don't think I ever introduced myself."

"Nice to meet you." I smiled half-heartedly.

"I went with Sam Watson," she said in a voice not much more than a whisper.

Her manner reminded me of girlfriends telling secrets to one another on the school bus. She tilted her head to the side and rolled her eyes.

"Oh . . . the barbeque . . . I forgot." I felt my cheeks get hot. I'd totally forgotten the barbeque. "I didn't feel well." Nor do I now, I thought.

She was undaunted, enraptured by her story.

"Sam hadn't called me in six months, and out of the blue he called and asked me to go with him. Have you met him?"

"Sam? Yes. I have a dog."

"Isn't he wonderful? And gorgeous? He's a gorgeous man. You'll have to excuse my going on and on. I can't stop thinking about him." She giggled.

I stared at her. Could my discomfort get any worse? I hadn't expected a let's-be-girlfriends chat from the woman, especially not one about Sam.

Please Lord, make her shut up, I thought.

Uncle Bill opened the door, stepped out, and said quietly to the receptionist, "I don't want to be disturbed."

"Yes, sir," she said, regaining her poise.

"Come on back Lily Rose." He escorted me into his office and stood behind me with his hand on my shoulder until I sat down in the chair he'd pulled close to his desk.

"Thank you, Uncle Bill, and thank you for seeing me on such short notice."

"Certainly. Can I get you something to drink before we get started?" He opened a bottle of water and gulped half of it down in one big swallow.

"No, thank you. I'm fine."

Neither of us spoke for a minute. I watched as he arranged a legal pad and black pens in front of him.

"I'm sorry, Lily Rose. I'm sorry the privacy of your home was violated. I'm sorry we didn't prevent it."

I took a deep breath and closed my eyes.

"That's behind you now. We'll do all we can to keep you safe. Tell me what you'd like me to do."

"I need a divorce. I should have had you do this when I first came here."

"We'll have to fill out some paperwork. It's little more than that. Are you up to it?" He was matter-of-fact and kind.

I nodded, and he continued.

"Where does your husband live?"

"Detroit."

"And that's where you had a home together?"

"Yes, sir."

"I'll give you these forms, and you can fill them out and give them back to me. The process will take several months. It's a bit more complicated since you are here now. There's a residency requirement, but I'll take care of everything. Mr. Valenti will be notified to sign the paper-work as well, and then it will be filed."

"What if he won't sign?"

"Well, it will get more complicated, could get nasty, and expensive."

"Uncle Bill, I don't want him to come near me. How can we fix it so he can't?"

"I'm not sure we can." Uncle Bill leaned across the desk toward me. "Do you have reason to be afraid of him? Has he hurt you?" I stared back at him.

"I was afraid of that," he said. Without waiting for an answer, he calmly continued. "I will set up a restraining order, for what good that will do. I am sorry he got in your house against your wishes."

"It's my fault, Uncle Bill. I left the back gate open, and he drove on around. No one could have seen the car."

And then, my voice cracked. Through the tears, I told him about Manny's violent outbursts, about his slapping me, about his forcing himself on me when he stayed the night.

Uncle Bill shook his head slowly, a grim look on his face. His lips pressed together making a thin line.

"And there's more." I blurted out the story about Cynthia Moore.

"Two weeks before I left Manny, a woman came to our condo. She basically told me they had been having an affair and that I should give him a divorce. Manny was irate that she'd spoken to me, said she was ruining his life, and ten minutes after she left the condo, he left after her. A week later I heard on the evening news that she was missing. I don't know if she is still missing or not. I never told anybody."

"That's not something we can keep to ourselves, Lily Rose. I need to find out if this woman is still missing. If she is, the proper authorities have to be informed."

"I know, Uncle Bill. I'm sorry. It's terrible that I didn't contact the police, isn't it? Oh, Uncle Bill, I've been stupid and self-absorbed. I wanted to run away and never look back. At the time, I couldn't deal with all that on top of everything else."

"It's understandable, honey. We'll get you through this," he said, and pushed back from the desk. "Just sit here, Lily Rose, and take a moment to calm yourself. I'll be right back. I'm going to make some calls."

Within a matter of minutes, Uncle Bill confirmed that Cynthia Moore was still a missing person. I began to shiver as we drove over to the police station. After writing an official statement, I answered question after question until my insides trembled. Uncle Bill stayed near me the entire time. When it was over, he helped me walk to the car and drove me home. He stayed with me until he was sure I was all right.

I spent half the next day in bed before I made myself get up and take a shower. I pulled the sheets off the bed and threw them into the washing machine. Then I felt compelled to get outside. I wanted to see flowers, smell their sweet fragrance, hear the birds tweeting, and feel the sun on my skin. I'd already walked a block before I realized where I was going. The little church would be open.

The quiet stillness inside the sanctuary permeated my soul. I slid onto the pew and let the peace saturate my mind. Calmness wrapped around my shoulders like a soft shawl. It was like I could feel all the prayers that had been poured out in that place. They whispered to me. *God is near.*

I knelt before the altar.

Oh God, help me get through this. Please forgive me for the mess I've made of my life. Please forgive me for all my mistakes. Help Manny too, Lord. He needs you so much.

I prayed before the altar. Then I moved back to the pew aware of the sense that I was not alone.

I sat there an hour or more until my bones began to ache against the wooden pew, and then I returned home. But, I didn't want to waste a minute of the sunshine, so I got the bicycle from the backyard.

"Let's go Peppy. We're going for a ride." I secured him in the basket on the handle bars. He lifted his nose to the breeze, the hair on his little ears quivering. My hair, back to its natural golden brown, felt good blowing back from my face. We rode through the neighborhood and around the town square, and then stopped at the city park. Sitting in the grass, rubbing Peppy's stomach, I felt refreshed, but I couldn't quite identify the feelings. Free. Yes, I felt free, and it had nothing to do with whether I was married or not. It was bigger than that. There was something about the place. Here, I felt alive. In Detroit, I would have hunkered down in the condo, alone, stifled and dying inside. There, I never felt free. I felt caged. Here I wanted to be out in the light amongst familiar faces and places.

I continued my musings, searching my soul, gaining clarity. I'd suffered a setback. Nothing more. The last few days had been upsetting, but Manny couldn't spoil what I'd regained. My resolve had not changed. I was stronger.

I was tying Peppy in the basket when Officer Barkley pulled up to the curb and stopped beside us.

"Hey, Lily," he called. "Everything all right?"

"We're fine, Jeff, thank you."

"I'm really sorry we didn't see your husband come in here the other night."

"It couldn't be helped," I said. "I don't blame you."

"We'll keep a closer watch from now on," he said, "but be sure to close and latch your gate at all times."

"Yes, I will." I nodded.

"That was a mighty good meal you made for us the other day. Thanks again for having me."

"You're very welcome."

We waved good-bye, and he drove on, but he had helped me realize I have friends who care. I'd never be alone again. And tomorrow, I'd be home in time for one of Annie Ruth's home cooked meals. She was expecting me for supper.

Chapter Twenty-Four

When I was finally packed and in the car with Peppy, we made a beeline home, stopping only to get fresh corn and vegetables from the produce stand.

Annie Ruth was waiting for me on the front porch. I saw her stand and hold her hands together in front of her. Tears stung my eyes. We visited for a while on the porch with Mama, then the two of us walked to the pond with Peppy. While we ate the delicious meal she'd prepared, I told her about the dinner I'd had the week before for my friends in Wilcox Station. She didn't ask questions, only listened while I explained. When I started talking about Manny and our marriage, I said things I never thought I'd be able to say to anyone, realized things I didn't know I knew, felt things I'd never even admitted to myself. We both cried a little, but she was so relieved I was back in Georgia that she quickly forgave and reassured me.

"Lily Rose, you can't let the memory of how things used to be, or for that matter, how things might have been, stand in the way of you living the life God gave you," she said quietly. "There ain't no roads back to yesterday."

All I could do was look into her sensitive eyes. Her words resonated in my heart.

"Don't let dark clouds from the past cast a shadow on today," she said. We hugged for a long time. This time, trusting her would be enough.

After she went to her house for the night, I went upstairs to my old bedroom, said my prayers, and slept like a baby. In my dreams, I walked with Daddy in misty moonlight. When I awoke, it was like I'd dreamed in a room full of roses and woke with the scent still lingering on my skin. Then I knew. My soul knew. I had walked with him in heaven. But now, all I can remember of that is the amazing sense of assurance that I could get on with my life. I still had Daddy's blessing.

It was a good visit. Annie Ruth promised to come see the house at the end of the summer. I promised to come for Christmas when James Michael and his family would be home. We'd all be together for the first time in years. Mama actually had color rise in her cheeks when we talked about his upcoming visit.

I got back home to Wilcox Station before dark and looked at all the flowerbeds. I broke off the dead flowers and pulled some weeds. Brushing the dirt off my hands, I walked across the street and told Miss Grace I was back. Officer Barkley drove by as I was crossing the street.

"Back home already?" he called.

"Yeah, I'm home already." And tomorrow, I thought, tomorrow I'll call Sam.

***

Even with so much work still to be done on the property, I woke up with the desire to write. I went to the desk and rifled through the stories I'd written in Michigan. I found the notes and the beginnings of the story that kept running through my mind. With notebook and sharpened pencils in hand, I went downstairs to get a cup of coffee. Sitting at the kitchen table, I wrote like a person desperate to have her say. The words kept spilling out. Before I knew it, sun was shining on the back terrace. Maybe the time was just right for me to start writing again, because as soon as I had lunch and put my writing away, I got a call.

"Hello, is this Miss Cates?"

"Yes, this is she."

"Hi there, this is Mrs. Conner at the magazine office. We'd like for you to come in for an interview."

"That's wonderful," I said. "When would you like for me to come?"

"How about tomorrow morning, ten o'clock? Is that too soon?"

"Not at all. That's perfect."

"We have your resume. Please bring some samples of your work as well," she said.

"I look forward to meeting you."

As soon as the call ended, I dialed the clinic. I wanted to share my good news with Sam and thank him for the pretty flowers he'd brought me. He was the only man to have thoughtfully chosen lilies and roses to match my name. I smiled, thinking about him.

"Doc Watson's Veterinary Clinic."

"Hi, Lisa, is that you? It's Lily."

"Hi, Lily," she replied.

"Lisa, I was hoping to speak to your brother. Is he around?"

"Well, Lily, he is, but I don't think you should speak to him." Lisa's voice was cool and aloof.

"What's wrong, Lisa?" Her tone puzzled me.

"You should know," she replied sharply. "Apparently Sam just now found out that you are married. By the look on his face the other day when he came back from your house, I'd say he was stunned by the news."

"Oh, my. Was that it?" I muttered.

"I'd say that's something you should have informed him about. You've been here how long? You certainly should have told him if you were going to start a relationship with him."

"A relationship? Well . . . I intended to tell him about it. I simply haven't had the opportunity. It really wasn't . . . "

"Lily, I can't talk," she said in a flat voice. "We're busy. But, for your information, Sam is a good man. He deserves honesty. And I don't want to see him hurt again." She abruptly hung up the phone.

I stood there looking at the receiver in my hand, a bit dazed, slightly aggravated, and insulted. She hadn't let me finish my sentence.

"Geez," I said aloud. "She doesn't want to see him hurt. Well, that makes two of us." I hung up the phone like it was a hot potato.

Lisa had jumped to some negative conclusions about me. I didn't like the thought of losing a friend before I even got to know her, and I liked even less the fact that Sam thought I'd lied to him. It wasn't a pleasant feeling. But in reality, it was my own fault, plain and simple.

"Hi, I'm Lily Rose Cates," I'd said to everyone I met. Why had I done that? It was my cowardly way to avoid all discussions about my current situation and my

marriage. Because I didn't want to deal with the unpleasant realities, I'd allowed false impressions. I resolved to
clear up the misunderstanding the next time I ran into
Sam. I certainly couldn't hold it against Lisa. I'd jumped to
enough conclusions myself. Of course she'd want to protect
her brother. I would see him within a week or so, I felt
sure, and then I'd set things right. In the meantime, I had
plenty to keep me busy and enough worries to keep at bay
without adding Sam to the list.

Sure enough, a few days later, as I was coming out
of the magazine office, I noticed Sam walking in my direction.

"Hi Sam," I called, lifting my hand to wave, but he
stepped inside Uncle Bill's office without even slowing his
pace. Had he not seen me? Of course he had. He was staying away from the "married woman." In spite of the rebuff,
I made one last attempt to explain. I left a message on his
answering machine, but he didn't return the call. I felt embarrassed and disappointed. Maybe one day he'd understand, maybe not. Just the same, serves me right, I
thought. I remembered Annie Ruth's saying, can't worry
about what might have been.

"Not now anyway," I said to myself, remembering
Sam's sweet smile.

As it worked out, I landed a part-time job writing
on assignment for the magazine. It would be a start, and
I'd still have time to work around the house. Quite unexpectedly, I threw myself into writing the novel. It kept my
mind off Manny. That situation was so daunting I kept
busy to keep myself from thinking about it. I'd turned everything over to Uncle Bill who advised me to put it out of
my mind as much as possible. For a few short weeks, I
lived in a kind of mindless denial, but to my dismay, some-

thing more had come of the night Manny had forced himself on me. Something more that would change everything.

***

Before it was confirmed at the county health office, I knew I was pregnant. As soon as I missed my period, I knew. For three days I vomited. Not because of pregnancy, but due to my mental state. Everything I swallowed came back up. I experienced agony at a new level. Not physical pain or sorrow, but a maze of confusion and disappointment so deep I was in misery. My thoughts looped round and round. Was this some kind of cosmic joke? As much as I'd wanted Manny's baby, why would this happen now? It was looking more and more like Manny was crazy. Maybe even a murderer. I'd failed as a wife. But what could I do? I couldn't save him. Didn't I have to save myself? And now I was going to have a baby. I cried out to God night and day. More than a week passed with my soul in turmoil.

"Miss Lily," Sugar said, "what on earth is wrong with you? You don't look so good." He stood in the back door, looking at me with a scowl on his face. I moped around the kitchen but sat down at the table when he walked in.

"You haven't finished the flower boxes. Do you need me to do it?" He appeared baffled. I'd been making big plant arrangements to set on the front walk, and I'd stopped with the pots half done in the backyard. It occurred to me then that I hadn't watered them.

He stood still, looking at me. I couldn't look at him. Normally every few days Sugar and I chatted, and we always talked when he came to work in the yard. I hadn't spoken to him in a couple of weeks.

Without waiting for me to ask, he pulled out a chair and sat down across from me. I knew he was looking at me hard, but still I looked away.

"I'm not leaving until you tell me what's wrong," he said quietly.

I frowned and shook my head "no."

"How about a glass of sweet tea?" he asked. After a silent pause, he got up, fixed two glasses, and brought them over to the table. I picked mine up and sipped. My eyes were stinging. A tear rolled down my cheek and dripped on the tablecloth, absorbing into the homespun fabric. I glanced up at Sugar to see if he'd seen it. Our eyes met.

"How about we go for a ride?" He stood and lifted the keys from the hook where I kept them. "You haven't let me drive that car but once since you been here. You've been hogging it for yourself. And I'm the one who does the maintenance." He shook the keys. "What do you say?"

I still said nothing.

"Miss Martha and Aunt Izzy used to take a drive in the country every week. If I was lucky enough to be here, I'd go with 'em. They'd buy me a Co-Cola and a big Baby Ruth candy bar," he said. Then he chuckled. "I'd eat it real slow to make it last the whole ride while I looked out the back seat window."

I cut my eyes at him and pursed my lips. He'd made me remember the Sunday drives I'd taken as a child. I stood up then, and we walked outside together. Peppy skipped around us and jumped into the backseat. We drove out the city limits, into the country, and Sugar talked about fishing and farming—who had pretty corn and who didn't. He talked about Aunt Martha and his Aunt Izzy, and before we made it back to the house, I told him enough about my husband and the pending divorce that he finally under-stood my sadness. And I told him about the baby I was go-ing to have next spring. Somehow to him, that was all plain ol' good news.

"And doesn't that just make up for all the bad," he said. "You'll be right here in Wilcox Station, and there'll be a baby in the house." By the time I got out of the car, we were laughing about silly things, unimportant things, life.

The next day I went to see Miss Mae and spent the day. She even gave up watching her shows so we could talk. After all, she said, they were only soap operas, and she'd much rather talk about real life. She'd told me her whole life story; it seemed like the right time to tell her mine. With her kind heart, she listened. With gentleness, she spoke. Mostly, she held my hand. When I walked through her door, I grappled with torn emotions. When I left her house, I could breathe again. I promised to go see her eve-ry day until I was "back to myself."

Her words left an impression. As soon as my head hit the pillow, I thought about what she'd said. "I want you to come see me every day, Lily Rose, until you're back to yourself." Had I been "back to myself" since I'd come to Wilcox Station . . . ever been back to myself since Daddy died? Maybe I had been getting there. Answers would come, but then, that night, after so many sleepless nights, I slept.

Within days I'd incorporated work for the magazine into my routine. I thought about the pregnancy and some-how knew this baby would be born. It grew like a hidden seed taking root deep down in my body and my heart.

I hired a team to paint all the rooms in the house before cold weather set in. They started in the kitchen with a fresh coat of yellow, and then proceeded to the other rooms downstairs with the lightest rainwater blue. While the painters worked downstairs, I had time to tackle Aunt Martha's bedroom and the baby doll room.

Aunt Martha's room smelled of menthol, talcum powder, and stale perfume. Although it was huge, every time I stepped foot in it, I felt smothered. So, I decided to wait for Annie Ruth's help. The baby doll room I could manage. I sorted the dolls first and gently washed and ironed the tiny clothes. Basically, I played dolls.

Because of the baby, I couldn't help thinking of Manny, but the things I thought about were good—his shiny hair and satin skin, his intelligence and passion. I threw myself into the projects I'd started trying to occupy my mind with anything besides him. And every now and then, I remembered Sam's smile.

Chapter Twenty-Five

The first Monday in October brought a cool freshness in the air, and the Greyhound bus brought Annie Ruth. When I pulled up at the station, she was stepping off the bus. She wore her royal blue Sunday dress, coffee colored stockings, and high-heeled black pumps. The dress's large white collar framed the narrow face that peeked from beneath a pale blue pill box hat. She wore her pearl ear bobs. Annie Ruth had said she'd never seen the point of going anywhere if she couldn't get back home to sleep in her own bed at night. She'd held to that principle her entire life, until now. Coming to see me was an adventure and an even grander gesture of love. I was proud of her. Back at home, Mama stayed with Aunt Rachel for the week.

I carried the red Samsonite suitcase to the car and put it in the back seat.

"How was your bus trip?"

"Nice," she said. "The seats were comfortable, and the bathroom tolerable even if it weren't no bigger than a sardine can."

"Good," I said. "You weren't scared, were you?"

"Naw," she said. She was looking at the car. "My goodness, Lily Rose. What kind of car is this? Is this one of those Rolls Royces? I'll feel like a movie star getting in that car."

I laughed. "You're better than a movie star. You're practically my mama." I gave her a hug. "You like the car?"

"Well, of course, I do," she said, still eyeing it.

"It's not a Rolls Royce. It's a 1950 DeSoto. Amazing, isn't it? These aren't even made anymore, and this one's like brand new. I've been told Aunt Martha used to wipe her shoes before she'd get in. It was her baby."

Before I took her to the house, I drove Annie Ruth through town, pointing out the sights and telling her who lived where. When I turned into the driveway, she turned around in the seat trying to take it all in.

"Where you going, Lily Rose?"

"Home," I chirped.

I drove on back through the gate and stopped right in front of the carport. I looked at her with a big grin on my face. Surprise had frozen on hers.

"Well, aren't you going to get out?" I laughed as I opened my door. She slowly emerged from the passenger side. I waited at the back of the car with her suitcase. Peppy welcomed us by running back and forth at high speed. When he tired of that, he licked our ankles. Annie Ruth knelt and rubbed his belly.

"Lord 'a mercy, Lily Rose. The house is so pretty. And just look at your flowerbeds." She walked over to the flowers. As we walked around the yard, I pointed out the new plants we'd put in and told her about all the work Sugar and I had done. She admired the heirloom plants. Annie Ruth was delighted.

"Just wait until you see inside," I said.

She loved both the house and yard, but mostly, she loved my kitchen.

"Sunshine yellow. I love this yellow kitchen. I can't wait to start cooking in here," she said. And she didn't wait. By suppertime, she'd already made a chocolate layer cake, and chicken and dumplings were in the pot. I hadn't had any in years, and I thought I would hurt myself I ate so much for supper.

"Annie Ruth, you're going to have to help me walk upstairs tonight," I teased.

"You'll be helping me, too." She laughed. "I'm so glad I'm here. I had to come see for myself how you was doing. And you're doing fine, ain't you?"

"Yes, ma'am, I am. After I came home from my visit in July, I started doing a lot better. You're better than a B-12 shot, Annie Ruth." She laughed at that since she swears that B-12 shots are the quintessential feel good remedy.

"Well, pregnancy looks good on you. You look so pretty. I always say, some women just glow when they're expecting."

She had a way of making me feel good about everything.

Annie Ruth would be sleeping in the room used to be Daddy's. She seemed especially touched by that. The polished furniture gave it a lemon scent, and I'd washed the prettiest patchwork quilt and embroidered pillowcases for the bed. When we said goodnight, I grabbed her and hugged her hard.

First thing the next morning, Annie Ruth insisted that we get to work cleaning Aunt Martha's room.

"Got to make this place all yours," she said. "Can't have no mausoleum in here."

I pushed open the door and the flowery scent of old perfume lingered amongst the musty smells. My eyes fell immediately on the hollowed out place in the bed. A dusty rose chenille bedspread draped its tired fringe onto the floor. All the bedding would have to go.

"I'll have to buy more mattresses," I said. Annie Ruth had already started pulling nightgowns and under garments out of drawers.

First, we went through all the drawers and closets and packed clothes in boxes to take to the nursing home and give to charity, and then we packed another box for Annie Ruth and Mama. Some of the clothes and knick-knacks went into the trunk of the car to take home on my next visit. We packed one of Aunt Martha's suitcases with all the things Annie Ruth would take back home on the bus. She wanted to give some things to her friends. My aunt hadn't worn much jewelry. Besides a set of pearls and a brooch, which I kept for myself, I gave the vintage neck-lace and ear bob sets to Annie Ruth.

Sugar helped haul out the faded area rug and the mattress set. A few odd pieces he kept for himself. After the windows were opened and a breeze flowed in, the dreaded chore was done. With Aunt Martha's things gone, I could make it my own. I wondered why I'd let those lingering scents keep me out. I sprayed some lavender water completing the transformation.

Every day Annie Ruth and I took a walk to the town square.

"Well, I declare, Lily Rose," she said. "This is the prettiest little town." Peppy skipped at her heels. They had bonded with that first belly rub.

"He likes to have his stomach rubbed 'bout as much as Rascal did," she said. At the mention of the name, I turned my eyes away and resumed walking.

We'd just returned from our stroll that Friday morning and sat down, when a big green pick-up truck drove up the driveway. When I recognized the truck, I almost stood up, but instead tightened my grip on the chair arms and rocked a little harder.

Sam jumped out and brought a large pumpkin up to the steps and set it down. Then he went back to the truck, reached over into the back, and hauled out a bushel basket. About halfway up the steps, he paused with a timid smile on his face.

"Hey, ladies." He nodded at Annie Ruth. "Good morning ma'am," he said, and then his blue-green eyes rested on me.

"Well, hey Sam, how are you?" I barely smiled, and I've been told that I had a what-in-the-world-are-you-doing-here look on my face. It had been over three months since I'd seen him.

He cleared his throat. "I'm fine, Lily. I've been to the Farmer's Market this morning."

"I see. Sam, I'd like for you to meet Annie Ruth. She's the woman who raised me."

He smiled at Annie Ruth.

"It's very nice to meet you," he said as he stepped over and stuck out his hand. Annie Ruth stood up slowly and took his hand. They stood smiling at each other, for what seemed like a long moment. Then, she looked at me and smiled.

I wanted to ask, "What the heck? A mutual admiration society?" but instead, I smiled.

"Well, my goodness. What did you bring?"

"A pumpkin, Charlie Brown." He chuckled a little. "It is October already. And I brought you a bushel of apples."

I think that's about when my mouth dropped open.

"You know," he said. "Applesauce, apple fritters, apple cake, apple pie."

Annie Ruth laughed. I shut my mouth and ran my tongue over my teeth, in a lame attempt to downplay my inability to speak.

"Oh, ho ho," I pretended to laugh, remembering how he'd once done the same. "I see where this is going."

"I'll even help you peel 'em," he said sheepishly.

"Sounds like a fine proposition to me," Annie Ruth said. I cut my eyes at her.

"Sounds like a good one to me, I guess." Then we all laughed.

"Well," he said, "I reckon I'd better get on back to the clinic. How much longer will you be staying, Miss Annie Ruth?"

"Lily Rose is taking me to catch the bus at one o'clock this afternoon. This has been the shortest five days of my life."

"We've had a good time. It's been better than Christmas," I said.

"I hope you have a safe trip home," Sam said.

"I'm sure I will," she said, and nodded her head slightly. "That bus was surprisingly comfortable. But if'n it hadda been as uncomfortable as an ole mule wagon, I would have been glad to take it to get over here to see my child." I smiled, and let the joy and gratitude fill my heart.

"Well, you did a good job raising her," Sam said softly. "I'm happy to have met you."

"You, too," she said.

"Can I call you Lily, to see when you need my help with these apples?"

"Sure, that's fine." I felt my cheeks get warm as we said good-bye. We watched him drive away, and then Annie Ruth turned her eyes on me. I didn't have to look at her to feel her watching me.

"I declare your cheeks done turned as red as them apples. Tell me about that fellow. The way he carries hisself, for a little bit, he reminds me of your daddy."

So, with that, I told her about his saving Peppy's life and letting me sleep on the cot, and picking blackberries, and the yellow lily and rose bouquet, and when I was done talking, just like that, she said, "Lily Rose, he sounds like a fine man to me." She nodded her head slightly. "Uh-huh," she continued, "shoo' does."

She had dubbed Sam a fine man. I sighed. And for a long solemn moment, I was pulled back to the day I took Manny home to meet Annie Ruth and Mama. I remembered how she'd sized him up as well upon first sight.

***

Annie Ruth's visit was a godsend. Her gracious life-force inspired me. I felt joyful about the baby. I was sure now I wanted to stay in Wilcox Station and make this house my home. Annie Ruth was pleased about that. The only dark clouds looming were the fact that Manuel refused to sign the divorce papers and the fear that he'd be back.

While Annie Ruth was en route home that afternoon, I poured out my heart in a long letter to him. Somehow, he'd have to sign the papers. Although I knew, with the baby coming, we'd always be connected. I also knew I couldn't bear to stay with him—especially after that last night together. Somehow, I'd make this work for the baby, but I felt nothing but despair when I considered the things that had happened and all the bleak unknowns.

As soon as I finished the letter, Peppy and I walked to the post office. I sent it on a prayer that the words would touch his heart and work a miracle. The phone was ringing when I walked in the back door.

"Hello."

"Lily, it's Sam."

"Hi Sam," I said softly. It was quiet on the other end. He hadn't wasted any time, I thought.

"I'm sorry, Lily."

I don't know what I had expected him to say, but I didn't expect that. Something about those words coming from him made me want to cry.

"I was hoping you'd let me come over for a few minutes," he said, "so we can talk. I want us to be friends."

"Friends?"

"Yes, like we were before," he said. "Can I come over?"

"Uh . . . I guess so . . . sure."

"I'm coming on over now," he said.

"Okay, come on." I put the phone down, took a deep breath, and sighed. Only then did I realize how much the breach between us had hurt. It hadn't plagued my thoughts, but it had been lurking below the surface all along as another reminder of how badly I had managed my life and relationships.

I stepped outside on the terrace and snipped a bunch of pink roses from the trellis. Their subtle sweet fragrance perfumed the back entrance. I was arranging them in an antique porcelain vase when Sam tapped at the back door.

"Come on in. It's open." Sam walked in, and we stood still looking at each other for several seconds. Before I knew it, he moved close and wrapped his arms around me. I closed my eyes and settled against his chest. For a tender moment, we embraced.

"I couldn't help myself," he whispered. I remained still and quiet.

"I'm sorry, Lily. Will you forgive me?"

I nodded my head, and held on a minute more. He kissed the top of my head, and then I looked at him. He had the most serious look on his face. His mouth was so close. I rose up on tiptoes and lightly kissed him before taking a step back.

"That's for speaking to me again."

"I'm sorry I ever stopped," he said. I didn't know what to say, but I couldn't just stand there and stare into his eyes.

"I'm the one who should be sorry, Sam. I didn't mean to lead you on or deceive anybody. I thought there'd be time to explain. I didn't think. It was just easier not to go into it."

"I understand that," he said. And when he smiled it was like nothing had ever happened to spoil our friendship.

"What brought about your change of heart?" I asked, and sat down at the table. "Please sit down Sam."

"Aunt Mae. One day she started me talking about you. She knew exactly what she was doing. Before I knew it I'd told her my feelings, and how I had brought the flowers that day and found out you were married. I'd assumed that you weren't. The fact that there was another man in your life, I didn't see that coming. Well, I was hurt and jealous, and mad. Pride got in the way. Quite frankly, I felt like I'd been sucker punched."

It was hard for me not to tremble in the presence of his naked heart. I struggled to keep my emotions inside. In spite of myself, tears welled in my eyes.

"She told me why you came here, and some of what you've been through, and about that last visit."

I looked away and swiped a tear from my cheek.

"She's very fond of you, Lily, and so am I."

I attempted a smile, but I couldn't pull it off.

"I suspect, she'd like to bring us together," he said. "Play match maker if possible."

"We still have a long way to go before we will really know each other. And it will be a long time before I'll be a match for anyone."

Peppy was looking back and forth between the two of us.

"I'm a good match for Peppy, of course, and this baby I'm carrying." We laughed.

"Yeah. Still, we both could use a special friend."

Again, there was silence. I looked down at my hands resting on the table. My hands, without rings. The flashy diamond had been stashed away upstairs since I'd arrived.

Sitting there with him, listening to our breathing, something good began to settle down inside me.

Then he said, "Is that chocolate cake I see in the cake stand?"

I laughed. "Yeah it is. Annie Ruth made it. Can I cut you a piece?"

"I'd love some."

"How about a cup of coffee to go with it?" He nodded, and smiled his beautiful smile. So I put on a pot of coffee, and we ate cake and talked until dusk. The comforting friendship we'd started months before rekindled. We'd missed each other.

"But what about Sherry?" I raised my eyebrows and smiled a silly smile.

Sam slapped his forehead and looked up to the ceiling. "You know about Sherry?" He chuckled.

"Uh-huh, I do. I recall her being one excited lady to have gone to Uncle Bill's barbeque with a certain gorgeous man." I pursed my lips. "Yep."

"Oh, no," he moaned. "She told you that? We did go together to the barbeque. I didn't want to face you there alone, but you weren't there after all. And we had lunch together the next week. In fact, it's your fault I took her to lunch."

"Oh, do tell," I said sarcastically.

"Well, I was in town on business, and there you were, walking out of the magazine office. I ran in the law office like a scalded dog so I wouldn't have to speak to you. There was nothing I could do but ask her to lunch," he said. "Sorry, I behaved badly."

"And that's all?" I shrugged my shoulders.

"She's a nice person. She's cute. But, she bores me to death. I can't stand spending two hours with her. I asked her out about a year ago, too. I'm done. There's just nothing there for us. No magic. No chemistry. Although she'll make someone a fine wife."

"Just not you," I said.

"No, not me," he whispered, and shook his head, gingerly reaching for my hand.

"And I'm in no position to be thinking about an 'us together', or about magic and chemistry, you know," I said, turning my head to the side. "It's been devastating . . . my love for Manny, our awful marriage. And now, with the baby coming . . . ."

Sam kissed my hand. "You don't have to explain that to me," he said softly. "I understand and I know your heart. And besides that, I'm not going anywhere. You know where I've been for the last thirty years. Right down the road a piece."

"And I'll be right here in my father's house."

When he said good-bye, we hugged again . . . one of those magical melding together kind of hugs that satisfies me better than chocolate cake, or roses, or anything else I can think of.

Chapter Twenty-Six

Bright summer days faded into soft golden ones of fall. The temperature was mild with periods of light rain, and the leaves were glorious. God's paintbrush, I've heard it said, because what other explanation could there be besides the Creator's hand?

I continued daily walks in the neighborhood and town square, stopping at the magazine office a couple times a week and dropping by the law office from time to time to speak to Uncle Bill. The front porch dwellers retreated indoors more and more as the days grew cooler, preferring to sit inside at cozy kitchen tables or by crackling fires. We were friends now. I'd become part of their community. Can a neighborhood nurture you? Can a house care for you? Some days when I neared the house after one of my walks, I sensed a subtle pull, like strong arms reached out to me. I almost heard a whisper, *come on home.*

The baby growing inside me had made its presence known. For the longest time, I wasn't showing, and then overnight my belly popped out. One morning while I was kneeling beside a flowerbed, dead heading the burgundy and gold chrysanthemums, a bump, then a thump followed by a tiny tickle caused me to suck in my breath, straighten my spine, square my shoulders, and wait in wonder. I drew in a slow deep breath, held very still, and waited for that little butterfly to move again. I knelt there for a long time before I got up, and then practically tiptoed around all day not wanting to miss its next tiny flutter. I didn't feel movement again that day, but before long it was a regular occurrence. A little tickle of a "hello" that never failed to inspire joy in my heart. Sometimes my eyes got misty with tears of gratitude at this transformational thought—in the midst of the mess I'd made of my life, God created a sweet new life in me.

I hadn't seen Sam for almost two weeks when he called again.

"Hey Sam. How are you?" I smiled at the sound of his voice.

"I'm good," he said. "I've been thinking about you. I wondered if you might like to take a trip with me this weekend up to the mountains. I need to go up to my parents' cabin and make sure everything is in order before winter. I usually go about this time so I can see the fall leaves. It's beautiful and peaceful up there. The cabin is right beside a little creek."

"That sounds nice."

"Well, the thing is, I'd like you to come with me. We can bring Peppy. It would be fun."

"Oh Sam, that does sound like fun," I said brightly.

"But the thing is," Sam said, "we'll need to stay the entire weekend for me to get everything done."

With that added detail, my excitement subsided. "It's nice of you to ask, Sam." My voice dropped off. "But I don't think so.

"There are two bedrooms. You'd have your own private space," he said.

"You know good and well that we can't go off together for the weekend. Me, a pregnant, married woman, and you the town's most eligible bachelor. What will people think?"

"They'll think we're good friends, and to tell the truth I don't care what they think. I don't like the idea of going out of town and leaving you here alone. Under the circumstances, I think it is fine for you to go."

I grimaced and rubbed my fingertips across my forehead. I could tell he had thought it through.

"I'm not so sure," I said softly.

"Do you want to talk to your uncle about it? He approves of our friendship."

"I would like to go, but I don't want people thinking badly of us."

"The few people who'll know won't think one bad thing. I have a good reputation round here. Everyone would agree our friendship is a good thing. Don't you think?"

"Yes, of course." We were silent for a moment. I waited for him to speak, but when he didn't, I said, "Okay, then. I'll go if Uncle Bill doesn't object."

"Then, it's as good as settled," he said. "I don't want you to worry about anything. And if you change your mind, well, that's okay too."

"It's a woman's prerogative," I muttered.

"I'll bring everything we'll need. You'll need some hiking boots or good walking shoes, and a warm jacket. It gets chilly." His voice betrayed his excitement.

"Okay." I smiled.

"Could you get away on Friday afternoon?"

"I think I can manage that."

"Then I'll pick you up at two and we'll be there by supper time. Sound good?"

"It does," I said. "I guess I'll see you then."

"Goodbye, Lily."

"Bye, now." I put down the receiver and wrinkled my nose. That invitation was out of the blue, I thought. The baby fluttered.

"That was out of the blue, too." I placed my hands on my belly in a caress. "I'll take that as your blessing, little one. You feel safe too with Sam by our side."

I called Miss Grace to let her know I'd be out of town for the weekend. If I didn't see Sugar before I left, I'd write a note and leave it on the back door for him. He hardly missed a day coming around to look in on me, especially since that one day he'd failed to come back for dinner and Manny had walked in instead.

After Sam's call, I skipped upstairs, sat at the oak desk, and wrote all afternoon. I completed the assignment for the magazine and wrote pages and pages of my novel. Early the next morning, I walked to the magazine office to turn in my work, and then stopped at Uncle Bill's office.

"Hi, Sherry," I said. "Does Uncle Bill have a client with him?"

"No, he's alone right now," she said.

"Could you ask if I can speak to him?"

She buzzed him. "Mr. Hollister, your niece is here. She'd like to speak to you if it's a convenient time. Yes, sir."

She put the receiver down, and then looked at me. "You can go on in."

I noticed her subdued manner. There'd be no small talk today.

"Hi, Uncle Bill." I smiled as he came around the desk. I put my arms part way around his side then he gave me one of his bear hugs.

"Lily Rose, you look well. Really well. You must be feeling better."

"Yes, sir, I am. Annie Ruth's visit did me good." I sat down, taking an audible deep breath. Uncle Bill tilted his head, waiting expectantly. I hesitated a minute before asking the question.

"Have you heard anything from Detroit?"

"No, honey," he said, slowly turning his head from side to side. "It could be a while."

"I wrote Manuel a letter," I said softly. "I was hoping he might sign the papers if he understood how much it means to me to stay here and why I can't be a part of his life anymore." Regret for him rolled over me like a storm cloud. I hadn't expected that, but my emotions continued to surprise me with displays as changeable as the sky. I looked at my hands fisted together in my lap, like Annie Ruth held hers when she worried.

"Lily Rose, it's out of your hands," he said. "Leave it in mine and God's."

"Okay." I nodded. He looked kindly at me like a father would. We sat silent for a few seconds, and the dark thoughts lifted. I felt blessed to have Uncle Bill.

"I came by for another reason as well. I want to let you know I might go out of town for a couple of days," I said with a lilt in my voice. "Sam Watson asked me to ride up to the mountains with him. He's going to check on his parents' cabin. It's the perfect time to go see the fall leaves. What do you think about that?"

"He mentioned it to me. I think it's fine." He lifted his eyebrows, while nodding his head slowly in approval.

"Oh," I said quietly. "I should have known he had." After a silent pause, I stood up.

"The mountains are beautiful this time of year," he said as he walked around his desk and to the door. "Sam's a good man, and you certainly don't need my permission. Y'all have a nice time. Enjoy the peace and quiet."

He stood in the open doorway as he spoke. When I walked out into the waiting area, Sherry's head snapped around to face me. She scowled, a how-dare-you look in her eyes. If looks could kill, I thought, I'd be full of buck-shot.

"See you soon." I glanced from one to another and waved good-bye.

"You and Sam have a good time now," Uncle Bill said as the door closed behind me. He seemed genuinely pleased.

On the other hand, Sherry looked annoyed. I hated that. Bless her heart. I was sorry for her discomfort, but there was no way to explain. Then in the next second, I wondered how long it was going to take her to tell everyone she knew. Julie had warned there'd be gossip. I determined not to give it another thought. After all, no one could really understand how much I looked forward to a couple of days of the peace and protection promised by Sam's presence.

***

When Sam arrived at the house on Friday, it wasn't quite two o'clock. Peppy and I heard the truck pull up and rumble to a stop. Moments later, his boots hit the porch. Peppy sprinted for the front door. I put the last piece of clothing into my bag, zipped it, and then cringed when I remembered the trek of that traveling tote. I definitely have to buy some new luggage, I thought.

I skipped down the stairs barefooted and swung open the front door. Tanned and ruggedly handsome, Sam stood smiling at me in a halo of light.

"Hey, I'm early." He grinned. "Is that all right?"

"Come on in. I've almost got everything together."

"I didn't want you to go to any trouble. I've already picked up fried chicken and a gallon of sweet tea from Miss Molly's, and got the cooler packed. I tried to think of everything."

"It sounds like you have." I smiled, more than a little impressed, and walked back to the kitchen.

"Yeah, you just need to put something on those pretty feet, grab a jacket, and we'll hit the road." He laid his hand on my shoulder and walked behind me to the chocolate and coffee scented kitchen.

"I baked cookies. Chocolate chip." I held up a Tupperware container full of cookies.

"Real cookies, not store-bought? Yum," he said. I looked at him and giggled.

Every now and then on the drive up, Sam stopped so I could take snapshots with my Polaroid, but the instant pictures couldn't do justice to the vibrant colors. The mountain views were spectacular. Finally we turned off the highway onto a narrow winding road that appeared to lead nowhere. Dense woods formed walls on each side of the road. Then suddenly it opened up into a little clearing. The cabin sat nestled in a wooded cove beside a creek which circled around two sides of the cabin.

Sam's daddy had designed the genuine log cabin and helped build it himself when Sam was just a boy. Porches ran along both the front and back of the cabin. The large center room was flanked on one side by two small bedroom suites. The den was furnished with a sleeper sofa, and two deep leather recliners in front of a large river rock fireplace. A bar separated the small galley kitchen from the den. As soon as we'd unpacked the car, Sam made a blazing fire.

"This is wonderful, Sam."

"Yeah. I've always loved the place. I had quite a few busted thumbs before we got through building it. Dad gave me a hammer and bag of nails, and even though I wasn't old enough to be any help, he made me think I was."

Looking out toward the creek, he smiled a wistful smile. When his eyes shifted to mine they seemed to reflect something sad and deeply personal, and I turned away before he could see the emotion in mine. We both missed our fathers.

Before night fell, we took a walk along the fast moving creek. Peppy lifted his feet high as he pranced along the edge of the icy water. Sam reached for my hand and led me to a small ledge. We watched the water tumbling over the rocks as we stood in the seclusion of its babbling lullaby. We walked back to the cabin with our fingers intertwined. Then, sitting in front of the fire, we talked or just watched the flames, sharing its warmth and the warmth of companionship. As the hours passed, we relaxed and eased closer. I felt mindlessly content, like I could sit there with him forever, completely safe and warm.

A log burned in two, sending a burst of sparks up the chimney. Words came to me from the Bible.

A man is born to trouble as the sparks fly upward.

Normally I would have pondered those words, *born to trouble*, but with Sam so close I could touch him, trouble seemed far away. Too far away to trouble me.

On Saturday, while Sam cut enough wood for a frontier family's winter, I sat near the fire and read the book I'd brought along. But not before I'd stealthily taken a picture of him. He looked handsome in jeans, and a blue flannel shirt which pulled taunt over the muscles in his back with each strong movement. I couldn't help notice his agility and strength as his muscles flexed with every swing of the ax.

When he came back inside, he insisted on making the vegetable soup for supper.

"In addition to everything else, you cook? I'm impressed."

"I'm a man of many talents," he teased.

"You can make supper on one condition," I said.

"And what might that be, Julia Child?"

I playfully swatted him with a dish towel. "Let me make cornbread muffins."

"Good. I love cornbread muffins."

The hot soup was filled with a medley of summer vegetables that Lisa had put up from her kitchen garden. Butter melted on the warm muffins which produced a delicious aroma. We ate in silence, but every time our eyes met, they smiled.

The following afternoon we again found ourselves snuggled in front of a warm fire. We'd already eaten lunch, straighten up the cabin, and packed our bags for the trip back to Wilcox Station.

"Let's sit here a while longer," Sam said, his voice a husky whisper, "until the fire burns out." His arm rested on the back of the sofa. He took my arm and gently tugged me closer to him. With a sigh, I slid close to him and let my head fall against his chest. His arm dropped around my shoulders.

"I could sit here like this forever," I sighed. A cozy warmth filled my body.

"Every time I'm with you," he said softly, then stopped mid-sentence and sighed. "This weekend has been wonderful, you know. I hate for it to end."

I felt a little catch in my throat. "Me too, Sam."

But it did end. We returned to Wilcox Station without much conversation. The easy peace lingered. I learned some things about Sam that weekend. His kind steady nature made him easy to be around. He accepted me just like I was. I respected him and he never made me feel intimidated. He seemed to be able to do anything. He took charge without being the least bit overbearing. Besides being a kind person, he had dignity and deep respect for people and nature. He was as solid as the mountain on which the cabin was built.

I learned all that about him that weekend. And without realizing it, a quiet gentle love had begun to grow.

Chapter Twenty-Seven

When I returned home around suppertime that Sunday, the misery I had felt so acutely for much of the previous two years had been forgotten, at least for a while. Even when my thoughts turned to Manny, the memories didn't hurt so much as they once had. I suppose the memories were being stored away in my own inner version of Daddy's army trunk. I'd expected life with Manny to be good. Instead, stomach churning anxiety and pain marred our marriage. Now, I needed to believe that misery such as that didn't have to be mine for a lifetime.

The next day the letter arrived. My breath caught in my chest when I saw the familiar writing. My hands trembled as I removed the single sheet of white stationery from the long envelope. I could almost hear his voice as I read.

My dear Lil, I love you. You are the only woman I've ever loved. I want you to know that. I will give you a divorce, only because I must. My heart is not in it. Cir-

cumstances spun out of control due to serious misjudg-ments on my part. I never intended for any of this to hap-pen. I'm truly sorry. Please forgive me. Love always, Manny

Tears slid down my cheeks as sadness welled up in-side. For a long time I sat, staring out my bedroom win-dow. Then I knelt beside my bed and prayed for God's for-giveness for both of us. I had asked for the divorce, but my body seemed to cry out against it. Heaviness ached in my limbs all day. My stomach churned souring the taste for food. I didn't go out. I was glad when the sun went down. I lay in bed for hours with the quilts pulled over me, clinging to bits of conversations with Manny, remembering the hopes and dreams. I'd thought the sheer force of our pas-sion would make a marriage, would make our dreams come true. How wrong I had been. And I wondered, could Manny ever be happy now? I held my head in my hands and willed myself not to think about it. Now our story, my story, seemed like a bizarre aberration . . . a tangled mess. Incomprehensible. Yet somehow I'd muddled through. Sadness for the failures and the loss of our marriage seized my heart. The pain felt new again. I needed it to be over, forgotten, and buried in the past.

***

My pregnancy monopolized my thoughts while the restora-tion of the house and gardens gave me a great deal of pleasure. The writing provided an outlet for my strangled emotions. Manny and the divorce—I couldn't allow myself to think about that, refused to allow it to drain me of vitali-ty and confidence. So I buried those thoughts as quickly as they arose. Uncle Bill had said, "Leave it in my hands and God's." Those words became my mantra.

Sam and I talked every week or two. The magical time in the mountains had been forgotten for what lay right before my eyes. Lisa remained cool on the occasions when we ran into each other. Unbeknownst to me, she and Sam had had words about me. They had argued before that weekend in the mountains. Sure enough, Sherry had called Lisa when she heard I was going and they had partnered up to protect Sam from me. In fact, they had hoped that Sherry would accompany him to the mountains, and when Sherry heard differently, she was mad. She fired up Lisa, who in turn confronted Sam. He never mentioned one word about it to me. I only became aware of all those go-ings-on when Lisa called in November to invite me to their house for Thanksgiving dinner.

"Despite my misgivings, Sam assures me he knows what he's doing," Lisa said, after her hasty first-let-me-have-my-say speech. "I thought Sherry was a safe bet. She's been trembling at the gate for a long time."

I cringed at the horse analogy. "My goodness. I had no idea."

"Sam and I have talked. He has a good heart and he cares about you. To put it bluntly, he wants the two of us to be friends." She paused for a second before going on. "Be-sides, I no longer have any use for Sherry. She speculated that the baby you are having is Sam's. She knows Sam bet-ter than that. And we knew about the baby before. It was downright lowdown of her to say that."

I realized then her protectiveness of Sam. She had been so nice when I first met her at the clinic, but then she had an entirely different side when her instincts called for watching out for her brother.

"Well . . . " I hesitated.

"Now, come on Lily, please say yes. Sam will never forgive me if you don't come."

"In that case, I'd love to," I said.

***

Sam picked me up on Thanksgiving morning. Lisa said there was no need for me to bring anything, but I couldn't go empty handed.

"What have you got there?" Sam lifted his chin and sniffed the air.

"It's a pecan pie." I beamed with pride. "You just wait until you taste it. It is delicious."

Before we headed to the farm, we stopped to pick up Miss Mae. At Sam's house, his six and eight-year-old nephews ran around, happily oblivious to us. Lisa had made so much food it looked like she was trying to hold us over until the next harvest.

Mark was a bit hefty. He wasn't as large as Uncle Bill, but he was big. He looked every bit the former football player. He made me stand by his side to compare bellies. His made my pregnant one look like a cantaloupe, which got a big laugh all around. He was a jovial guy. He had been enthusiastically watching football when Sam and I walked in, but he even more enthusiastically ate Thanksgiving dinner.

It wasn't long after we sat down to eat that I saw why Lisa had cooked so much. I sat beside Mark with Sam on my left. Aunt Mae sat across the table on the end near Lisa. I couldn't help rolling my eyes when I saw the hearty portions those men dipped onto their plates. Sam, unlike Mark, was tall, sinewy, and in good shape, in spite of the amount of food he ate. Even the children ate well. As soon as they came to the table, they folded their chubby hands and waited quietly while grace was said. No one had to say to them "mind your manners." Then they followed their father's lead and ate like there was no tomorrow. Lisa noticed me watching them, and chuckled.

"You see now why I couldn't think of Sam's favorite food?" she asked, arching an eyebrow. "He likes everything." We burst into laughter.

"Yes, I see."

"Well, you ain't a man if you're a picky eater," said Mark. I pursed my lips and passed the cornbread dressing.

Sam and Mark entertained us with rowdy renditions of sporting events in high school and at UGA. Harmless endearing stories about childish pranks and adventures. Lisa interrupted from time to time to add colorful details they failed to mention.

The food was delicious, and Lisa was a gracious hostess. The children were dismissed from the table, but we adults lingered. Lisa obviously adored all the men in her life, and she was very attentive to Aunt Mae. I realized then what a great friend she could be. Her loyalty was fierce, maternal, and protective. I smiled to myself and began to appreciate those qualities in her.

"Lily, when is the baby due?" Lisa asked. She was clearing the table, and I rose to help.

"April 8th," I said, and instinctively looked down at my belly. Everyone looked at me and smiled.

"That's Easter," she said.

"Yes." I smiled.

"Who is your birthing coach?" Lisa, holding a stack of dirty plates in her hands, paused for my answer.

"I don't know," I said. "I haven't thought about that yet. I guess I don't have one."

"Didn't I volunteer to be with you?" Sam said. "I'd be a good birthing coach."

"You stay out of this Sam." Lisa scowled. "Helping a woman give birth is a bit more delicate that pulling a calf." She turned and looked at me. "Can I be your birthing coach?" Her eyes lit up like sparklers.

I giggled a little. Then I glanced at Sam. He smiled and puckered his lips to kiss the air. Unexpectedly, tears moistened my eyes.

"I'd love for you to be with me Lisa. That's so nice of you. Thank you."

"Good," Mark said. "Maybe that will get her mind off of us having another baby." We all laughed.

"And thanks anyway, Sam," I said, "but your big sister asked first." And with that said, I put on a pot of coffee.

While the coffee brewed, desserts were served. Cakes, cheese cake, pumpkin pie and pecan pie starred on the dessert menu. That was when I learned the secret of the children's excellent table manners.

Lisa asked the boys if they'd like some dessert. They promptly reclaimed their seats at the table. While we placed slices of cake on the plates, she quietly explained, "If they don't behave at dinner, they don't get dessert. They don't know if they've been good enough until I call them back to the table. That's why they behave so well until we finish up."

Sam winked at me, and I smiled as I handed the boys thick slices of chocolate cake. Then I sliced the pie and served Miss Mae. She gave my arm a gentle pat. I sat down, unexpectantly joyful, and thought about how grateful I was to have been included in this family's Thanksgiving.

***

The weather turned colder, and I reserved walks for the sunnier days. In the meantime, I sat at my desk for hours every day, writing. The further I got into the story, the more driven I was to get it done. Writing was an escape into imagination. At a time when I most needed it, I breathed new life along with my fictionalized folks and focused on their joys and pain.

The week before Christmas, Peppy and I loaded up the car and drove home. My brother and his wife and their little boys stayed for a week. I hadn't seen my brother in years and I didn't really know his wife, Janine, before that visit. She was thrilled that I spoke French, saying that I was the first person she'd met in the states that she could talk to. Since I spoke her language, we were able to get to know each other well.

Annie Ruth was in and out since she and Mr. John had their relatives to visit for the holidays. Mama sat quietly observing with a smile on her face. She showed more interest in the grandsons than I ever expected she would, saying how they reminded her of James Michael when he was a boy. More than once, without realizing it, she called Jimbo "Daddy." Hearing her say that made us miss him so much our hearts hurt.

We gobbled up our time together like so much needed nourishment. I was enjoying the visit so much I forgot about Manny, until my brother wanted to talk to me about my marriage and the pending divorce. One night after everyone else had gone to bed, James Michael, Janine, and I sat in the living room together. I watched the colored liquid bubble in the antique lights on the tree and thought about my childhood Christmases.

"Lily Rose, you know what the Bible says about divorce." James Michael launched in, his voice somber.

"Of course I do, James Michael." I swallowed a lump in my throat. "I've searched the Scriptures and read and reread them. You know I have."

"I'm opposed to divorce under any circumstances. 'Whosoever God has joined together . . . '" Janine frowned at him when he said that. At that point, she seemed about as uncomfortable as I was.

"I know," I whispered. "That's what I've always believed. And that makes it even more painful. I haven't made this decision lightly." After a pause, I added, "No one can understand but God and I know he does."

"Well, help me understand," he said. Janine placed her hand on mine and looked at the floor.

I didn't want to talk about it, certainly didn't want to reveal any particulars. I shivered as I gave him some sketchy details of the abuse that scarred my marriage. Then, tears threatened to spill out.

"No, I'm not going to go into this with you. I'm not talking about it anymore." I got up and walked out onto the front porch. I squeezed my eyes shut and took a deep breath of the cold night air. I didn't want to relive the pain and humiliation, or be reminded of my failures. I wanted to remember the treasures of the past, my childhood with Daddy and my big brother who hung the moon.

He walked out and came to my side. He put his arm around me, and I leaned my head against his shoulder. A memory came into my mind.

"Jimbo, remember when you'd stand out here and read from the black family Bible?"

"Yeah. You'd sit on the steps as quiet as a mouse, and Mama would add the 'Amens.'"

"I thought you must have looked like Jesus talking to the multitudes."

"And I thought I was more like Billy Graham at the crusades we watched on TV." He chuckled then, and I managed a slight smile.

"Daddy said you were preaching off the porch." James Michael squeezed my arm and pressed me to his side.

"Even then, you knew what you were going to do with your life." I shook my head a little and swiped away a tear. "It was all laid out before you."

"I guess it does seem that way," he said. "It's been easy for me, by God's grace. All things aren't equal though, you know. No two paths are the same."

"What do you mean? We both started out right here."

"Yes, but I had both Mama and Daddy. By the time Daddy was gone, I was well-established, a grown man with a loving wife by my side. You were still just a child, and Mama wasn't able to give you much. I know you had Annie Ruth, and thank God for her. But you still needed a father."

"I miss him." Tears filled my eyes and spilled down my cheeks.

"I know you do." He held me a little closer, and looked down into my face. "Don't be too hard on yourself. I'm sorry I was just now. It does seem sometimes that one has to choose the lesser of two evils. I'm not going to put any more condemnation on you, Lily Rose. There'll be enough of that from the world."

We hugged then. I couldn't speak for the tears.

"You're still the best little sister anyone ever had. I'm sorry I haven't been there for you."

I shrugged my shoulders. "It's okay."

"No it's not," he said. "I know I'm far away, but I'm going to make a better effort to reach out across that distance between us. I call and talk to Mama every week. After you went off to college, you and I stopped talking. I'm going to start calling you too."

"I'd like that," I whispered. "I can make an effort too."

"You should definitely come visit us in France," he said, "when the baby's big enough."

"And you all could stay with me in Wilcox Station. There's plenty of room, even for Mama and Annie Ruth."

"Let's talk with Janine about it. She'd love for us to come visit." So, the evening ended on a kinder note.

***

When I returned home to Wilcox Station late in the evening of December 30th, I drove past Sam's place on my way into town. I hadn't been home ten minutes when someone knocked on my front door.

"Why, Sam," I said. "How did you know I was home?"

"I saw your lights on," he said, grinning with his hands behind his back. We stood there smiling at each other.

"I just now got in."

"Are you going to invite me in or not?"

"Of course, come in Sam."

When I said that, he backed up and side stepped around the corner of the porch. When he returned he was carrying a huge red box tied with a big satin bow.

"Sam Watson, what are you up to?" I giggled.

"I've been waiting to be your Santa Claus." He laughed. I stood on my tiptoes and put my arms around his neck. He stooped to put the gift down, and then wrapped his arms around me.

"I missed you so much, Lily," he whispered. "I like having you close by." He kissed my cheek.

"Oh Sam."

He looked down into my face, and as I looked into his eyes, he kissed me. Not a friendly quick brush of a kiss, but a real slow kiss full of longing and tenderness. For a few breathless moments I melted in his arms. When we pulled away from the kiss, he held me tightly to his chest and stroked my hair. His heart pounded against mine.

"I missed you," he whispered.

"You really did," I said, and giggled again. Then he laughed too, and brushed my hair back from my forehead with the palm of his hand. "I brought gifts," he said in a playful voice.

We went into the living room, and he maneuvered me to the sofa. Then he brought over the large red box and set it before me.

"I can't imagine what this is," I said before clasping my hands over my mouth.

"Well, have at it."

After carefully untying the ribbons, I tore off the shiny paper and opened the box to reveal the cutest dappled rocking horse. The pony was white plush with brown spots. The rockers were made of natural maple. It was the perfect size to sit a toddler.

"Oh, Sam, it's absolutely adorable," I cooed. "Where ever did you find it?"

"I know some real horse lovers. A friend hooked me up. I had a rocking horse when I was a kid. Of course it was much bigger than this one, and I loved that thing. I called it Scout like Tonto's horse. Every child needs one, before he gets the real thing."

"I love it." I smiled at him and reached forward to lightly touch his face. "The baby will love it too. Thank you."

"Open this one," he said, handing me a small square box that looked like a jewelry box. I hesitated.

"Go ahead, baby, it's all right."

When I took the box from him, for a moment I was mesmerized by the sincerity in his blue-green eyes. I opened the blue box to reveal a gold necklace—a dainty gold heart, cut out in the center, dangled alongside a tiny key.

"Oh Sam. It's beautiful."

"Here, let me put it on for you." He gently brushed aside my hair, and then reaching around he clasped it. I reached up and held his hands in mine, and then I leaned forward and kissed him.

"Sam, you're so sweet. These gifts are so meaning-ful. They touch my heart."

"You have the key to mine," he whispered.

I bit my lip to keep it from trembling. I stood up, blinking a bit in surprise, and walked over to the Christmas tree. I grabbed the box wrapped in plaid paper concealed behind the tree, and handed it to him.

"Now, it's time for your gift."

"Ah, Lily, you shouldn't have," he said. "I didn't ex-pect a thing."

"Open it, open it." I waved my hands impatiently towards him, so excited I didn't know what to do with my-self.

He unwrapped a framed picture and held it up at arm's length.

"Lily, this is wonderful," he said as he admired the painting. "How did you do this? It's the cabin. The colors are perfect."

"I hired the artist at the local gallery to paint it from one of the snapshots I took. Do you like it? It's a watercolor on canvas. A remembrance of our special weekend."

"It's perfect," he said. "I'll never forget that weekend." He looked at me longingly for another touching moment, then leaned forward and gave me a tender kiss.

"One more gift," he said, holding up a bottle at arm's length. "I was hoping we could drink some of this bubbly tomorrow night to celebrate the New Year."

"Champagne? That's a nice idea, but you know," I paused, taking a closer look at the bottle.

"Yeah, alright, it's just sparkling grape juice," he said. "Since you can't drink the real stuff, we'll toast the New Year together with this."

"Sam, that's so sweet of you. What a nice gesture." I marveled at his thoughtfulness. He made me feel special.

"There'll be other times for champagne," he said.

On New Year's Eve Sam came over and made a big fire. He'd brought a pizza and buffalo wings, which I couldn't eat because of the horrible indigestion I was experiencing. Instead, I ate potato soup. We sat on the sofa and watched a movie on the small portable TV. Then watched the ball drop, topping off the evening and toasting the New Year with a wine glass of sparkling juice.

"Chin chin," we said in unison. At the stroke of midnight, we drew close together and looked into each other eyes for a very long moment before the warm tender kiss that sealed the evening and our relationship.

But as much as I enjoyed being with Sam, I felt a catch in my heart when he tried to get closer. I'd run ahead of God once before in matters of the heart. I didn't want to do that again. So I kept a tight rein on my fledgling emotions, and Sam just seemed to know to give me time.

Sam had more plans for us on New Year's Day, but since I'd already promised Miss Grace, I went over and spent the day with her and Mr. Ralph. Their adult kids had visited at Christmas, then returned to their homes, and she was missing them. We ate black-eyed peas for health and collard greens for prosperity, and while Mr. Ralph watched football, Miss Grace and I talked about babies.

My belly was as big as a basketball, and people had started predicting the baby's gender. Miss Grace thought it was a boy; Annie Ruth thought it was a girl. I for one couldn't imagine either and prayed that I'd be brave enough to have it naturally. I told Miss Grace about the birthing class that Lisa and I were attending and demonstrated the pant-pant-blow breathing method. She listened intently, and then shook her head. When she burst out laughing, so did I.

"You'll do fine, Lily Rose," she said. "Whether you remember to breathe right or not. You'll do fine. God built it all in, and that natural urge and force to bring a new life into the world will take over at just the right time." She squeezed my hand.

I sighed. "I can do this," I said.

"You can. It's gonna be wonderful." And I knew she was right.

***

Sam's thirty-second birthday was just before Valentine's Day, and he asked me out.

"Let me take you out for dinner," Sam said. "And how about a movie too?"

"Sam, uh, let me remind you, I'm about eight months pregnant. Quite as big as a barrel," I said matter-of-factly. I leaned slightly back and rubbed my belly round and round for emphasis.

"You're not so big," he said. "You should have seen Lisa when she was carrying those boys. She was as big as a barrel for real. You're beautiful," he continued. "I want to take you out. It's my birthday."

"Ah . . . I didn't know. Someone should have told me," I said. "How old will you be?"

"Thirty-two. Won't you celebrate with me? I want a big juicy steak and a cold beer, and a date with the prettiest girl in town."

"Oh you do want tongues to wag." I lifted my eyebrows and pursed my lips.

"I can take it," he said.

"Since it's your birthday, of course, and since you don't mind being seen with a cow," I said.

"If you're a cow, honey, you're one I wouldn't mind being seen with every day of my life."

"Oh, stop it," I said. "When is our date, birthday boy?"

"Pick you up Friday at seven."

"I have one thing to say to that Sam Watson." I paused, and then startled the both of us with the biggest, "Moooooo" ever heard from human lips.

"Whoa," he said. "I can't believe you just did that." I laughed so hard I cried.

***

True to his word, Sam ordered the biggest porterhouse in the restaurant, and I ordered a tender petite filet mignon. Sam had reserved a table in the cozy dining room by the

fireplace. It shouldn't have seemed so romantic and intimate, but it did. He was warm, reserved, a real gentleman.
My skin practically tingled when our hands or arms
touched. I thought pregnancy hormones were to blame.

When we left our table, the waiter wished us a good
evening. In parting he said to us, "Is this your first?"

My eyes got big. I hesitated, and looked down shyly,
but Sam simply wrapped his arm around my shoulders and
pulled me close.

"Yes, it's our first," he said. I looked up into his
smiling eyes. I didn't have to say a word. I couldn't have
anyway if I had tried. My heart was melting a little.

As soon as we got back home, we made ourselves
comfortable in front of the fire. Sam went into the kitchen
to get us each something to drink. Peppy darted to the
door, barking. Then we heard a knock on the front door.

"Sam? I wonder who that could be. It's eleven
o'clock." A sudden chill ran through me.

He laid his hand on my shoulder. "Just relax, Lily.
I'll get it."

When I heard Uncle Bill's voice, my breathing
stopped.

"Uncle Bill . . . what?" I stammered. My mind went
blank, frozen in fear.

Sam hurried over to my side with Uncle Bill right
behind him.

"Lily Rose, I didn't mean to scare you," Uncle Bill
said. "I wouldn't have stopped tonight, but I saw Sam's
truck."

"Is everything all right with Annie Ruth? Is it Mama?"

"They're fine. It's nothing like that. Please calm
down," said Uncle Bill. "I'm so sorry to bother y'all, but I

thought I needed to let you know something." He paused, and then looked at Sam, like he silently asked for his support.

"Y'all sit back down," he said. I sank down on the corner of the sofa, still tense and anxious.

Sam kissed the top of my head, then kneeled beside me and drew his arm around my shoulder. I didn't speak.

"What is it, Mr. Bill?" asked Sam. "Tell us."

Uncle Bill wiped his hand down the side of his face, and took a deep breath. "They've found the body . . . Cynthia Moore's body."

I gasped and pressed my hand over my mouth.

"Dead?" Sam asked. Uncle Bill barely nodded.

"I'm sorry Lily Rose. It was found in the basement of an abandoned building in Detroit. The building had been scheduled for demolition. Due to another crime being committed there, the demolition was halted. While investigating the other murder, her body was found."

"Oh no," I moaned and doubled over. "Oh no." I felt like I'd been stabbed in the stomach.

"She was wrapped in a jacket or sweater, or something that might have belonged to your husband. It's being investigated as a murder. He's being investigated."

"Oh God, no," I cried. "Please no." My mind broke down somewhere between demolition and dead.

Suddenly I felt very tired; my whole body went weak. Nausea washed over me and anxiety obliterated any joy I'd felt that evening. I buried my face in my hands.

Sam eased onto the sofa beside me, wrapped his arms around me, and pulled me to his chest, my face still buried in my hands.

"I don't want to believe it," I moaned.

Sam stroked by hair and whispered soft words to soothe the tears. "Shh-h, I'm so sorry, darling."

He held me for what seemed like a long time. At some point, Uncle Bill left, unnoticed. Sam made hot tea and brought it to me. After a few sips of the warm liquid, I didn't tremble as much. I tried to speak but words wouldn't form. Sam walked me upstairs and helped me get undressed. He pulled the covers back on my bed. I could only sit there stunned, unable even to open my eyes. He lifted my legs onto the bed, then pulled the sheet and quilt up under my chin. I was dizzy with grief.

"I'm not leaving you tonight, Lily Rose." I heard him whisper. "I'm going to stay with you." I felt him lie down beside me. My shoulder touched his chest, and he laid his hand over mine. He would protect me as much as humanly possible from the cares and despair of the world, but that night there was no protection from the turmoil going on in my mind. I fell asleep imagining the cold dark place where her body had lain all those months.

Sam stayed for another night after we got the horrible news. He would have moved into the room across from mine if I would've let him.

"Sam, I wouldn't have made it these last two days without you," I said. "But now I'm okay. Thank you so much, but you really can't stay."

"Please Lily," he said softly.

"No, really I'm fine now," I said. "I am. Go home please. You have work to do. I'm able to stand on my own two feet. And I'm not afraid."

"If you need me . . ."

"If I need you, I'll call," I said firmly.

He came by the house every day after that, sometimes bright and early, and sometimes in the evening, but he never failed to come check on me. He'd call during the day as well. Almost always, when he stopped by, he'd find me writing. Living in that fictional world over which I had complete control. Unconsciously drawing strength from lives I created.

"What's your story about Lily?" Sam asked.

"It's the classic hero's tale . . . about a woman and a man, of course," I said quietly, then rolled my eyes and smiled. "You might say, it's a chick lit kind of story."

Sam nodded and raised his eyebrows knowingly "A chick lit kind of story, huh?"

"But, it's also about second chances, renewal, and forgiveness."

"Then, it's autobiographical?"

"No, not at all," I said curtly. I squinted my eyes and frowned thoughtfully as I considered his comment.

"Sounds like it could be," he said, like he wanted to draw more from me.

We looked into each other eyes for a few seconds, and I understood his point.

"Not in actual events," I said softly, "but maybe the themes . . . the themes are similar."

"I can't wait to read it." He leaned forward and kissed me on my forehead.

"We all have to wait, it seems," I said, rubbing my round belly. "Which reminds me." I raised my eyebrows. "*Wuthering Heights* . . . I've had this question I've wanted to ask. Did you really read that novel or not?" I leaned toward him with a silly grin on my face.

He threw back his head and laughed.

"In ninth grade, Becky Martin was reading it, and what better way to get the prettiest girl in the class to notice me, besides be seen reading the same book?" He grinned. "Gives a regular feller something to talk about."

"Oh, you under estimate yourself," I teased, nodding "You're a sly one. And did it work?"

"What do you think?" With that he playfully grabbed me, and when we found ourselves wrapped in each other's arms, all playing ceased. Our lips met and we melted into a seriously breathtaking kiss.

I sighed, reluctantly pulling back. "I think Miss Martin would have noticed you, whether you ever opened a book or not."

He touched my face and then his arms were around me again. Apparently he intended to hold me close for another kiss, but I pulled away, suddenly self-conscious at the awkward contortions necessary to get around my baby bump. Sam only chuckled.

Chapter Twenty-Eight

Maybe it was because of so much more than the weather and the flowers that made me feel so alive that spring, the most beautiful one in my memory. The flowers were bouquets for a queen. The golden forsythia came early and stayed to welcome the shy crocus and friendly daffodils. A large swath of daffodils cloaked the side yards in yellow. I'd stroll through them picking big bunches to bring inside. The showy pink azaleas came next. The purple irises were majestic. I joined the garden club that year. I wanted my father's house to be included on the tour.

One afternoon towards the middle of March, I had my final say in the lives of my characters. I wrote "The End." When it was done, I looked at all the pages stacked on the desk and I thought, *I can't believe I really did it*. And then I cried because I was overcome by actually having completed it. I felt euphoric. I wondered if I'd ever show the manuscript to anyone. Julie came to mind, so did

Sam. But, that didn't matter. Here I had obsessed over it
for weeks, sometimes getting up before dawn, often staying
up late at my desk. But when it was done, I was content to
have finished it and fulfilled a dream. I'd be satisfied to revisit it some other tomorrow. And that was all I needed at
the time.

The next day I worked in the flowerbeds, but after
having taken a walk, nine months heavy with child, I was
bone tired. I took a long warm bath early in the evening,
and then sat at the kitchen table, gazing out the back door.
Peppy perked up and barked. Then someone knocked on
the front door. It was about time for Sam to come by. Still,
I hesitated a second before putting my hand on the knob.
It's probably Miss Grace, I thought, and then I opened the
door. Manny stood there, looking drawn and stricken. I
gasped and stumbled backwards as he rushed in.

"Manny." My voice was barely audible. "Please . . . I
don't want you here." Bile erupted in my throat.

He shook his head and held up his hands in a gesture of surrender.

"Lil, please. Give me this chance to talk to you.
Please, a minute . . . that's all. I need this." The voice I
heard belonged to a broken man.

I sank down onto the sofa and crossed my chest
with my arms, grasping the tops of each arm, and slowly
rocked back and forth. Seeing him like that, hurt. Grief
welled up inside me for the man I had loved, while at the
same time I wanted to turn away from him. His voice, so
drained, cut to my heart, and at the same time it terrified
me.

"I'm going to be arrested. I don't have much time."

I covered my face with my hands, wanting so badly to block out all the words and the reality of what was happening.

"Listen to me," he yelled and pulled my hands away from my face. "I didn't kill her. I didn't. I hated her. God, how I despised her, but I didn't mean for her to die. I didn't mean for her to fall and hit her head."

Hot tears pooled in my eyes and blurred his face. I squeezed them closed.

"I have to tell you this, you have to hear this from me. Then I'll leave and I won't be back. Look at me!"

I opened my eyes and nodded while looking into his. "I'm listening, Manny."

"I screwed around with her before I knew you. I used her for all she was worth . . . to get ahead in the firm. After I met you, I didn't want to play that game anymore. I swear, Lily. I didn't want anything to do with her, and I told her." I put my hands to my face again, pressing my fingertips to my eyes, and rocked.

"I'm sorry, Lil. I love you. I wanted our marriage to work. I told her, and she kept after me. She didn't care that I was in love with you. She considered me bought and paid for. The day I slapped you, I'd argued with her. It was she I wanted to hurt. She made me crazy."

Even in the dim light of the room, with him kneeling down in front of me, I saw his tears. He grabbed my hands and held them tightly. For a long moment we looked into each other eyes. For that moment we remembered the love we had for each other now tangled with the anguish in our souls. I didn't pull away.

"Please forgive me, I never intended to hurt you. The night she came to the condo, I followed her. A cab had dropped her off several blocks away. She didn't call one when she left, that's why I saw her walking on the street. I stopped. She got in. How I wish that had never happened. We stopped near some abandoned buildings. We argued furiously and she jumped out of the car with me right behind her. She spun around and rushed at me, had raised her hand to hit me, but she never did. Her shoe caught on something and she fell hard on her face without catching her fall. That's when I saw—her eyes were open in a horrible glassy stare. I touched her. There was blood on her head, on my hand. I panicked. I didn't know what I was doing. I wrapped my jacket around her head, picked her up, and put her in the car. I was out of my mind. I carried her to one of the abandoned buildings scheduled for demolition . . . it should have been torn down . . . I thought she'd never be found. Now, it will be impossible to prove I didn't do it. Impossible. I was a fool. She ruined my life."

He stopped talking abruptly and turned his head toward the street. Only then did I hear sirens from multiple patrol cars approaching.

He grabbed me in his arms and crushed me to his chest for one heart-stopping embrace. Then he jumped up and ran out the back door. I heard car doors slamming and loud, angry voices, while lights flashed on the living room walls. Someone ran inside and grabbed the phone off the wall in the kitchen.

"Get over here right now, Sam!" Officer Barkley shouted into the receiver. "No, it's not the baby. It's her husband. Come now."

"Lily Rose, are you okay, honey?" the officer asked. He'd knelt by my side, his hand resting on my shoulder.

"I'm okay," I murmured, instinctively rocking.

"Stay right here. Don't you move until Sam comes. Stay right here on this couch. You hear me?"

"I won't move." I held my face in my hands and sobbed.

Have mercy Lord. Please have mercy. That's all I could pray. Nothing else could help.

Shouting continued outside. I thought I heard Sam's voice. For a second, I feared for him, but then he was by my side.

"Oh my God, Lily, you poor baby." He took me in his arms.

"Sam, hold me," I whimpered. He gathered me in his arms and rocked me for I don't know how long.

After some time, Officer Barkley stepped in and said something to Sam. Then he left and everything became still. Peppy stopped his frantic yapping and pacing and lay down at my feet.

"Oh Sam, will this nightmare ever end?"

He brushed the hair back from my face. "It ended tonight, darling. Don't be afraid anymore. It's over." I turned my head into his hand and kissed it.

"I've never had the courage to face real life."

"You've been brave . . . you're the bravest person I know," he said. "And if ever you need me, I'm here. I'll be your strength."

When I awoke the next morning the sunlight was already bright in the room. I raised my head and eased myself up on my elbows. Peppy was not in his bed. I remembered what had happened then and lay back on my pillow. I placed my hand on my belly and rubbed across it. I needed to go to the bathroom, but I didn't want to get up. I heard Sam talking to Peppy downstairs and it warmed my heart and made me feel like crying. Then I heard him coming up the stairs.

When he walked into the room, the morning sun lit his face, so solemn and full of concern. He came around to the side of the bed and sat on the edge with his arm propped over me. Silently we looked at each other. He stuck out his bottom lip like a pout, and I reached up and touched his lips with my fingers. He kissed them before kissing my forehead. He rested his face there, his warm breath on my skin.

"I love you so much, Lily," he whispered.

And without even thinking, I said the words that my heart must have known for some time.

"I love you too, Sam." He pulled back and looked at me. His blue-green eyes sparkled.

"You love me?" he asked in a tiny voice, as if in amazement. I got misty eyed. Peppy lightened the moment by jumping up on the bed.

Sam took a deep breath and sighed. Then finding his voice, he said, "I could get in there with you . . . or should I go make us some breakfast?"

"Humm. That's a tough one." I hesitated while lifting my hand to his face. I ran my fingers lightly across his chin. "But I have to say . . . I'm so hungry . . . I could eat a horse." My hand lingered on his cheek. "While you fix us some breakfast, I have to go to the bathroom. I've got to go pee pee real bad." I rolled to my side, cautiously slid out of bed, and waddled toward the door.

He pretended to cough and laughed a little. "Pee pee? Did you say pee pee?"

I laughed then, and something warm run down my leg. I hurried toward the bathroom, but before I got there, I stopped and stared at my feet.

"Something's happening, Sam. Sam!" He almost hurt himself rushing to get to me. At the time, it was not funny. Afterwards, in the retelling, it was.

"I think my water broke."

He helped me into the bathroom, all the while talking softly to me. Fluid was still leaking out.

"This is normal, Lily. And it's not too early. Are you in pain?" At the same time, he kept his hands on me, soothing me, supporting me. Maybe he was bolstering his own courage as well.

Tears moistened my eyes, but I giggled and shook my head. "I'm not in pain. I'm really not." That would start in the next couple of hours and obliterate the day.

Sam helped me get myself together and grabbed the new suitcase I'd packed for the hospital.

"Will you call Lisa for me?"

"We're going to get you to the hospital first. Then, I'll call her," he said. "Are you okay, baby?"

I nodded.

"Sam, I can't remember a thing they taught me in birthing class."

"Don't worry. It's nature. It'll come back to you."

Sam stayed with me. When Lisa didn't come, he told me that she'd had a minor emergency and would be delayed. One of the boys needed some stitches from a playground accident, he said.

"Oh no, I hope he's okay." I barely ground out the words before another contraction claimed all my focus. My legs had begun to tremble.

Sam stayed. At first I told him no, I'd rather he not be there, but after the contractions started coming in earnest I needed him. In fact, I clung to him, even clutching him around the neck from time to time. Even if he'd wanted to, he could not have moved away from my side.

After what seemed like hours, I heard Lisa speak to Sam. "How is she doing? I'm glad I finally made it."

"Lily, are you doing okay? I'm sorry I wasn't here for you sooner."

"It's okay," I whispered. "How's little Mark?"

"Just a tiny gash, an accident on the swings," she said. "Sam, I'll take over now. You can go on out."

"No! I mean, it's okay. I want him to stay." I clutched Sam's wrist. He leaned close and kissed my forehead.

And as it turned out, it took all of our efforts to bring that baby into the world. It was a long and arduous labor. When my strength was gone, Lisa and Sam helped support my back, and then helped me push, one on either side of me. When the baby took its first squalling breath, we all cried.

She was an astonishing eight pound baby girl with her daddy's black hair and olive coloring, but she looked just like me.

"What a precious little beauty," Sam whispered. From that moment on, she wrapped him around her little fingers—every one of them.

I named her Julianne for the two women who meant the most to me. Pure joy dawned in my heart that day and my life has never been the same.

The following morning, just after sunrise, Sam tiptoed into the hospital room.

"I'm awake, no need to tip-toe," I whispered. "I don't think you can wake her." He gently tended to us, kissing me on my cheek and stroking the baby's tiny hands.

"You were magnificent, Lily," he said. "You made it look easy."

I smiled. "I was delirious."

"And now you're exhausted," he said. "You look frail. What can I do for you?"

"Would you please go get Annie Ruth? She wants to be here so bad. I hate for her to ride the bus."

"I'll be happy to. I'm sorry I didn't think of it. I'll stay with you this morning, then go right after lunch. I'll have her here by tonight. When I bring you and the baby home tomorrow, she'll be there waiting for y'all."

"Thank you, Sam. Thanks for staying with me, thanks for the flowers, for everything."

So, Sam brought Annie Ruth to the house. She stayed a week. Between the two of them taking care of me and the baby, I'd never felt so loved. All my attention went to the baby. I never knew I could love so much. My sadness and despair were totally laid to rest, and Sam would not let me revisit them.

"That man dotes on you, Lily Rose," Annie Ruth whispered. "Uh-uh-uh. He is a fine man."

"Annie Ruth, is he as fine a man as Daddy?" I frowned a bit, pretending to be serious.

"You know, Lily Rose, I think maybe he is."

I couldn't help grinning when she said that. "I think you're right, Annie Ruth. I'm so happy."

"Me too, child. Me too." She squeezed her eyes shut and tightened her grip on my hand.

After Annie Ruth went back home, Julie came to visit with little Chloe. When she wasn't helping me with the baby or doing things around the house, she and Chloe walked Peppy in the neighborhood and charmed all the

302   Rose Chandler Johnson

neighbors who kept bringing us all kinds of delicious casseroles and gifts.

Chloe played with the dolls. She and Julie took some with them when they visited Miss Mae. Julie read my novel and predicted bestseller status. At least she laughed and cried at all the right places. She promised to come back in the fall when the leaves changed.

"Or, I'll come back sooner if some other momentous event should occur." She beamed. I knew what she was implying—she too had been smitten by Sam.

"I'm learning patience is a virtue, my dear," I said. "And some things are really worth waiting for."

"You took the long way around, Lily Rose, but I believe you found your way home."

"I believe I have."

"Who could have even imagined a year ago how happy you'd be now. There's not a trace of those tattoos. Your hair has grown out." She laughed. "And don't even let me get started talking about that amazing man."

"I know. I never could have imagined. And I have my precious baby. I'm so glad you came to be with us, Julie. Thank you for coming."

She tilted her head and nodded. I swaddled the baby close to my chest and Julie put her arms around the both of us. But still, she couldn't fool me. Although she wouldn't say it, I knew she feared what would come of the horrible situation with Manny. But, the joy of new motherhood was already washing away the pain of the past, and I wouldn't lose out on those joys by dwelling on circumstances beyond my control.

When it was time for them to leave, Sam took Julie and Chloe to the airport promising to take them horseback riding on their next visit. When he returned, we were alone for the first time in weeks.

"Now you'll have to make do with me," he said as he nuzzled my neck.

"Don't let Miss Grace or Miz Walker hear you say that," I cautioned. "You know they come in and out over here all day. They're in love with this baby."

"I'm in love too, and I'm going to get as much time with my girls as I possibly can. Hope that's all right with you."

I caressed his neck. "I should say so. Have as much time as you need," I whispered. "You deserve it." He leaned close to give us both soft kisses.

***

On a beautiful day in early June, I strolled down the shady street to the magazine office. Peppy pranced along beside us. Julianne smiled up at me from her Pram. We garnered lots of *hi's* and *hello's* from everyone eager to get a glimpse of my adorable daughter.

The magazine editor had been clamoring to read my novel ever since I'd first mentioned it, so I took it to her and picked up my first assignment since the baby's birth.

We were already headed back home, having left the town square, when Sam drove along beside us and hung his handsome head and shoulders out the truck window.

"Hey there, pretty girl," he yelled in a leering voice, waving his arm. "You pretty thing, wanta ride?"

I giggled, a bit embarrassed at his antics.

"Shhh, Sam, stop that." I shushed him and waved my hand at him dismissively, all the while grinning from ear to ear. I realized exactly what he was doing.

He kept whooping and hollering despite my giggly protests, having too much fun to easily give up the reenactment of my infamous trek into town over a year before. I played along.

"Stop that," I shouted. "My friends are picking me up at the church." He gunned the engine, then swerved along the curb, and stopped on the street up ahead. When he jumped out the truck and walked towards me, my heart soared. Butterflies fluttered in my stomach.

"Hey, Lily," he purred as he kissed me on the cheek. "I'm heading to your house. How're my girls today?" He leaned in to take a closer look at the baby and brushed the edge of her bonnet with his fingers. "Oh, she is precious, just like her mama," he whispered.

He looked at me with smiling eyes and nodded toward the truck. "You wanta hop in with me?"

I shook my head, still smiling up at him. "I'm heading straight home . . . we'll walk the rest of the way." I made a kissy face at him, wanting so much to kiss him right then. He took my chin between his thumb and forefinger and looked down into my face.

"Well, hurry home," he said softly, talking close to my face. "I have surprises. Good surprises."

"Surprises?" I whispered close to his lips and raised my eyebrows. "For what occasion?"

"Oh, you mean besides spending the day with the love of my life? No occasion. I just feel like cooking steaks. I brought the steaks and a grill."

"Umm . . ." I smiled.

"And I have more surprises, but you'll just have to wait for those."

He kissed me then, right on the mouth, a kiss full of tenderness and promise. I watched him walk away, amazed by him and his love for us. He opened the truck door, and then turned back toward me.

"Lily Rose, you're gonna to be all right," he hollered. Then he hopped up into the truck.

For a moment, I held my breath, looking at him, seeing him, but no longer hearing him. I was caught in a magic time bubble. My daddy's voice echoed in my mind.

"What did you say?" I yelled back to him.

He waved his arm out the window and hollered. I barely caught the words.

"You're going to be all right, Lily Rose." He drove away, still holding his arm out the window.

My eyes filled with tears as so many emotions burst forth from my heart. I lifted my face to the sky and let peace settle over me. My heart overflowed with joy, restored, as love rushed back to me. I knew again that long forgotten serenity from so many years before.

"Yes, Daddy." I spoke to the heavens. "Yes, I am going to be all right."

Then, I looked down into the face of my precious child.

"Oh, Julianne. Isn't it the most wonderful day!"

At that moment we walked past a row of yellow daylilies in full bloom bordering the sidewalk. They nodded their pretty heads like well-behaved children— riotously happy children. And I couldn't help myself. I laughed out loud . . . and the joyful sound floated up into the summer sky.

Works Cited

Page 15.

Levin, Eric. "The New Look in Old Maids." *People Magazine*, 31 March, 1986, vol. 25, no. 13. Web. 10 February 2016.

Page 174.

Lee, Harper. *To Kill a Mockingbird* (New York, NY: Grand Central Publishing, 1960) 1.

Acknowledgements

I should like to thank everyone who has helped me through the years on my journey, so to speak, since no novel is written without drawing on the life events that happen around us. Since that is not possible, please permit me to be selective and brief.

I owe a debt of thanks to those who read and critiqued early chapters of the story – Eva Marie Everson, Anne Marie Keith, Pamela Harrison, Vanessa Gravelle, and Tiffany Colter. Without their encouragement I would not have completed this work.

I am humbly indebted to those who graciously read and reviewed the early drafts of the manuscript – Elizabeth Cane Crabbe, Anne Marie Keith, and Pamela Harrison. Without their keen perceptions, suggestions, comments, and edits, *My Father's House* would not be nearly as winsome as it is.

I want to acknowledge the contribution of my talented editor, Heather McCurdy, who worked tirelessly with patience and dedication to detail. Her enthusiasm for *My Father's House* made all the revisions a joy.

I'd like to thank my fellow author friends who have encouraged me in all my writing and publication endeavors – Janie Dempsey Watts, Cassie Dandridge Selleck, Bryce Gibson, and Kathleen Ruckman.

My sincere gratitude to the authors who read *My Father's House* as it was readied for publication – Alice Wisler, Ann Tatlock, and Susan Reichert. The gifts of their time, kind words, and encouragement were much appreciated.

Finally, I was immensely blessed by my three daughters, Anne Marie, Melanie, and Katie, my daughter-in-law Cory, my granddaughter Cameron, and my sister, Darlene, who listened attentively as the characters and story evolved. Thank you for believing in me. It was my pleasure to share the process with you.

About the Author

Rose Chandler Johnson is the author of the award winning devotional, *God, Me, and Sweet Iced Tea: Experiencing God in the Midst of Everyday Moments. My Father's House* is her first novel. She happily makes her home near Augusta, Georgia.

To connect online, visit her website or author page.

www.writemomentswithgod.blogspot.com
www.facebookrosechandlerjohnson/author

51009305R00192

Made in the USA
Lexington, KY
31 August 2019